INVIDIA

SHADES OF SIN

INVIDIA

COLETTE RHODES

ILLUSTRATED PAPERBACK ISBN: 978-1-7386107-2-3
DISCREET PAPERBACK ISBN: 978-1-7386107-3-0
HARDCOVER ISBN: 978-1-7386107-4-7

COVER BY: COLETTE

INVIDIA IS A MONSTER ROMANCE BETWEEN A HUMAN AND HER NOT-QUITE-HUMAN PARTNER, SUITABLE FOR READERS OVER 18.

CW: SEXUAL CONTENT, PREGNANCY

"YOU ARE DAMAGED AND BROKEN AND UNHINGED. BUT SO ARE SHOOTING STARS AND COMETS."

\- NIKITA GILL

TALLULAH

CHAPTER 1

Being nice was exhausting.

My cheeks hurt from smiling, my heels were pinching my toes, and I'd been ready to leave this ball at least an hour ago, but I didn't want to look rude by making an early escape when clearly, this whole thing had been put on for the benefit of myself and the other single Hunters—former Hunters?—who'd moved here to the shadow realm.

It suited some of our personalities better than others.

Verity laughed loudly, lounging elegantly in her chair, surrounded by admirers and holding out her goblet for a refill. Striving to emulate her bright, relaxed demeanor, I batted my eyelashes and smiled coyly at the Shade offering to top up my own wine, wondering if I was pulling off effortless grace the way Verity was.

Fake it 'til you make it. Fake it 'til you make it.

"It seems a shame to see you dressed in shadows," a Shade next to me murmured, their claw drifting over the top of the shadow dress Phileas had formed for me. "When you're such a vision in color. You always wear such beautiful garments."

"Thank you," I said earnestly, grateful for both the compliment and a chance to talk about something that I was actually familiar with. "I make them myself. I love to sew."

"You make them yourself?" he asked, sounding suitably impressed, and I puffed up slightly in my seat. I was wearing a gorgeous strapless emerald green number beneath the shadows, which I was hoping I'd get a chance to show off at some point to make the suffering the boning in the bodice was causing me worthwhile. "Where did you learn such a skill?"

"It was something my grandmother taught me." The tension eased out of my stiff neck and shoulders ever so slightly as we chatted about it, the conversation leading me back to the few fond memories I had of visiting my grandparents' grand home when I was young.

Eventually, the chat petered out, through no fault of the Shade valiantly trying to flirt with me. I was overstimulated, overtired, and floundering in my attempts to sound like the sultry, funny, personable ex-Hunter everyone seemed to assume I was.

I didn't know if I was good at lying to them or lying to myself that my scent didn't give away any hint of discomfort. Maybe it was a little of both.

"Would you excuse me for a moment?" I said with my most sunniest of smiles, standing up and making my way through the crowded room, my heels clicking against the stone floor with every step. Someone had thrown open a usually shut side door, letting some air into the stuffy room and allowing guests to access the overgrown circular courtyard in the center of the spiral-shaped palace.

Perhaps because it was so overgrown—and a little creepy—the courtyard was blessedly empty, and only just illuminated enough to prevent

Shades from shadow walking into it. Or maybe it was the faint chill in the air, keeping everyone inside near the warm glow of the open flames dotted around the dining hall in towering metal torches.

The shadows I'd been wearing vanished the moment I moved out of whatever the magical distance was between myself and Phileas, and even though I'd wanted to show off my dress, I suddenly felt overexposed in the night air with my shoulders and arms on display.

At least there was no one to see me out here. I made my way farther into the overgrowth, letting the sounds of the ball grow muted behind me. I'd always liked the dark. I let it wrap around me, hiding my tomato-red cheeks and ostentatious dress.

You're being ridiculous, the nagging voice in the back of my head reminded me. *This event is for the ex-Hunters. It's for you. They've made an effort, you need to do the same. You're supposed to be getting to know the Shades, you're supposed to be making connections. Maybe even finding The One.*

But what if I didn't find The One? What would The One even look like? I didn't even know what I was looking for. I didn't understand the culture, or the history, or the seemingly rigid class structure that appeared to go unexamined. I was intrigued by Shade features—and I found them beautiful in an aesthetic sense—but I'd never fantasized about monster fucking the way some of the others who'd moved here had. I didn't *dislike* the physical differences between us, but I couldn't pretend I wasn't intimidated by them.

I definitely hadn't had an instant belly-fluttering-panties-soaking reaction to anyone yet. And what if I never did? What if I *couldn't* feel attraction to anyone? Honestly, I hadn't had a great track record of it in the human realm either. I'd assumed the worst of every man who'd ever so much as glanced at me.

None of this is going to improve by you hiding out here all alone, I told myself sternly. *You need to put yourself out there. Flirt more. See if a connection develops.*

There was a circular waist-height stone wall in the center of the courtyard, with overgrown, haphazard bushes planted at even intervals, almost hiding the wall completely.

I slipped my feet out of my heels, almost moaning at the cool sensation of smooth stone under my aching feet, and carefully lowered myself to the ground, trying not to snag my outfit as I wriggled back between two of the bushes to sit against the wall. The dress was a formfitting number and not the most comfortable to curl up in, but I was cold enough that it was worth the extra effort to wrap my arms around my knees.

It wasn't ideal—I'd have preferred somewhere a little more confined and a whole lot warmer to curl up and talk myself down, but beggars couldn't be choosers.

Five minutes. I just needed five minutes to collect myself, and then I'd head back inside and be *more* charming and *more* flirty and *more* vivacious. But for right now, I didn't need my scent broadcasting that I wasn't as confident as I appeared.

"Sorry to interrupt, but should you be out here?" a low, soothing voice asked, making me startle so hard that if the snagging branches hadn't been in the way, I would have cracked my head on the stone wall.

I clutched my chest like I could physically grab my heart and stop it from beating at such an alarming rate, squinting through the leaves and scanning what I could see of the courtyard in front of me.

"Who are you? Where are you?" I winced a little at my own bluntness. Apparently, my goal for this evening was to make as many poor first impressions as possible. Then again, I was already sitting in a bush. What were a few unpolished words at this point?

"On your left."

I startled, realizing the voice was coming from beside me. Peering through the leafy charcoal-colored bush I was sitting by, I found a pair of glowing navy eyes staring right back at me. To my surprise, I didn't immediately shriek and run away, which is probably what a sensible person would have done at finding a pair of glowing monster eyes staring intently at them through a bush.

Maybe I was acclimatizing to life in the shadow realm better than I thought.

"Should you be out here?" he repeated, sounding oddly amused by the awkward situation we'd found ourselves in.

"Should you?" I countered. I mean, *yes*, I was hiding in a bush. But that was because my nerves would probably make me throw up if I didn't. What was his excuse?

"Doubtful," he replied easily. "But I don't like crowds, and crowds don't like me. I'll leave if I'm making you uncomfortable—I'm a member of the Guard, if it helps. If I cause you so much as an ounce of distress, the captain will publicly execute me in front of the entire court."

"That's not necessary," I said hastily, wondering if I should be a little more wary about Captain Soren. "I'm not distressed. My name is Tallulah, by the way."

"I'm Evrin." He paused for a long moment. "So, why are you sitting in the bushes?"

"You first."

He made an endearing sound that might have been amusement. "I usually don't... attend these things. I'm not used to them. They aren't used to me being here. Your turn."

I opened my mouth, intending to give him a generic answer about the warm room and fresh air, but that wasn't what came out. Perhaps because there had been a thread of vulnerability in his voice, and it had reached out to pull on the many vulnerabilities that were swirling around in my head.

"Sometimes, when I'm talking to people I don't know very well, my skin feels too tight for my body and my head gets fuzzy, and I kind of want to throw up, but I don't want anyone to *see* that because that would be humiliating. And my face is sore from smiling and I feel like everyone can tell that I'm faking it? But they all think I'm so happy and confident, so maybe they *can't* tell. I don't know anymore. So I came out here to just take a minute to pull myself together so I can go back in and be more convincing next time."

I sucked in some oxygen, my face growing increasingly hot as the realization of just how much I'd said out loud slowly hit. Oh my god, I'd just totally trauma dumped on a total stranger in a dark garden in the middle of the night. Maybe this was an arrested development thing. I'd never gone to parties in college, gotten drunk on seltzer, and unloaded all of my emotional damage on strangers. No time like the present, apparently.

My face was hot, but the rest of me was cold, and my teeth chattered in the extended silence, my breath coming out in awkwardly loud shudders.

"Your coldness is extremely distracting."

There was some rustling, and I squeaked in surprise as an enormous Shade suddenly crawled around the bush toward me, swearing under his breath as a branch snagged on his slightly overlong, floppy hair. I did a double take, not having seen that kind of hairstyle on any other Shades in the realm.

"What are you doing?!"

"Your teeth are so... rattly," Evrin replied distractedly, squeezing into the tiny gap to my right, carefully not touching me. "I'm shielding you from the wind."

"Oh. Okay."

Objectively, it was a very high-handed thing to do. And an invasion of my personal space. And, especially considering the empty courtyard and the discreet spot I'd tucked myself into, it should have made me feel deeply uncomfortable to have a strange male—Shade or human—squeezing in *right* next to me.

Especially after my impromptu confessional.

I waited for those objections to form on my tongue, but they never came. Presumably, my scent wasn't doing anything off-putting either. Evrin's nose didn't even twitch.

"Um, thank you."

A branch had gotten tangled in his hair, and I reached up in the free space between us to tug it loose. Evrin leaned away, glancing at me in shock, and my face heated all over again as I shot him a sheepish smile.

"Sorry. There's, um, a branch..." It came free with a gentle pull, and I wrapped my arms around my waist, tucking my hands beneath my elbows before they went wandering and freaked him out again.

"It's fine," he said gruffly. "I thought you were looking at something else."

I nodded as though I understood, though I absolutely didn't. He was blocking the breeze more than I'd expected though, which was lovely. Honestly, I kind of wanted to wriggle closer, to see if I could steal a little body heat, too. The fact that he was more interested in plucking vines and leaves out of his hair than looking at me probably helping. Honestly, he seemed pretty ambivalent about my presence, if anything.

"Am I able to move a little closer?" I asked tentatively. "For warmth?"

Huh. Weirdly, in all of my *actual* attempts at flirting since I'd arrived in the shadow realm, this was the only time I'd felt that sort of self-conscious, giggly, *shy* flirty energy. Historically, that was more authentically me than the bold, eyelash-batting, coy-smiling flirting I'd been doing here, but I also didn't like being authentically me, so it wasn't exactly a win.

I *liked* people thinking I had my shit together.

"Sure."

I scooched over slightly, until my bare arm pressed against his solid one, the shadows he was cloaked in tickling my skin. His arm felt *massive,* and solid as a rock, and while I didn't *think* that was something I'd been particularly attracted to, there was the faintest hint of a belly flutter at the contact.

"You've stopped trembling," Evrin noted, relaxing slightly next to me.

"Have I?" I hadn't even noticed, though the cold didn't feel quite as bitter as it had a few moments ago. "Thank you. I really appreciate you taking pity on the weird lady you found in the bushes."

Evrin snorted. "It's a vast improvement on how I imagined the night going."

I blinked in surprise, which reminded me that I'd subjected my eyelids to false lashes—another layer of overstimulation to deal with. "Why did you come? Was it mandatory?"

"Yes and no. So many members of the Guard wanted to attend as guests—to try to impress the ex-Hunters, I assume—that they were short of guards on duty. Usually, I don't patrol outside of my own area, but I agreed to tonight. I did warn the Lieutenant that I'd spend most of the night out here."

"Lurking in the bushes," I teased, nudging his arm lightly.

He laughed—a rusty, and somehow adorable sound. "Something like that, yes."

"It sounds like you've got quite a lot of freedom in the Guard?" I hedged, trying to make sense of it. I'd assumed that the Guard were all much of a muchness below Captain Soren and Selene, the Lieutenant. Maybe there was more of a hierarchy than I'd thought.

"I suppose. They need me more than I need them," Evrin replied simply. Confident, but not arrogant.

It made the whole confined space situation infinitely more dangerous— mostly for my self-control. Evrin had a sense of ease about him that I'd only ever encountered a few times in my life—the girl in middle school who used to link our arms and drag me around the playground singing Céline Dion at the top of her voice. What was her name again? Or Kaia, in high school, who'd dressed like an anime character before it was cool and let negative opinions run off her back like water. Evrin possessed the same unbothered energy that they did, and I'd always gravitated to those kinds of people, hoping some of that self-assurance would osmosis its way over to me.

"You weren't eager to get flirty with the ex-Hunters tonight?" I joked, mostly to show him that I was capable of being cool and funny, and not a walking, talking ball of neuroses like my anxiety speech had probably indicated.

"Flirty is not a word usually associated with me," he replied, with such perfect dryness in his voice that I couldn't help but laugh. "Though, I was curious about all of you. I'll admit that."

"About us ex-Hunters? That's a very reasonable thing to be curious about." I settled in a little more, Evrin's arm warm and solid where it pressed against mine. I was suddenly desperate to drag this conversation out, to get him to stay out here with me just a little longer. "If you have any questions, I could answer them for you."

"That's very accommodating of you," Evrin said after a pause, gently tucking some vines into the bush next to him before resting his head back against the wall. He was so much taller than me that the top of my head only reached his shoulder. "I guess you're not in a hurry to get back inside and resume faking enthusiasm for the ball."

Looks like he'd been paying attention to my ramble after all.

"I'm not in any rush, no," I agreed sheepishly, wondering what Hunter embarrassment smelled like to Shades, since they could apparently sniff out all of our feelings, and negative ones were supposedly an unpleasant scent.

I didn't have a degradation kink personally, but my mind wandered off on a side quest, contemplating how much it would suck to be enjoying humiliation and then start smelling like rancid milk midway through the act.

"I had assumed from watching you all in there that all Hunters were social creatures."

"All Hunters—*ex*-Hunters—aren't any one thing, as I'm sure all Shades aren't either," I replied, before softening my words with a smile, knowing that I didn't always come across as warmly as I intended to.

"A very reasonable point," Evrin replied, a hint of amusement in his voice. At least he didn't get offended by my correction and call me a snob. "Hm, what was I curious about when it came to Hunters? I'll admit, this entire interaction has thrown me slightly. You're already shifting the image I had in my mind."

"In a good way, I hope?" The history between our kinds was never far from my mind. Hunters had spent centuries actively killing Shades, and the rediscovery of the old dynamic that used to exist between our kinds— one where we co-existed—was new and fragile. While I hadn't encountered anyone at court who wanted me gone, those Shades did exist, and I didn't blame them for it.

There was a very good chance they'd lost loved ones at the hands of my kind.

"Yes. In a good way." He went quiet for a moment before speaking again. "I've only ever encountered your kind in *your* realm, where Shades are so defenseless. It didn't occur to me how much more... fragile you would seem in this realm."

That thought had occurred to me almost hourly since I'd moved here, though, not while I'd been out in the courtyard. "Should I be nervous?"

"I'm not going to hurt you."

I didn't have any real reason to believe him, and yet I did. Maybe it was just that he had such a settling presence about him. Maybe it was because of how carefully he'd disentangled himself from the vines and branches, gently tucking them back into the bush without breaking them.

That had to be a green flag, right?

"Do you believe me?" he asked, twisting slightly to look at me. "I'll leave if I'm making you uncomfortable."

"No, no, I believe you. You'd smell if I was nervous. Or any other kind of heightened emotion. Do I smell unpleasant?"

It sort of sounded like I was fishing for compliments, though it had been a genuine question. Whatever chemicals we put out that made our emotions smell obvious to Shades weren't detectable to human noses.

"No. You smell fine."

Okay, I *hadn't* been fishing for compliments, but I wouldn't have complained if he'd slipped one my way. Maybe living in the shadow realm was going to my head—I was getting too used to being complimented every second of the day just for existing. This was different. This was the first time I'd actually *wanted* a Shade to flirt with me since I'd arrived here.

Maybe I just wanted what I couldn't have.

"Why did you come to the shadow realm?" Evrin asked, moving right along.

I shrugged, mirroring his nonchalance. "I needed a change. I hadn't been part of the Hunters for a while. There was no love lost there on my part. I guess I felt like I was getting one over on them by coming here."

I doubted anyone cared, aside from my immediate family perhaps, but even those relationships had been strained in recent months.

The other reason that I'd come here—that I'd had nothing going on in my life, and desperately wanted to crawl out of my own skin and everything that had ever touched it—was less cute, so I kept that one to myself.

"You don't have parents?" Evrin asked bluntly.

"I do. They're Hunters first. Parents second."

"Ah." He didn't apologize for bringing up what was clearly a difficult subject. I wondered what that would be like, walking through life without second guessing every word that came out of your mouth and whether they'd been offensive to someone, even unintentionally. "I'd offer to answer your questions, but I presume you have some kind of welcoming committee of Shades to do that for you."

"Not quite. We have Ophelia—who is amazing, of course—but she's answering questions from a human perspective." Honestly, it would have been really helpful to have a Shade we could speak to privately, but I guess the king was worried that we'd feel too much pressure and leave if there was so much as a single Shade in our presence at Elverston House.

"You can ask me," Evrin offered, tipping his head back against the wall, one leg bent and his arm draped over his knee. He was the very picture of languid ease, and I kind of wanted to crawl into his lap and absorb that sense of calm through my pores.

My scent might start making things awkward soon, because I was definitely starting to have a physical reaction. The more unbothered Evrin was, the more I contemplated having rabid, filthy sex with him.

I was glad there were no therapists in the shadow realm, so I didn't have to feel guilty about not going.

Should I... try to seduce him?

The idea had never occurred to me before. I honestly wasn't sure I had it in me. Verity ate Shades for breakfast, but she was drop-dead gorgeous and a ray of sunshine no matter who she was speaking to.

Still, I could try. Right? There was no one around to witness my humiliation if Evrin rejected me. And he said he wasn't usually at these things, so I'd never have to see him again.

I could do this.

I could channel my inner Aphrodite, and try to get laid in this courtyard. Or at least do the Shade equivalent of getting his number.

Just... be sexy. It can't be that hard. Right?

"I don't know that the questions I have are appropriate for strangers," I said with a slightly hysterical giggle that I didn't quite tamp down in time.

Oh god, I was terrible at this.

Evrin angled himself to look at me better, and I forced myself to be brave and hold his gaze, admiring the sharp planes of his cheeks and the kind of jawline that humans paid good money for. To be honest, I'd never had a good memory for faces, and with Shades, their facial features were humanoid, but also very much not at the same time.

Aside from the dark blue eyes—which weren't an uncommon color at court—and floppy hair, I wasn't sure there was anything that would particularly make me remember this dude's face again if I ran into him around the palace.

"Hmm, not appropriate for strangers... It wouldn't be about our anatomy, would it?" he asked lazily. "I'm sure we're all curious about yours, and this supposed compatibility between us."

Alright, this was heading in the right direction. Maybe I wasn't as terrible at this as I'd assumed.

"It's hard not to be curious about that," I admitted, glancing at his claws. "We're very... fragile, compared to you."

"Everywhere?"

I *felt* his gaze on my bare legs.

"Everywhere," I confirmed. "Your claws would, um, shred us. You know. Down there."

"Well, of course. We don't use those on female Shades either. Down there."

Oh. That was reassuring to know. I'd sort of assumed female Shades' lady bits were made of more durable stuff, and I'd been worried that would make me vulnerable with a Shade partner who might not comprehend how delicate I was.

There were no human doctors here, and I didn't want to have to stitch up my own vagina.

"Is it true you can take a knot?" Evrin asked eventually.

"Is it true you *have* a knot?"

He laughed, a rich, warm sound that traveled down the length of my body. "It is."

Can I see it?

I didn't say that, of course. I just thought it. I had to work the conversation in that direction in a natural, flirtatious way that definitely involved both of us getting naked in this bush.

In the back of my mind was a small voice valiantly trying to remind me that I, a) wasn't an exhibitionist, and b) was probably just ovulating. But I ruthlessly silenced that little traitor because I didn't want to hear it.

Evrin's inhale was shamelessly deep. "What does that scent indicate? If it's mere curiosity... well, it's certainly enticing."

"It's a little more than curiosity," I admitted raspily. "But there is that, too. I won't pretend that I haven't been nervous about the logistics of it all. I'm very... intrigued about how it all works."

There was another low, rumbling laugh that seemed to come right from the depths of Evrin's chest. "That makes two of us. This is probably an incredibly inappropriate suggestion, but if you wanted to see, just for exploratory purposes—"

"Yes."

Way to play it cool, Tallulah.

My new friend—surely we were friends if he was showing me his dick—swept aside his shadows like he was opening curtains, revealing a thick, semi-hard penis lying against his thigh. I did my best to tamp down my reaction, not wanting to freak Evrin out, but I'd always been a very *visual* person.

And it was so *smooth*, disrupted only by ridged veins that I wanted to trace with my tongue.

It was the prettiest dick I'd ever seen.

"The knot forms here," Evrin said, circling a claw oh-so gently at the base of his cock. "It swells once we reach completion. With Shade partners, we pull back so that the knot is on the outside as it causes them pain without adequate preparation. But there are rumors that the Hunters can... accommodate that part of our anatomy."

"I suppose we're kind of stretchy," I replied absently, still admiring his dick. I'd been *desperate* to see what all the hype was about since the moment I got here, just not desperate enough to actually get naked with any of the Shades courting me to make it happen.

My control-top panties were growing alarmingly damp, but Ophelia had warned us that we produced extra lubricant around Shades to accommodate them. While my brain was still catching up, my vagina knew exactly what to do.

Evrin froze, his cock hardening right in front of my eyes. When he inhaled this time, there was no languid playfulness to be found, but the intensity that replaced it seemed to work just as well for me. "Your scent..."

"It's a little more than just 'fine' now?" I hazarded with a breathy laugh.

The sound he made wasn't quite a growl, but it was certainly close. It caused a faintly cramping sensation before another flood of arousal saturated the gusset of my panties.

"Can I move closer, Tallulah?"

Fuck. Me.

Just the way he said my *name* did strange things to my ovaries.

"Yes."

Evrin pushed the foliage over my head out of the way, angling his body slightly over mine, and dipping his head down while I tipped mine back so his nose could settle at the crook of my neck. His hair brushed against my jaw— the leathery texture of it oddly erotic against my skin. It was a reminder of just how very *un*human he was.

"That is..." Evrin took another long draw of my scent like he was settling down to his favorite meal at the end of a long day. "...exquisite. That answers a lot of my questions all on its own."

I laughed breathily, hyperaware of my body now that it was in such close proximity to his. The tight boning of my dress, the sudden achiness of my nipples, the increasingly sticky fabric of my panties. How long had it been since I'd had sex? Since I'd even been *touched* by someone—sexually or otherwise?

The incessant overthinking buzz in my head was blessedly quiet.

I parted my legs slightly, pheromoning all over the place, entirely aware of what I was doing. I was horny, I was attracted to Evrin's no-fucks-given attitude, and that was as deep as I needed to get.

Evrin groaned, nuzzling in a little closer. There was a faint tickle of something on my bare leg that may have been shadows, and I found myself arching into it, desperate for more.

"That's... really something," he rasped, his hands ghosting over the fabric of my dress, following the curves of my body as though he wasn't sure whether he was allowed to go any further.

"You are single, right?" I asked, squirming slightly against the cold, hard wall. I probably should have led with that question.

"Yes. Very."

"Then *please* touch me before I lose my mind."

I wasn't a small lady. I never had been, and I was completely fine with that. But it certainly sent a rush of *something* through me at the ease with which Evrin wrapped an arm around my waist and lifted me onto his lap facing him like I weighed nothing. I didn't know being tossed around was something I'd even wanted until that moment.

Evrin peered intently at me, clawed hands resting lightly on my hips as I batted vines away from our heads. "Are you sure about this?"

The fact that he *asked* only made me want him more.

"Yes. You're curious, I'm curious. I don't... expect anything from you—"

Evrin's hands were pushing my dress up over my thighs before I'd even finished speaking, and my brain went to that blissfully quiet space that I so rarely got to spend time in. There was no room for thinking when his claws were gently scraping my thighs, tugging my plain black cotton panties carefully to the side, one knuckle brushing near my clit until my hips started taking over, angling him in the right direction.

I was vaguely aware of a haze of darkness settling around us like someone had drawn a curtain of shadows for privacy. It was like a mini orgasm for my brain, which had always sought out small, dark places to relax in.

"This is incredibly disrespectful of me," Evrin murmured, not sounding entirely sorry about it. "We're mere feet away from the entire court. In public. On cold, hard ground."

"I don't mind being a little disrespected," I breathed, the tight seams of my dress stretching perilously with each movement.

Evrin made a rumbling noise of approval, watching my reactions closely as his knuckle explored. In general, it took me a few times with someone to feel confident enough to make demands of what I wanted in bed. But with Evrin, it felt like I'd skipped that first step, somehow. I boldly grabbed his wrist and guided him where I needed him, my eyes rolling back slightly the moment he brushed my clit.

"Right there," I gasped, circling my hips as I found my rhythm, vaguely aware that I was blatantly using him for my own pleasure. "A little harder."

He did exactly as I asked, watching me with a look of heated curiosity on his face that had me feeling like a goddess writhing above him. It helped that his other hand was kneading my thigh almost desperately, his smooth, dark cock standing at attention between us, the fat head of it glistening with silvery precum.

He kept inhaling deeply too, like there was nothing more satisfying than my scent.

Everything about his body language screamed that he wanted me, and it made it all feel so *easy*.

"I'm so wet," I whispered, which might have been dirty talk if I'd managed to say it in an even somewhat sexy way. Instead, I sounded confused and a little alarmed, because Ophelia's warning about "extra lubricant" really hadn't done justice to the waterfall situation that appeared to be happening between my thighs. It was *sliding* over his knuckles.

"It's your slick," Evrin replied in awe, tipping his head down to watch his hand work. "I didn't realize humans produced it."

He glanced up, his demeanor changing from obsessively horny to reassuring when he saw the look on my face.

"It's good, Tallulah." His voice was low and soothing, and the way he said my name sent a flutter through my stomach. "It means you'll be able to take me. Maybe this sweet little cunt will stretch around my knot after all."

I bit down on my lip to stifle my moans as an orgasm I didn't know I'd desperately needed bore down on me, briefly making my vision white out. The cold, hard ground and the vines determinedly tangling in my hair didn't exist. There was only Evrin, and me, and pleasure. So much pleasure, I thought I might die from it.

"I want to be inside you, Tallulah."

I made some muffled noise of agreement, clumsily pulling the fabric of my dress up over my hips—acutely aware that my underwear went up to my ribs to smooth everything out under this dress—and lifting myself up on my knees so he could line himself up at my entrance. Evrin was still holding my panties to the side, his claws perilously close to my sensitive flesh.

I'd never had sex anywhere other than on a bed, with the lights off, suitably disrobed and perfectly comfortable. Everything about this felt so... *rebellious*.

Evrin pulled me down a little, sliding the tip of his cock inside me. Even that was enough to be alarming. He was so inhuman, so *thick*.

"Easy," he murmured, one hand moving around to grip my ass, encouraging me to let gravity do the work, and I felt myself relaxing again at the smooth calmness in his voice. "Take your time. Fuck, you feel incredible. You're so slick for me. You're taking me so well."

For every quarter inch I moved, there was another compliment, and I hoarded them all greedily, hoping I'd remember every single one.

My vision blurred once I finally took all of him, the stretching sensation *just* on the right side of the pain-pleasure dichotomy.

Evrin groaned, writhing slightly beneath me. "The power coming off you... I've never felt anything like it. You're so... *decadent*."

It was borderline too many compliments. This was about sex—I didn't need to start swooning.

My fingers tightened on his shoulders as I began to move, and in the confined space, there wasn't enough room for me to do much more than roll my hips, grinding my clit against his pelvis with every motion. Evrin's hands were everywhere, the faint scrape of his claws alerting me to his movements. As addictive as his words of praise had been, the ragged, desperate attempts at keeping quiet were just as sexy.

"I shouldn't knot you here," he whispered brokenly, though the grip he had on my ass cheeks belied his words. "Someone could walk out. They could hear you. I'd kill them. I'd have to."

I clenched around him at the show of possessiveness. Why was that doing it for me? I'd never liked high-handed guys before.

"Don't pull out," I breathed, digging my blunt nails into his shoulders. "I want you to knot me. I'm on birth control. *Please*."

Evrin said something in a language I didn't recognize, though, I was pretty confident from the inflection that it was a curse word.

"Stay quiet," he growled, punctuating his words with the tiniest prick of his claws, even though he was the one who was making all the noise.

I did as I was told though, biting down hard on my lower lip to muffle the moans I couldn't let free.

I slipped a hand between us, circling my clit with practiced ease to push myself over the edge. Evrin cursed again the moment I clenched around him, roughly pulling me down as he thrust up, lodging his knot in place. At first, it wasn't *too* noticeable, and I couldn't help but wonder what all the fuss was about.

But then it kept growing.

I let out a squeak of alarm, but Evrin was entirely relaxed, tugging me forward so I was laying against his chest, my head resting on his shoulder.

"S'good," he slurred. "You're so good. Relax. I'll take care of you. Relax."

Despite my uncertainty, I found that I was able to sink into the warmth and strength of Evrin's body.

And then immediately tensed up again, because the slightest movement seemed to set off a chain of orgasms that I was helpless to stop. The thick, solid knot rubbed against my hypersensitive inner walls so perfectly that it felt like he was always meant to be there.

I hadn't *got it* before when the others talked about having their minds blown by Shade sex.

I got it now.

I totally got it.

My eyelids felt like they weighed a ton each, but I forced them open so I could stare blearily up at Evrin's face in repose. God, he was gorgeous. And the chemistry was unreal. And he had such a soothing presence and didn't seem totally put off by my high-strung nature, even though I'd made almost no effort to hide it the way I usually did.

Maybe I'd been as lucky as Ophelia had been, and met my match—the Shade who would become my mate—right away too. It was more than I had even dreamed of hoping for.

TALLULAH

CHAPTER 2

Oh my god, I need an ice bath for my lady bits," I sighed, sliding down the sofa until my legs were hanging off in a slightly ungainly manner, taking the weight off the achy parts. "We're not ever returning to the human realm, right? Can we make a pact or something? I miss Wi-Fi and I'd sell a kidney for some chicken nuggets and an icy soda, but the *sex*. I'm not going back to regular sex after that."

I fanned my face dramatically, reveling a little in the shocked looks I was getting from Ophelia, Verity, and Meera. Astrid had disappeared somewhere as she was wont to do, slinking off like an aloof house cat whenever she was in the vicinity of social interaction.

"Oh!" Ophelia said, trying to make a quick recovery. "Um, I didn't realize someone had caught your attention—"

"Who did you fuck?" Verity interrupted bluntly, dark eyes shining with interest. She didn't outright *say*, "I didn't think you had it in you," but her expression pretty clearly conveyed that sentiment. Not that she'd ever pressured me or Meera to keep up with her voracious appetites, or anything like that.

It was more that Verity seemed slightly confused about why we wouldn't just *want* to sample all the goods on offer.

And now that I'd had Shade sex, I could sort of see why. Last night had been incredible. Evrin and I had the kind of chemistry that couldn't be replicated.

It wasn't like me to be dreamy and irresponsible and hope for something as permanent as a mating bite right away, but my dreams had been filled with visions of it last night.

"I'm not going to kiss and tell," I replied primly, though my motives were a little less respectful of Evrin's privacy than I was making out. Mostly, I just wanted to keep him to myself. He wasn't a name that had come up at court, and he hadn't been one of the Shades who had congregated around us like moths to a flame in the dining hall.

He was mine, and I wanted to keep him that way.

Verity grinned at me like we were in on the same joke, and Ophelia looked so excited for me that I couldn't help but flush with pride.

I was one of *them*. I was fitting in. We were bonding.

"Fair enough." Verity grinned. "Maybe you'll see him at dinner tonight?"

"Absolutely." I smiled back, filled with confidence. He'd come so hard that it had taken us close to an hour to leave our little hidden spot in the courtyard last night, and he'd seemed practically drunk on power after feeding from me.

Evrin had made me an even more elaborate shadow covering than the one I'd arrived in, and helped me discreetly get out of the palace and back to Elverston House through an exit only the Guard used. And he'd seemed super reluctant to say goodbye. I'd gone in for a hug, and I'd definitely had something very hard and eager pressing into my stomach.

Of course, I'd see him at dinner tonight.

There was a slightly niggly feeling in the back of my mind, reminding me that I didn't actually know that much about him. He was in the Guard, and he'd indicated that he had a unique role there, but he hadn't said what. And I'd never seen him in the dining hall or anywhere around the palace.

But that was all just regular getting-to-know-you stuff that we hadn't had a chance to get to last night because I'd been busy ripping his shadows off. We'd have time for those conversations later.

"What about you?" Verity asked Meera, leaning forward in her seat. "Did anyone catch your eye?"

"Nope." I could have sworn Meera's face looked a little flush, but no one pushed her for more information. It had been clear from the moment we met that Meera was intensely private, and I trusted she'd confide in us more when she was ready. Compared to Astrid—who straight up vanished half of the time—Meera was practically an open book.

The day was a lazy one as we lounged around, debriefing after last night, and Verity lamented the pitfalls of having more than one glass of wine at a time now that she was over thirty. Eventually, the sky darkened, and the jittery nerves that had been on a low simmer all day bubbled up to the surface as we went our separate ways to get ready for dinner.

How much effort was too much effort? I didn't want to be overdressed and embarrass myself, but I did want to look *nice*.

In the end, I opted to style my hair into an updo, leaving a few loose tendrils down to frame my face and hopefully draw attention to my neck. The swishy silk skirt I picked out was the same color as the dress I'd worn last night, and I paired it with impractically sparkly heels and a pale top for more neck-emphasis action.

I was totally overdressed. I attempted to keep my makeup on the more subtle side, but I wasn't even sure I pulled that off.

It was extra—*I* was extra—but I just wanted everything to be *perfect*. For the first time, I'd found someone that I actually *liked*. The pressure was dialed all the way up to eleven not to screw this up.

"Look at you." Verity whistled as I came down the stairs, dressed from head to toe in pale pink tulle, looking like a tall, sexy glass of whipped marshmallow. "You look gorgeous."

"So do you," I replied instantly because she did—as always. "Where's Meera?"

"Waiting outside."

"Ah, right." I didn't even know why I'd asked. Meera spent more time outdoors than indoors. I didn't even bother asking where Astrid was—if she wanted to be here, she would be.

We grabbed Meera on the way to the palace, filing into the crowded dining hall and taking our usual spot all together at the front of the room.

"I think your outfit is a hit," Verity whispered, grinning at me.

"It's definitely drawing attention," I mumbled, my face warm. Why had I worn the sparkly heels? I had no choice but to own it now, but the regret was potent on the inside.

The tables were long, with benches on either side, and we had a steady rotation of Shades vying to sit close to the three of us each night. There didn't seem to be any rhyme or reason to it, but I imagined there were some internal politics at play. Like it probably made some kind of difference who your family was, and how strong you were, as if those were things that *we* cared about.

There was some jostling around us as Shades debated who was going to get the prime spots, and I discreetly glanced up through my lashes, looking for Evrin. I couldn't imagine him debating with someone for the privilege of sitting next to me, not with the cool confidence he'd displayed last night.

He'd just claim his rightful spot, and then check that it was fine by me in the sexiest way possible afterward.

But he wasn't doing that. Because he wasn't here.

He could just be running late. Don't spiral.

I smiled like I didn't have a care in the world as Phileas sat down next to me, falling over himself to compliment my dress and how pretty my hair looked tied up like this, and had I done something different with my makeup? Based on the looks they were giving me, Verity and Meera both thought Phileas was the mystery guy from last night, and I held my tongue even though I was desperate to correct them.

Most impressively, I repressed the slithering, insidious chill of rejection so thoroughly that not one Shade present so much as hinted at a sour note to my scent.

I turned to Meera midway through the meal, my cheeks aching with the effort of holding my smile in place. "Would it be super rude if I snuck off, do you think? I'm not feeling great."

"Oh! No, I'm sure that would be fine. Here, I'll walk you back—"

"No, no, that's not necessary, I promise. Stay. Enjoy the meal. I just have a headache. I think I need a lie down."

"Did you have too much wine last night, too?" Verity asked from across the table. The knowing glint in her eye made me think she was giving me an easy out on purpose, though I didn't think she knew why. She probably thought I'd just changed my mind on Phileas.

"Yeah. It must have been that," I laughed, excusing myself. Phileas stood so I could climb off the bench, gently taking my elbow to steady me, since all the Shade furniture was designed for far-taller beings than myself. "I'm so sorry to run off like this. I'll see you all later."

I scurried off rather than hanging around to hear their answer. I was already going to have to do a walk of shame down the length of the dining hall. The sooner I could get it over and done with, the better.

"Here," a member of the Guard said quietly, waving me over to a side door. "You can leave this way. I'll walk you around to the front."

Thank you, universe.

"You don't have to do that," I assured him, practically leaping for the escape from all the eyes on me, and slipping out into a corridor.

On second thoughts, he might have to show me the way out. I didn't recognize this part of the palace at all.

"I kind of do," he said sheepishly. "You're not strictly allowed in this corridor, but I'm sure the queen would argue in your favor if anyone questioned it. I'm Verner, by the way. If you'll follow me?"

"Okay, thanks. I really appreciate you helping me out."

Verner inclined his head, his mouth tilting up in a small smile before he headed off down the hallway, leaving me to power walk in his wake in my stupid, embarrassing shoes.

"I hope you enjoyed the ball last night?" Verner said politely.

"I did, thank you. Did you attend?"

God, I hoped this was a short walk because I wasn't sure I had anything left in the tank to be charming with. The urge to ask Verner if he knew fellow member of the Guard, Evrin, was overwhelming, but I managed to tamp down the impulse in an attempt to preserve the last few shreds of my dignity.

"I did," Verner replied, looking straight ahead, his tone not particularly inviting further conversation, which was just fine by me.

Maybe Evrin is working right now. Not all members of the Guard were stationed at the palace, and I'd never seen him around the place.

Or maybe he was tired after the ball and didn't feel up to socializing again so soon. He wasn't a social guy, he'd said as much.

Or maybe, Tallulah, he's just not that into you.

But no one wanted to admit that to themselves, right? The utterly despairing level of rejection that came with the thought was almost too much to bear.

Especially because I'd only met him *last night*. God, it was so like me to get hung up on a guy I'd literally just met, who'd probably forgotten my name by now.

My face burned hot at the memory of how cocky I'd been this morning. Why hadn't I just kept my stupid mouth shut? If I hadn't blathered on about what a great night I'd had with a great Shade, the others would be none the wiser. They'd be tactful because they always were, but the humiliation was going to haunt me in the early hours of the morning for the rest of my life.

Verner left me at the border of Elverston House with another discreet nod before heading back to the palace, and I grabbed my stuff from my bedroom before making a beeline for the thermal pools under the house.

It was a whole bathroom complex down here, with private water closets built into the walls around the edges, and enormous steaming pools in the middle, with only just enough orb light to illuminate the space.

I wanted this outfit off me. I wanted to scrub the makeup off my face and pretend this stupid updo had never existed. I wanted to wallow in the hot pool and my shame.

Maybe I wanted to cry a little bit, too.

Not over a guy I'd only met twenty-four hours ago. That would be stupid.

Right?

Right.

I was crying for other, unrelated reasons. Probably.

By the time I emerged from the bathing chamber, Verity was already back from dinner and on her way down to wash.

"There you are! How are you feeling?" she asked, pulling me into a hug on the landing.

"Much better, thank you. Maybe I was just feeling overstimulated or something."

She nodded sagely. "Was the guy from last night at dinner? I thought at first it was Phileas, but you didn't seem that jazzed to be talking to him."

"Didn't I?" Shoot, I'd probably offended him as well, and Phileas was perfectly nice.

"No, I mean, you were your usual bubbly self," Verity said hurriedly. "You just didn't seem *into* him."

If only. If only I could like someone as straightforward and readily available as Phileas.

"Unfortunately not. The guy from last night wasn't there." I laughed brightly, batting my eyelashes playfully at her. "Guess I was just too much for him to handle."

Meera wouldn't have been convinced by my bravado, but it worked a treat on Verity. Probably because she *was* a bright, bubbly force of nature, and undoubtedly had been considered too much to handle by lesser mortals plenty of times in her life.

She wore that like armor, though. I wore it like a hair shirt.

Verity grinned. "Then, no great loss, right?"

"Right," I agreed, impressed that my voice didn't waver. "No great loss."

CHAPTER 3

How was the ball?" Caius asked, blowing a smoke ring before finally handing the pipe over, the show-off.

It was absurdly cold out here in his overgrown garden at the base of a mountain, but he never invited me inside the small cottage, no matter how frigid the air became.

I suspected he was ashamed of it. A one-room dwelling in a cold, damp, miserable area of the realm hadn't been what Caius had envisioned for his future.

It was probably what he had envisioned for mine.

"It was good." *Excellent. Best sex of my life.* I wasn't telling my brother that, though. I wasn't telling *anyone* about that. That knowledge was just for me.

There weren't that many ex-Hunters in the shadow realm. It wouldn't be difficult to figure out who I'd spent those blissful few hours with, and I'd feel like a real prick if Tallulah's reputation was hurt by association. Especially when she'd so generously used me to sate her curiosity, not to mention feeding me so well that I'd had to go siphon at the energy stores last night before the jittering got out of control.

Caius stared at me while I took a long drag of the pipe, letting the flux moss blunt the edges of the desperate desire I had to see her again.

"Good? How could it have been good? Wasn't it a ball at the *palace*? Surely, you didn't show yourself inside. You'd send half the guests running in fright," he added with a scoff.

"I was mostly outside, keeping watch from the courtyard."

"Staring longingly through the window, you mean?" Caius asked snidely. He hadn't always been like this. The Caius of my childhood had been distant and aloof, but fair. "Was *he* there?"

"I didn't look."

I'd diligently *not* looked. Our middle brother would be expected to attend these events, having won the family seat, but I went out of my way to avoid him. It wasn't as though we'd been close before, but I was still saddened to see what Roan had become. To see what the once good relationship between Caius and Roan had become.

Undoubtedly, Roan felt pity when it came to me and the position I'd chosen in the Guard, but I'd never had the luxury of choices that they'd had. The Guard gave me somewhere to live, provided for all of my needs.

I had plenty to be grateful for.

"Fuck him," Caius muttered under his breath, glaring into the middle distance. We both knew he was waiting for the herbs to kick in and transport his mind away from those unhappy memories. Away from the life he'd been denied.

I hummed in agreement because it was easier, as though Caius had any interest in spending time with me before he'd fallen out with Roan.

"Are you going to start going to court stuff now?" Caius asked, his voice laced with suspicion. "You never bothered with the events before. Is this because of those Hunters that came over? You know none of them will want you, right?"

You're curious, I'm curious. I don't expect anything from you.

"That goes without saying." She'd laid it out explicitly, and I was more than grateful for what I'd had.

Grateful, and a little guilty. Tallulah hadn't been able to see in the low lighting, obscured by the bushes, how malformed I was. If she'd known just what kind of Shade she was letting touch her perfect body, she'd be horrified. In hindsight, I almost wished I'd given her a different name, on the off chance she asked about me and someone told her how repulsive I was. Or worse, insinuated that somehow *she* was repulsive for letting me touch her.

On the other hand, I couldn't stomach the thought of her calling me by any other name.

Caius nodded absently, the flux moss finally kicking in. "Good. Obviously, I don't need to tell you this, but absolutely nothing good in life comes from wanting more. Settle for what you have, Evrin."

While I didn't disregard Caius's words—he'd seen firsthand what life was like living with the fate I'd been handed—I couldn't bring myself to stay away from Tallulah entirely. I wasn't hoping for more. I *was* settled with what I had.

I just needed to see Tallulah sometimes. After she'd confided in me— perhaps in more detail than she'd intended—about how she felt in front of others, I couldn't help but worry almost every single second that I wasn't with her that she was struggling.

Logically, I understood that she didn't want my support. That she'd just been sating her curiosity on me.

And yet, I couldn't stay away.

I lingered as far away as I could outside the palace while still being able to see the front steps where Tallulah would exit after breakfast to head back to Elverston House.

The mere proximity to her seemed to help with what I could only describe as withdrawals. It was not a sensation I'd ever experienced before—I didn't depend on others. But I'd also fed incredibly thoroughly on Tallulah, which perhaps had created this strong *need* to be in her presence. Power was intoxicating, after all.

Usually, Tallulah emerged arm-in-arm with one of the others, laughing loudly, her blue eyes sparkling. She had a laugh that was somehow delicate and robust all at once. I could have listened to it all day, but I never forgot that it might be a front—she'd admitted at the ball how much worry was hiding beneath that cheerful expression. But I suspected that when she was with the other Hunters, her smiles were mostly genuine. It was from my fellow Shades that the expectations came.

Today, Tallulah didn't emerge with the others. She didn't emerge at all, not until the breakfast crowd had cleared entirely, and even then she seemed to be dragging her feet, twisting the fabric of her dark purple dress before seemingly forcing herself to release the material and smoothing it down.

Tallulah paused at the top of the stairs, her fingers flexing restlessly at her sides, looking around as though she was searching for something. My mind supplied an image of the small gap in the bushes she'd discovered at the ball to squeeze into.

She'd looked like this then too, the moment she'd come out in the courtyard while I'd been watching her from between the leaves.

My feet were moving before I'd even consciously made a decision to speak to her. Fortunately, since the breakfast crowd had dissipated, no one saw me approach her. Tallulah was clearly having a tough enough time without *that* indignity on top.

"Do you need a moment?" I asked her as gently as I could, though she still jumped when I saw her. I braced myself for her rejection—especially seeing me as I was in broad daylight—but Tallulah just gave me a strained nod, her eyes wide and a little frantic. Her scent wasn't quite signaling alarm, but it wasn't entirely content either.

I ushered Tallulah down the steps, intending to lead her into the mazelike gardens that extended out in front of the palace, spreading out toward the barracks. They were perfectly manicured, and the plants were cut low—no good for a Shade wanting to hide away from the world, but Tallulah was significantly shorter than most Shades. I could find her a little spot to squeeze into.

"No," Tallulah rasped, grabbing my elbow and tugging me toward the portal. "Can we go in here? Just for a moment?"

"Into the in-between?"

Tallulah nodded. It would definitely be easier for her not to be seen with me if we were in the dark, though it pricked at the remnants of an ego I had thought long since dead.

Regardless, if that was what Tallulah wanted, that's what I would give her. I switched our positions, so I was gently holding her elbow instead, and guided us through the portal, plunging us into darkness. Although it had been her idea, I was still inhaling deeply, searching for the fear or discomfort that I was certain would come at being alone with a relative stranger in the dark, but it never came.

I navigated the dark expanse with ease, taking us to a spot that I rested at during my long shifts. The caspite that made up the in-between responded to me, pressing in close in a way that most Shades found oppressive, but I was used to.

Tallulah sucked in a breath, and I watched, entranced, as she reached out, her delicate fingers grasping at nothing. She could *feel* the darkness pressing in, expanding into every space it could fill, but it wasn't solid enough to touch.

"Here," I said, lightly tugging on Tallulah's arm, encouraging her to sit. This was a quiet area that wasn't on any main travel routes. I'd never been bothered here. To my shock, instead of sitting opposite me as I'd expected, the moment I was on the ground, Tallulah crawled into my lap. Then again, perhaps I shouldn't have been shocked. She'd liked the confined nature of the spot she'd found at the ball, and the in-between was anything but confined.

My arms weren't, though.

I pulled her crossways on my lap, cradling her in my arms, marveling at the way she seemed to fit so perfectly. Tallulah hummed softly, nuzzling her head into the crook of my neck as though it was always meant to be there, sighing happily when I cocooned us in a layer of my own shadows. We both shuddered at the sensation of my power brushing her bare skin. I didn't know how it felt for her, but for me it felt... possessive. Like Tallulah was mine, and I had the right to cover her in my shadows whenever I pleased.

I didn't, but in the peace and privacy of the darkness, with Tallulah's inferior human eyesight, it didn't matter that I was a damaged third son, or that half the realm was terrified of me. My arms were strong enough to hold her, and my shadows were dense enough to surround her, and Tallulah was content with that.

"It's not too much?" I asked, aware of just how dark it was here. Even many Shades would find it eerie.

"Not at all." Tallulah sighed peacefully, the sour edge of her scent slowly disappearing.

"Have you always liked sitting in dark places?"

Tallulah laughed, and I fought down a tremor of desire as she inadvertently rubbed against me. "Yes, actually. I have a very restless mind, and when I'm squished up somewhere and I can't see anything... I don't know. I can't explain it. Maybe it's just the lack of stimulus. It gives my head a break. Um, I'm sorry for climbing all over you. I didn't even realize I was doing it—"

"Don't apologize." My arms tightened around her reflexively. "You like confined places. This is confined. Did something happen at breakfast?"

"No. Not really?" Her laugh was a little more uncertain this time. "I don't know why I'm like this. Sometimes there's no tangible reason."

"That's okay. There doesn't need to be."

Tallulah's scent sweetened instantly, a soft smile lighting up her face as she peered up at me in the dark. She was so beautiful, it was almost painful to look at her.

"Won't the others be looking for you?" I asked, trying and failing to remember the other Hunters' names.

"It'll be fine. We don't, like, report on our movements or anything to each other."

"Perhaps you should?" I suggested mildly. "You're in a foreign land, after all. It would be best practice to have some kind of security measures in place to keep yourselves safe."

Frankly, I was disappointed that the king hadn't suggested such a thing himself, though, I suspected he was so eager to keep the Hunters here that he'd give them as much leeway as they desired to do whatever they wished.

"It's probably not the worst idea," Tallulah agreed thoughtfully. "Though I think we're all very conscious of not... being in each other's business while we adjust to life here."

The expression was a human one, but I got the gist. It was interesting that they felt the need to be reserved even with each other, given that they were all experiencing this strange change in circumstances together. Then again, perhaps they were all mingling with shamefully undesirable Shades too, and didn't want the others to know.

"Words are easy, but for what it's worth, you're always safe with me, Tallulah. Even out here. Especially out here."

I wished I understood the look on her face and the nuances of her scent—though it was so muddled today that I had no idea what to make of it. Oddly, there was something not unlike what her desire had smelled like. I wish I knew her well enough to ascertain what the other notes were.

"I know. I don't know *how* I know, but I believe that. You do have a very calming... aura or something. I can't explain it. I feel safe in your presence, for sure."

It was the highest compliment I'd ever received.

"Why did you say *especially* in here?" Tallulah asked after a moment's silence. I suspected that the chatter was also one of her techniques to find a sense of calm, and while I wasn't naturally verbose, I could indulge for her sake.

"This is my domain. I patrol the in-between."

"Alone?"

"Not entirely. But mostly, yes."

"Wow. That sounds... You must be really good at your job."

"I am." It wasn't arrogance, it was honesty. I didn't always get it right, but that I could even stand to be in here for as long as I was... Well, that was its own kind of achievement.

For some reason, it was *that* which had Tallulah's scent sweetening. And then sweetening a little more. Rather than lying still and relaxed, she was suddenly squirming slightly in my hold, though she seemed to be trying to get closer rather than to get away.

I inhaled deeply, selfishly, wanting to commit Tallulah's scent to memory. I couldn't let myself believe that it meant anything beyond a desire for a physical release, but if Tallulah asked for it, I would give her as many of those as she desired.

"I guess there's no point trying to be discreet about it since my scent is probably giving it away," Tallulah said with an awkward laugh. "But don't feel like you have to do anything. I can just ignore it. Or you can take me back if it's bothering you—"

"It's not bothering me," I interrupted, appalled that she would even consider that. "Did you want to... explore again?"

I wanted to get under that pretty purple dress more than I'd ever wanted anything in my life, but I wanted Tallulah to set the pace.

"Is that something you'd like to do with me again? Explore?" she asked slowly. Cautiously, even.

I blinked at the question. Was that not obvious?

"More than anything."

Tallulah hummed. "Me too. I just don't want our *exploring* to affect you negatively, you know what I mean? I don't want to get in your way."

"In the way of what?" The question *felt* like a trap, but I couldn't quite figure out where the spring was. Did she want me to say out loud that no one wanted me? It was the truth, but I also had some pride. Then again, that didn't seem like the kind of request sweet Tallulah would make.

"You know. A relationship, or whatever."

"I've never had a relationship before. I don't foresee that changing," I told her honestly. As far as Shades went, I was no prize. "It wouldn't be compatible with my job, anyway."

There was a long pause and Tallulah's scent grew muddled again.

"Okay," she said eventually, speaking slowly as though she was choosing her words carefully. "But you want to *explore* with me."

"If that's something you want, I will be available to you for as long as you're willing."

Tallulah hummed before settling back against me, which had to be a positive, didn't it? She was relaxing. Relaxed was good.

I wished *I* felt relaxed, but there was a weight pressing on my shoulders that I couldn't quite shake.

"Alright," Tallulah said with renewed confidence. "We could be, like, friends with benefits, I guess?"

"Of course. This way you can build your confidence with me while you continue to get to know all the Shades that are undoubtedly throwing themselves in your path."

I, in no way, expected any kind of exclusivity from a woman who was being courted by all the finest Shades in the realm. I'd take what I could get of her presence for as long as I could get it. I wasn't even sure how the situation had arisen that she was remotely considering *me* to sate her curiosity.

I had to assume that it was only because she knew there was no risk of me expecting anything more, as I was so clearly beneath her notice. Maybe that was why, with me, she didn't experience those sudden panics.

In a way I hadn't expected, I was *safe* for her.

"Okay..." She hesitated for a moment before clearing her throat, a burst of sexual confidence seeming to bloom out of nowhere. It was incredible to witness. "I don't suppose there are any beds in the in-between?"

Shit.

I couldn't take her back to the barracks. We'd have to go down a long corridor past every other Guard member's door. It would be disastrous for Tallulah's reputation.

"Unfortunately not, though I can do my best to make you comfortable here?" I said, expending a little more energy to shroud us more tightly in shadows before lying back on the ground so Tallulah would be spared the cold surface. She startled before laughing lightly, adjusting her position so her legs straddled my hips, hands planted on my chest.

"I'm not crushing you?" she asked. I did my best not to take the question as a personal insult to my strength. I may not have all the features that other Shades had, but I was still more than capable of carrying her.

"Of course not."

She hummed, her fingertips confidently exploring my chest in a way I wasn't sure she would have done if there was light in here.

"And no one is going to see us here? Isn't it basically a highway?"

"I wouldn't have suggested it if I wasn't one-hundred-percent sure of my ability to keep you safe," I assured her. "I spend more time in the in-between than anyone else in the realm. No one knows it better than me."

This particular spot was mine in all but name. No one came here but me.

I'd never brought anyone else here either.

"Well, if we're definitely alone..." Tallulah leaned in, her lips tracing the edge of my jaw before moving up, leaving a trail of soft kisses up to the corner of my mouth. "I wonder if Shades kiss like humans kiss."

I held myself perfectly still as she moved over my mouth, her lips soft and plush compared to my thin, hard ones.

"Tallulah..." I murmured. "My teeth."

"I'll be careful," she whispered against me, sucking my lower lip lightly into her mouth before biting down gently with blunt, harmless teeth. I bucked up against her, my hands gripping her hips the only thing preventing her from being thrown off.

"Give me your tongue," Tallulah demanded in a seductive rasp. I did as she ordered—I'd do anything she ordered—my shadows spiking eagerly, as her tongue stroked against mine. It was the most erotic experience I'd ever had.

In my bliss, I didn't notice as Tallulah's hands moved up the sides of my face, sliding into my hair. No. It was only when her thumbs brushed the stumps where my horns had failed to grow that I realized what was going on.

We froze at the same time, breaking apart. Tallulah's eyes grew wide in the darkness as she slowly moved her hands back down to rest on my shoulders.

"Sorry," Tallulah said awkwardly. She must have assumed that there was nothing beneath my hair in the way that human heads were entirely smooth.

"Don't worry about it," I mumbled, distracting her by kneading at the tight muscles in her back with my thumb knuckles.

"Oh, that feels so nice," she moaned, arching her back at my touch. "You're so good at that."

I tugged her dress up a little with each movement until my claws were catching on the delicate fabric of the panties stretched tight across her exquisite ass.

I'd wanted to distract her from the disaster that was my horns, to get her back to enjoying each other, and it appeared to be working.

But there was no pretending anymore. Tallulah knew exactly how broken I was.

CHAPTER 4

It was *deeply* unfair that Evrin's hands could feel this good, that his *tongue* could feel this good, that his body felt like it was meant to wrap around mine, but he wasn't mine and I couldn't keep him.

I mean, this was better than nothing, but with each kneading grasp of his hands on my ass, I was acutely aware that I was on the fast track to get my heart broken.

The sex might be worth it, though.

I sat back, carefully unzipping my dress and pulling it over my head with as much grace as I could manage.

"I want you all the way naked this time," Evrin growled, gently lifting me off him so I could undress. How good could Shades see in the dark? I felt like he wasn't getting my best angles lying prone on the ground while I yanked my panties off.

But the way Evrin grabbed me and pulled me back onto him like he was missing me already made me forget all about it.

I was dripping slick and immediately sought the friction I was craving, grinding my clit down on his hard length. Free from the tight confines of my bra, my breasts swung forward, and with a growl that rumbled all the way down to my toes, Evrin grabbed them, leaning up to toy with my nipples using his rough tongue.

This angle would be tricky if he had horns, I thought absently. Depending on the shape of them, there was a good chance he'd be impaling me in the throat right now.

I had no idea why Evrin didn't have horns, and I felt bad that I'd inadvertently drawn attention to something he was clearly self-conscious about, but his lack of them didn't bother me at all.

I gasped at the dual sensation of pricking claws and scraping teeth on my delicate flesh, coating Evrin in another gush of slick.

"Sit your cunt on my face, Tallulah."

I nearly fainted.

"I'll crush you—"

He didn't even let me finish making my excuses. He simply grabbed me by my hips and hauled me up his body until my knees straddled his head.

Another no-horns perk.

In the end, I didn't really need to lower myself enough to worry about crushing him, because Evrin's tongue was *so* long that he had no problem getting exactly where he needed to go.

I cupped my breasts, my hair tickling the middle of my spine as I tipped my head back, shamelessly grinding on Evrin's tongue like I owned it. The darkness helped, but mostly, it was just Evrin. There was just something about him that made me feel ridiculously at ease with myself.

The rough, insistent pressure of his tongue combined with the angle had me reaching my peak in an embarrassingly short amount of time. While I'd mostly gotten over my self-consciousness about the position we were in, it flared back to life in full force as I drenched Evrin's chin in slick, and I immediately climbed off him, shifting down his body on my knees.

"Are you okay—"

"I want you to do that several more times. But right now, I need to be inside you."

Sounded like a plan to me.

I threw my leg over his hips, not relishing the idea of being on top when my thighs were already jelly, but also not wanting to lie down on the hard, cold ground.

Fortunately, Evrin seemed more than willing to do the work as I slid down on his cock, lifting me easily, his claws digging into my hips. I braced myself with my palms on his chest, my own nails doing their valiant best to gouge his thick skin as I clung on for dear life, a vicious orgasm doing its best to drag me under despite my best efforts to hold it at bay a little longer.

I didn't want this to end. I wanted this to go on forever.

Unfortunately, there was absolutely no holding back the moment I heard Evrin's low, masculine moan. The sound of his pleasure seemed to travel directly through my ears and down my body, shoving me abruptly over the edge.

For a brief moment, the pitch black in-between seemed to glow. Even my skin felt supercharged—everything was too sensitive and just right all at once. Evrin's knot swelled as he came, and I sobbed slightly at the welcome stretch.

I felt so full, so connected to him in every way.

Evrin pulled me forward so I was draped over his body, and the movement set off another chain of orgasms. There was no post-sex awkwardness. There was no room for anything but the kind of pleasure that made us forget who and where we were.

"You're so addictive," I mumbled into his chest, immediately mortified at the slip.

"So are you," Evrin replied, claws tickling my back.

"Are you okay?" I asked when he shuddered beneath me, his jaw tightening for a moment before he relaxed again.

"I am," he assured me, stroking my spine again. "The power I get from feeding on you is... overwhelming. I'll need to go and siphon directly."

"Is it hurting you?" I asked, alarmed. "Ophelia didn't mention *that* side effect."

Evrin snorted. "I wouldn't say hurting, but I don't have room to hold this level of power within me. The king has a far deeper well to fill than I do. You don't need to worry about it, Tallulah. Once I siphon, I'll feel fine. And the realm's stores will be much healthier for it."

"Glad to be of service," I laughed. And I genuinely meant it, though, my motives for getting Evrin naked weren't exactly altruistic.

I suspected we were both lingering—probably for different reasons— but Evrin was clearly getting increasingly uncomfortable as the need to siphon weighed down on him, and he was due to start his shift soon.

"We really need to get you back before your friends send out a search party," he muttered, helping me to my feet. Although my clothes were obviously a foreign concept to him—especially my industrial-sized minimizer bra—he carefully pulled everything right side out and shook them flat before passing them to me to put on.

My underwear was ruined the instant I put it on, soaked through with slick and cum. I was going to have to go and wash the moment I was back in Elverston House.

"It's so nice in here," I said, stepping into my dress and pulling it up my body. "Like a little bubble away from… well, everything. Not that I necessarily *need* that," I added hastily, not wanting to come across like I was complaining. "I'm very grateful to have a home here in the shadow realm at all."

"A home seems like the least we can provide, considering what you're giving in return," Evrin scoffed. "And Elverston House is hardly luxurious accommodations—at least what I've seen of it from the outside. May I carry you?"

The question gave me whiplash.

"Can you?" I asked dubiously.

I couldn't see his face, but I could *sense* that the question offended him. Evrin made a show of sweeping me off my feet, scooping me into his arms bridal style like it was nothing.

I barely muffled my shriek of surprise, throwing my arms around his neck and holding on tightly. Though, as he began walking us through the darkness, it didn't *seem* like he was having any difficulty carrying me.

My scent was probably announcing loudly and proudly how much I was enjoying this.

"You're really strong."

"Yes," Evrin agreed. I was pretty sure there was a teeny hint of smugness in there, though he was being very gentlemanly about it.

He put me down gingerly as we approached the portal in front of the palace, his hands lingering before he pulled them away. I didn't quite experience the sting of rejection that I had when he hadn't appeared at dinner, but there was a little sliver of *something* unpleasant.

"I'll walk ahead," Evrin said. "That'll clear the way for you to follow."

"Why?" I asked, slightly alarmed. "Are you going to threaten them or something?"

Evrin let out a startled laugh. "No, nothing so extreme. Shades tend to avoid me, that's all."

It seemed too rude to ask why, so I kept my mouth shut, but I was definitely a little baffled by it. Evrin seemed friendly enough, albeit a little introverted. He was certainly a lot more even-keeled than many of the Shades I'd encountered here at court.

"So, um. Until next time, I guess?" I said with my brightest, most charming laugh.

"Whenever you want me," Evrin agreed simply, before disappearing out through the portal.

I waited a few seconds—just enough time to work myself up into a state—before following, finding the pathway completely empty, just as Evrin had predicted. It didn't quite feel like the walk of shame as I made my way back to Elverston House because I wasn't ashamed. I was maybe a smidge resentful, though.

What was wrong with me that it would be so terrible to be seen walking around with me? I wasn't some great beauty or anything, but plenty of Shades at court were interested in me. I wasn't a complete bridge troll.

I wanted Evrin. I wanted the chemistry we had, and the sense of peace I experienced around him, and the unfiltered conversations we had.

But I wanted him to want *me* just as much, and given how easily he'd agreed to a nonexclusive, sex-only arrangement...

I was definitely going to get my heart broken, and I wasn't strong enough to stop it.

Shit, shit, shit.

Austin was here.

My cousin had stumbled into the shadow realm—drunk and a little stupid—and I'd made such a poor impression in front of the royal Shades when I was explaining about his career and our family relationship. Plus, I'd probably offended Austin, who didn't deserve it, even if he was a bit rash and impulsive sometimes.

"Are you okay?" Meera asked, gently touching my arm. I startled back before pasting a bright smile on my face.

"Of course." I forced out a laugh. "It's just so on-brand for Austin to show up here like this. I can't believe I was surprised. I should have seen it coming."

Meera nodded, seeing more than I wanted her to see. "Why don't you go for a walk? That always clears your head."

If my face went crimson at the reminder of the almost daily "walks" I'd been going on, Meera politely didn't call me out on it. Instead, I just nodded and scampered away to the garden, knowing that if I just found a little corner in the garden to be anxious in, Evrin would find his way to me. He always did. I suspected he kept a closer eye on me than I realized he did, but just always far enough away that no one would see us together.

When we were together, that was fine. I wasn't thinking about anything except Evrin when it was just the two of us.

It was on my own that my head started to get all loud and questiony.

Like maybe I didn't entirely *love* being a dirty little secret. Maybe it would be nice to be able to walk into dinner with Evrin, hand-in-hand, the way the king and queen did. Or even just to walk next to each other, lovingly eye fucking the whole time, the way Soren and Astrid did.

But those things weren't on the cards for me and it would be stupid to dwell on them.

I huddled underneath something that vaguely resembled a small willow tree that did nothing to give me the sense of dark confinement I wanted, but it was as good as it was going to get in the palace gardens, which were always well maintained for security purposes.

"Hey." I exhaled in relief as Evrin poked his head through the hanging branches, giving me a bemused look. His hair flopped forward, hiding what I now knew to be stumps where his horns should have been. He was clearly self-conscious about it, and while it seemed a little crazy in hindsight that I hadn't noticed his lack of horns before I'd touched his head, I still struggled to be mindful of that fact.

He looked so attractive, just as he was. Who cared if he didn't have horns?

"This can't be working for you," Evrin said, his voice filled with a soft affection that made my heart melt as he gestured at the far too-open space I was attempting to disassociate in.

"Not even a little."

"Come on, then. I'll meet you down by the entry room by the barracks."

I all but squealed at the prospect of my Evrin fix, giving him a small head start before meandering down there myself.

The moment I had the door shut behind me, Evrin was on me. I squeal-laughed as he hoisted me into the air, pressing my back against the dark wall of the entry room and dipping his nose to my neck to inhale deeply.

Maybe this will be the moment he loses control and bites me, I thought hopefully, somewhat aware of how deranged the idea was, but not dismissing it from my mind.

"I missed you," he murmured, securing me a little tighter in his grip before pulling me off the wall and strolling into the in-between. I wrapped my legs as tightly around his waist as I could get them, slick already pooling in my panties just from the fact that he was holding me.

Not to mention the words. *I missed you.* That had to mean something, right? He wouldn't have said that to just anyone.

"I missed you too," I replied, my voice muffled as I hid my face in his neck, hoping the desperation in my voice wasn't as all-consuming as it was in my head. "I hoped you would come and find me."

It was a vulnerable admission—one I'd never made out loud, even though this was the way we always operated—but I pushed myself to make it. I wanted to be vulnerable with him. I wanted to show him that I was emotionally invested in him, and hopefully, he'd feel safe being emotionally invested in me in return.

"You don't mind that I seek you out?" Evrin asked.

"No, never."

I could have sworn he exhaled a little.

Evrin walked us farther into the darkness while I toyed with the hair at the back of his head, careful not to stray anywhere near the stumps of his horns.

He didn't give me a second to adjust once he found the spot he was looking for. The moment we arrived, he was lowering me onto my back, pushing both my dress and my knees up around my shoulders.

Lordy.

The next time I sought Evrin out, I was going to stretch my hamstrings first.

"Need to taste you," Evrin muttered roughly, his claws scraping over my hips as he shoved my panties to my knees, leaving my legs slightly bound. Historically—pre-Evrin—I'd considered myself pretty vanilla. Missionary with the lights off. Maybe on my hands and knees if the room was dark enough.

Now, I was wondering what it would be like to be bound up a little tighter. To have my legs pinned open, or my wrists tied above my head, or what the panties constricting my legs would feel like shoved in my mouth.

Perhaps it was because Evrin made me feel so safe. With him, I wouldn't mind trying things that I'd have found too risky and uncontrolled with someone else.

"Hold your knees," he ordered in a rough voice that sent my slick running. "Keep them out of the way so I can work."

Yes, sir, I said in my head, blinking up into the darkness.

My eyes rolled back in my head the second that long, slightly rough tongue made contact with my clit, the sounds of my slick adding to the general air of depravity. Evrin groaned, claws digging into the backs of my thighs.

"Your taste... you are exquisite," Evrin rasped brokenly before resuming his feast. I found myself reaching for his head automatically before remembering and pulling back at the last second, resuming my hold on the back of my knees.

Evrin ate pussy like it was his job. It almost set off my irrational-jealousy alarm, because how did he get this good? No one had ever eaten me like I was dessert before.

Maybe this was why I'd gotten so absurdly attached to him so quickly. The sex was *life-changing*.

The first orgasm was like sinking into a hot bath after a long day, but the second was almost vicious—tearing me apart and putting me back together all at once.

"Please," I sobbed, not caring how desperate I looked because it was precisely as desperate as I felt. "I need you inside me."

"One more on my tongue," Evrin demanded before sucking slightly on my clit, the wicked points of his teeth pressing against my most sensitive flesh without breaking it.

I was entirely lost to pleasure. I let out a somewhat undignified shriek before clapping a hand over my mouth, my legs kicking out as much as they could with my panties still around my knees and Evrin's hands pinning them in place. Maybe it was because I was so overstimulated already, but for a brief moment, I was worried I'd come so hard I was going to cry.

"That's it, that's it. You're okay, I've got you."

I clung to Evrin as he pulled me up and onto his lap, his cock thick and heavy between my thighs, though he made no move to do anything about it.

I did, though.

It wasn't just that I was horny. I fucking *needed* him. I needed to be connected to him. I needed to feel him inside me. It was the most visceral, intense craving I'd ever had in my life.

Mine. Evrin was mine. I felt that in my very bones.

I reached between us, barely able to lift myself on my jelly-like legs, and wrapped my hand around his cock, giving it a gentle squeeze.

The sounds he made were *so* gratifying. Evrin wasn't shy about letting me know if something felt good.

Gravity did the work for me as I sank down on his cock, my eyes rolling all the way back into the recesses of my brain at the sudden stretch. I wrapped one arm around his neck to keep myself steady, but couldn't quite drag the other one away from my clit, despite how overstimulated my nerves had been just a few seconds ago.

"You're so fucking sexy, Tallulah," Evrin growled, his eyes casting a faint dark blue glow over my steadily moving hand. "I could watch you play with your cunt all day."

That can be arranged, I almost said, before reining in my clingy thoughts at the last minute.

I lifted myself up on my knees, hoping my glutes played ball so I could ride Evrin the way he deserved after the best oral of my life, but I didn't even have to try. He immediately took over, claws digging into the flesh of my ass as he bounced me on his lap, setting a far-faster pace than I'd have ever managed in this position.

My already limited vision in the in-between went hazy around the edges as pleasure barreled into me from all sides. Evrin's body was warm and solid against mine, his arms around me giving me that confined feeling I always sought out. I was surrounded by him, *filled* by him, and dangerously at risk of falling in love with him.

And it was that terrifying thought that tipped me over the edge. Evrin groaned as I clenched around him, the base of his knot swelling instantly, dragging us closer together and keeping us that way.

If only I could keep him forever.

TALLULAH

CHAPTER 5

T hat was... really something," Meera laughed as we made our way back from dinner. Austin's arrival in the shadow realm—the first Hunter dude to show up here—had caused quite the stir. At one point during the meal, I'd half expected his admirers to serve him up on a platter to be feasted upon. "Has Austin always been so charismatic?"

"Yes," I responded instantly, my head filled with memories of all the performances he'd made us sit through over the years at family parties, right from toddlerhood. "Tonight was probably weird for him, and I wish he was staying at Elverston House so we could talk about it, but I doubt he had any trouble with the attention part. He's always handled that really well."

"That must be nice," Meera murmured a little wistfully.

"Right?"

She shot me a slightly bemused look. It was gratifying to know that I was pulling off my confident act so well that Meera hadn't even seen through it, and she was one of my closest friends here.

"Wait up!" Verity called, jogging to catch up with us after lingering in the dining hall to chat to her fan club. That she was running on an uneven cobblestone path in heels only held up by ribbons around her ankles was honestly one of the most impressive things I'd ever seen.

"Thanks," she panted as she caught up to where Meera and I were waiting for her, immediately linking arms with both of us. "My feet are fucking killing me. Hey, your cousin was on fire at dinner tonight, huh?"

"That's Austin," I agreed wryly. I wasn't jealous or anything. Or, at least, I wasn't jealous that he'd been surrounded by eager suitors. Maybe I was a little jealous that he'd literally stumbled into the shadow realm, drunk off his face, and immediately seemed to be right at home here.

"Are you alright?" Verity asked, tugging me up a little where our arms were joined. "Are you limping?"

"No," I replied, maybe a little too quickly. "I mean, I have a blister," I lied.

In reality, my inner thighs were burning from the "walk," I'd taken earlier, and I'd spent all afternoon trying not to hum to myself like a woman who'd just had the best sex of her life and couldn't tell anybody about it.

Not that I *couldn't* tell Meera and Verity. We were very different people, and we didn't always understand each other, but we supported one another. I doubted that either of them would judge my decision to have a low-key fuck-buddy arrangement.

The problem was that I was judging myself, just a little bit.

Which was stupid. I'd proposed the setup, and the sex was incredible, and Evrin was kind and considerate and attractive, and I liked being in his presence.

That was the problem.

I was just self-aware enough to know what they'd say if I vocalized all those thoughts out loud.

It sounds like you really like him.

Is this a good idea?

Aren't you worried you're going to catch feelings?

I just don't want you to get hurt.

They were all very valid points and I didn't want to hear them.

I would just dive in headfirst with the guy who'd explicitly said he didn't do relationships and hope for the best. It wasn't like I was going to try to change his mind or anything—that would be selfish of me. I just wanted to enjoy his presence for as long as I could have it, knowing I wouldn't be able to keep him.

And if he *happened* to fall madly in love with me in the process, well, I could definitely work with that.

Verity headed downstairs to bathe when we got home, and I went straight to the kitchen to get the fire going. I suspected there were vents of some kind piped through the house from the kitchen hearth, because the bedrooms were warmer when I got the fire going overnight.

Meera trailed along after me, which I hadn't expected. But maybe she was in the mood for more company than usual. I was happy to help with that.

"How was your walk this morning?" Meera asked as I pulled kindling out of the giant basket in the corner, stacking it in the hearth. "It's so great that you've been going out each day and exploring. So brave. I feel like I've barely been anywhere."

This was probably the point where I'd suggest she accompany me next time if I was actually going on walks and not sneaking to the in-between to have my brains railed out of my skull.

"It looks like you've been spending a lot of time in the garden," I replied instead, focusing a little harder than strictly necessary on nurturing the little flame I was getting going.

"I have been enjoying spending time in the garden." She cleared her throat almost a little sheepishly, though, I couldn't tell what could possibly be embarrassing about pulling weeds. "Was that Shade from the ball at dinner tonight? I keep meaning to ask if you've seen him around yet."

I choked on my own saliva. "I don't think he eats in the dining hall."

"Oh." Meera's face was full of understanding. If my mystery midnight courtyard lover didn't seek me out in the dining hall, it was because he wasn't interested in pursuing something with me. That was how it worked here.

"How are you feeling about that?" Meera asked with about as much tact as she could, considering the question. *How are you feeling about banging a Shade at a party and him avoiding you forever?*

Oh, totally fine, actually. He hasn't been avoiding me. We just sleep together in secret.

"The experience was a good reminder that I need to get better at separating sex and romance," I told her, which was the honest truth. "I really admire Verity's ability to just... have fun, then move on with her life. No strings attached. Especially here, where sex is intrinsically linked to feeding for a Shade. There's a biological *need* there that goes beyond just pleasure and, you know, reproduction or whatever. I can't fall in love with every hungry Shade who manages to seduce me," I added with an unconvincing laugh.

"Right," Meera agreed tentatively, perching on the wide edge of the hearth. "There's something to be said about that, but you're also *not* Verity. It's okay if you don't respond to things the same way as she does."

"No, I know," I mumbled, pumping the bellows to get the fire going.

I'd overheard it said around court that Meera was shy and lacked confidence, but the more time I spent with her, the less true that felt. *I was the* one trying desperately to fit in. It sure seemed like it took a lot more confidence to unapologetically move at your own pace.

"Well, forget that guy. He clearly doesn't deserve you if he's not making an effort to see you—that's the bare minimum." She didn't mean for words to hit me like a blow to the chest, of course. And in his own way, Evrin *did* make an effort to see me, but it was just in an extremely secretive way that made me feel vaguely ashamed of myself.

"Maybe someone else will catch your eye?" Meera suggested mildly.

"Maybe," I replied on a heavy exhale, though I knew there was no possibility of that happening while Evrin and I were doing what we were doing.

As much as I wanted to read less into sexual intimacy, I wasn't someone who felt romantic attraction easily. And when I did, I was entirely fixated on that person until it had run its course.

It was like I was cursed with Stage Five Clinginess, but only one percent of the time. Silver linings and whatnot.

"What about you? Anyone getting your motor running?" I asked Meera, hoping to move some of the scrutiny off me.

Meera shook her head, blushing faintly. I supposed Verner hadn't *technically* been at dinner—he'd been standing guard outside. Since that day he'd helped me make an escape from dinner, I'd spotted him hanging around almost constantly, but it definitely wasn't for my benefit.

"I might head up to bed," Meera said on a yawn, helping herself to a cup of water. "Are you okay down here?"

"Sure. I'll go up shortly. Goodnight."

She squeezed my shoulder lightly on the way past, leaving me alone as I fed logs into the flames, and my mind headed to the bad place.

If I was in the human realm, I'd be sending a "you up?" message right now.

But I wasn't, so I got the fire roaring and snuck out of the house instead. The charcoal gray sky churned restlessly above, and there was something soothing about how *different* it looked from the sky at home. I wasn't in Kansas—or Idaho Springs—anymore, but I was making a life for myself here, and that life was full of possibility.

The grounds surrounding the palace were always lit up like a stadium so that no one could shadow walk into the place without the Guard noticing, but even with the megawatt orbs of silvery lights, I knew it probably wasn't the safest option to traverse the gardens at night.

It was especially idiotic to head toward the barracks on my own when Evrin was trying to keep me a secret.

But I just...

I needed him. Not even for sex—though that would be nice, too. I needed his calm, steady presence. I needed him to wrap me up in those big strong arms and tell me everything would be okay. And objectively, I *didn't* need that. I was fine on my own, I knew if I'd just stayed in my room and waited out this incessant, itching need to feel his skin on mine and his voice in my ear that I'd make it through. But I didn't want to fight it. I wanted to *cherish* it.

I hovered outside the entry room, having a vague idea of when Evrin finished his insanely long shifts in the in-between. It wasn't the regular rotation that the other guards did, which meant there was no foot traffic going past, at least. I had no excuses at the ready for what I could possibly be doing here. I was really just relying on no one seeing me.

The moment Evrin came out of the entry room, his head swung in my direction, nostrils flaring. It was incredibly gratifying.

"Are you okay? What are you doing here?" he asked, keeping his voice low as he strode toward me, gently gripping my upper arms and rubbing them with his thumbs.

I opened my mouth before closing it again, lost for words in a way that I rarely was.

"Perhaps you were lonely?" Evrin hedged, tilting his head to the side.

"Yeah," I croaked, something settling into place at the recognition of what I'd been feeling. "I think I was. Which is so stupid, because I was just with Meera five minutes ago, and I don't really have any reason to feel this way."

Evrin pulled me into his chest, his enormous arms wrapping tightly around my shoulders as he squeezed the tension right out of me.

We stayed there for a long moment, my brain so blissfully silent that I was able to just enjoy the quiet nighttime breeze and the occasional rustle of fabric where my dress rubbed against Evrin's skin.

And then he made a noise that made us both jump. It started where my ear was pressed to his chest, and seemed to rumble up his body, and it wasn't a sound I'd ever heard him make before.

It was almost like a... purr.

"What was that?" I asked, leaning back to look up at Evrin's face, my arms still loosely wrapped around his waist.

"I have no idea. I've never made that sound before."

"I liked it," I told Evrin, patting his waist, because he seemed kind of self-conscious about it. "It was very soothing."

"I'm glad. Are you feeling better now?"

"Much. Are you okay? I hope I didn't interrupt your plans—" I said, suddenly realizing that I'd just imposed on him without warning.

"Not at all," Evrin interjected. "I was just going to grab some food and sleep. I'll walk you back to Elverston House first, though." A little bubble of hope swelled in my chest. "There shouldn't be anyone around this late, but I'll walk ahead if there is."

Never mind.

Don't get your hopes, I chided internally. *Don't catch feelings. Just relax.*

"How was your shift?" I asked as we made our way back through the garden. "Anything exciting happen?"

"No, thankfully." He looked over at me, and I could have sworn I saw the moment that he realized he wasn't giving me a lot of conversation to work with. "It's always quiet, especially with the human-realm portals now quiet. It's just Shades passing through on their way somewhere else. Most Shades struggle with the oppressiveness of it for long stretches of time, so the only member of the Guard actively monitoring it is me." He shrugged.

"Well, then, I'm definitely glad it was quiet if you don't have any backup," I replied worriedly.

"Even if something happens, I'm more than capable of handling myself." His voice was filled with so much confidence that I couldn't help but believe him.

"I hope so. Don't you get injured on me," I teased, though I wasn't really teasing, and it wasn't really what I wanted to say. Or at least not *all* I wanted to say.

"I won't," Evrin promised.

And that had to be enough.

CHAPTER 6

SEVERAL WEEKS LATER

O h fuck," I groaned, pushing forward to lodge my knot into place in Tallulah's snug, perfect cunt.

"Evrin!" Tallulah's nails sunk into the backs of my arms, her heels digging into my lower back as she yanked me closer like she couldn't get enough of me. It was a heady feeling having her clinging on to me like I was the only thing anchoring her to this world. A dangerously addictive feeling.

"What are you doing to me?" I groaned, bracing myself on either side of Tallulah's head and doing my best not to collapse on top of her as she squeezed tight around my knot.

"Nothing you're not doing to me," she replied, her voice so breathless I half wondered if I'd imagined the words.

The power that flowed through me from Tallulah was intoxicating. We were doing this almost daily—whoever was monitoring the stores must be suspicious about where all the energy was coming from, but I suspected the comfort and privacy of the ex-Hunters was too paramount for them to look into the matter.

"Are you okay?" I asked once my mind had returned to some level of coherent. "Are you comfortable? I can roll us—"

"Don't move me," Tallulah slurred. "If you move, I'll come again, and I'm legitimately dehydrated at this point."

I cursed quietly in my mother tongue. "I brought water for you, but I can't reach my bag."

"There are definite disadvantages to our secret trysts happening in a dark empty void," Tallulah laughed. Was it a genuine laugh? I was never sure.

The thing was, Tallulah had a *loud* laugh. It was much remarked on at court—Shades obsessed over its bubbly charm. But she didn't laugh like that around me.

"Do you ever not work?" Tallulah asked. "Like, do you go home for the weekend sometimes? You've worked every day since I've met you."

With a frisson of discomfort, I realized how little Tallulah knew about my life. She'd never asked, and I'd never volunteered the information. "This is my home. I'm happy to fill my days with work. I don't need a separate residence outside of the barracks. I don't go back to visit my family home."

"Oh, no, I totally get it. Don't worry, you don't have to explain it to me."

Didn't I? Because beneath the all-encompassing smell of sex that surrounded us, there was a discordant note to Tallulah's scent. It wasn't quite the intense sourness associated with negative emotions, but it wasn't *not* that either.

Worried I was making it worse, I fell silent until my knot was soft enough to pull out. I rummaged through the bag I'd started bringing in here with us, handing Tallulah a stoppered bottle of water and a washcloth while she straightened out her clothes.

"Are you looking?" she asked, narrowing her eyes in my general direction as she wet the washcloth to clean herself up.

I laughed, unable to help myself, considering all that I'd just seen. She had the most adorably fierce expression. "I'll turn around."

"Thank you," she said primly as I scooped up the blanket off the ground and turned away, busying myself with folding it back into the bag.

I looked out into the expansive darkness as Tallulah put herself back together, wondering when the in-between had started to feel lonely rather than welcoming. Usually, the vast emptiness felt like *possibility*. But with Tallulah here... I supposed it reminded me of all the things I would never have. All the possibilities I would never be capable of fulfilling.

"Ready."

I turned, smiling at her automatically before remembering she couldn't see me. Mostly, I preferred it that way, so she wasn't constantly reminded of my missing horns, but there were moments when I wanted her to see the nuances of my expression in the hopes that it would give her some comfort.

"Let's get going, then."

"Have you got a busy day planned?" Tallulah asked, moving toward me using the glow of my eyes to guide her as I shouldered the bag and reached for her. While it'd be faster to scoop her up and carry her back to the entry room, I wasn't in a rush for us to part ways. Instead, I wrapped my fingers lightly above her elbow, guiding her back in the direction we needed to go.

"I'll start my patrol in an hour or so," I said, realizing I hadn't answered her question. "That's me for the next twelve hours."

"*Twelve* hours?" Tallulah asked. I glanced down, catching her shocked expression. "Somehow, I didn't realize they were quite that long. Do you take breaks?"

"I don't leave the in-between, but I'll occasionally take a few moments to myself."

"Is the captain... *nice* to you?" Tallulah asked, sounding suddenly ready to march out to war. It was interesting that she had that much fire when it came to defending others, and yet she was eager not to make trouble for anyone when it came to herself.

"The captain works very hard to stay on my good side," I assured her. "Not many Shades cope well working in the in-between for extended periods of time."

"It's got to be at least a little hard on you, though, right?"

"My ability to spend extended periods of time here without it driving me insane is my one and only distinguishing skill. If it weren't for this, I'd have been relegated to Pit guard long ago—that's a far less prestigious position than any of the palace guards. The accommodations are far less glamorous too," I added, hoping to lighten the mood. "What about you? What will you do today?"

"This probably sounds really lame in comparison to what you do, but I'm fixing up some of the soft furnishings in Elverston House. Repairing upholstery. Sewing new curtains. That kind of thing."

"Why would that sound lame? That requires far more skill than wandering around in the dark, which is what I'll be doing."

"I don't know about that. I've been sewing since I was a kid. My grandmother taught me. It just requires a little patience, that's all."

"I'm afraid I must disagree—it's more than just patience. Just because you have honed a skill to the point where it no longer *feels* difficult doesn't mean that it *isn't* difficult. You're just good at it."

This was one of the few times where I'd felt confident that I'd said the right thing. Tallulah looked up at me with the brightest smile I'd ever seen from her. It wasn't quite the smile she gave everyone else, and I had no idea what that meant, but I hoarded it greedily all the same.

Every smile she gave me could be the last. Every day, we grew closer to her finding a Shade that she liked that was worthy of her.

And when that day came, I would be happy for her. Because no one deserved that more than Tallulah.

TALLULAH

CHAPTER 7

How did she even acquire all this?" Meera asked, untangling a necklace that had fallen down the side of what had been Verity's dresser.

She'd moved out with the Shade she was… seeing? Curing? Taking pity on? Honestly, I couldn't tell. But in her frantic rush to pack, she'd left plenty of small things behind that Meera and I were boxing up for her.

"I think half of Astrid's supply runs were just Verity's lists," I laughed, warily reaching under the bed, not entirely sure what I was going to find under there.

Fortunately, it seemed to be mostly an assortment of clothes—primarily socks in every length and texture under the sun, though, they were all in various shades of pink.

"Do you think she's happy?" Meera asked, her voice a little more subdued this time. "I know Damen said she was…"

"But would he really know?" I finished, having considered the same thing. "Verity has that flirty confidence that could probably convince anyone of anything."

"I also don't think she'd stay if she wasn't," Meera pointed out. "Verity is a force to be reckoned with."

I hummed in agreement, a small wave of jealousy that I hated washing over me. I didn't want to be jealous of my friend—I *wanted* to feel nothing but positive feelings where they were concerned. But the certainty with which Verity had made her choice to leave a couple of days ago, and the bemused way Damen had assured us that she didn't regret her decision...

God, I just wanted that for myself. I wanted that certainty. I wanted everyone in the realm to know about it.

"Aren't you going to go for your walk?" Meera asked suddenly. "You usually leave about this time."

I swallowed tightly, glad Meera couldn't scent my emotions. I *could* go. There was no one stopping me, except for the voice in my head that was suddenly and obnoxiously asking questions.

Questions like... *what the fuck are you doing?*

You want to fall in love. Is this how you're going to find it? Hoping for a relationship with someone who doesn't do relationships?

Are you actually keeping your feelings out of this like you said you would? Or are you already in too deep?

"I'm going to work on the curtains in the drawing room, actually. I really want to get them up, see what they look like."

"Do you need a second pair of hands?"

Probably. "I think I'll be okay."

I didn't want to inconvenience Meera, or force her to spend any more time indoors than she already had today. She was not an indoorsy kind of gal.

We set aside a couple of smaller boxes of things for Damen to take to Verity on his next visit before heading in separate directions. By midmorning, there was a very good chance Verity wouldn't have even been awake yet, but the house still felt so much emptier without her presence.

I felt cold all over at the idea of Meera suddenly upping and leaving me too, and that was definitely how this was going to play out, since the only guy I liked was emotionally unavailable to me.

The curtains somewhat worked as stress relief—and the idea that the heavy velvet fabric would provide warmth and privacy, and make Elverston House feel more welcoming, was incredibly motivating.

But they just absolutely wouldn't fall properly no matter what I did, and it would bother me every single moment for the rest of my life if they didn't look right.

A slightly hysterical corner of my brain that I didn't want to look too closely at was convinced that if only I could get the curtains right, all the other ills in my life would magically correct themselves, too.

"Those look great!" Meera said enthusiastically, coming to stand next to me while I examined them critically.

"They aren't hanging properly."

She shot me a bemused look. "Aren't they? I doubt anyone will notice that but you. They look stunning. Such an improvement on what was there."

Everyone would notice, though. Eventually. They'd notice, and they'd think that I was sloppy or that I didn't care about this house. And I did. I cared *so* much. I just wanted everything to be *perfect*, and for everyone to be happy, and for *me* to be happy. Was that too much to ask?

"I'm going to redo them," I announced, clambering back up the rickety wooden ladder. Meera made a sound of alarm, coming to the bottom to hold on to it.

"Were you up this by yourself earlier, Tallulah?! You do know the stone floor would be an uncomfortable landing spot for your skull, right?"

Coming from the usually even-tempered Meera, that was a real scolding.

"Sorry, I should have asked for help," I said, genuinely contrite.

She hummed, unconvinced, watching as I pulled the first hooks out of the loops, the curtains instantly sagging toward the floor. "I really think you should go for your morning walk. You seem out of sorts today."

I yanked out the next hook a little more aggressively than necessary before taking a deep, calming breath. I'd *really* lose my shit if I ripped the curtain now.

"I'll head out for a walk. It's a good idea," I agreed, though this time I was going to *actually* walk. Just meander around on my lonesome, and let the uncomfortable emotions I'd been trying to distract myself from fester a little.

Even if I wanted to hang out with someone, monopolizing Meera's time was my only option. Ophelia was busier than ever these days. Astrid's work schedule had picked up too, and Austin was rarely at court. Verity had been the one who was always available for socializing, but she was happily ensconced at her new estate, probably painting the ancient stonework pastel pink.

Evrin was the one I wanted to spend time with, but he was also the one I was trying to distance myself from. Not forever, I hoped. But I needed some time to pull myself together.

The heavy fabric pooled in a sad-looking pile on the ground that I would undoubtedly regret leaving there later, but couldn't be bothered tackling at that moment. Instead, I clambered down, gave Meera a quick hug, then let myself out of the house, traipsing through Meera's increasingly impressive vegetable garden until I got to the ex-Hunters-only border of the property. I didn't really have any direction in mind, but I found myself heading for the river opposite the property and sitting down against a thick tree on the bank, watching the calm ripples of the silvery gray water while I fantasized about sexy, sexy premade roller blinds.

They wouldn't solve *all* my problems, but it was the kind of obvious quick fix that made it *feel* like it would solve all my problems. Like when my last serious relationship had ended, and I'd been convinced all that I needed to feel better were blunt bangs and a little rose tattoo on my ankle.

"Hey."

I let out an ungainly squawk at the sound of Evrin's voice, scrambling awkwardly to my feet to find him standing a couple of feet away. He looked almost sheepish, which was a different look on him. Usually, he was the epitome of unbothered while I analyzed every single thing I'd done and said in his presence, wondering if I'd scared him off yet.

"You scared the bejeezus out of me," I panted, clutching my chest as he silently mouthed "bejeezus" to himself. "What are you doing here? Hasn't your shift started?"

"Yes, but you weren't in the garden. I came to make sure you were alright. I hope that's okay. No one saw me."

No one saw me.

My insecurities reared up like a lion, ready to take a swipe. I could see it happening.

This man—this Shade, rather—didn't claim me. He didn't want me to be *his*. I knew that I was all self-protective claws and get-ahead-of-the-pain teeth in that moment, but I was too far gone to pull it back.

"I'm surprised you sought me out in the daylight." *Stop talking,* I told myself in vain. *Don't say it. Don't let the unhealed version of you win.* "Given that you don't want to be seen with me."

Evrin's expression was absolutely unreadable. "Right."

Oh, I was definitely spiraling. I could feel it. I could *see* it happening right in front of me, like someone else was in the driver's seat. But it was all me. I'd said the words, hoping that he'd give me some kind of reassurance in return, some acknowledgment that I *wasn't* his dirty little secret.

And he hadn't.

"Is that not an accurate read of the situation?" I pressed, because apparently I was in the mood to hurt my own feelings today.

Evrin shifted his weight from one foot to the other, his shadows moving restlessly around him. "Yes. It is. I want what's best for you, Tallulah."

God, that felt like such a copout. *He* was what was best for me, only he didn't seem to agree.

My chest felt strange, and I was more than a little worried that I was going to burst into tears, which would be an additional humiliation I didn't really want to deal with right now.

Why had I even brought this up? Things had been going fine, so long as I didn't pay too much attention to the gnawing sensation in the back of my mind.

No, I knew why.

The Duke of Lindow had shown up and Verity had just... picked him. For reasons that literally no one understood, because he looked one gust of wind away from death and he seemed like an arrogant asshole to boot, she'd decided that she'd have him. And he'd immediately chosen her right back, albeit in an extremely bizarre way.

God, maybe I was a "pick me" because I absolutely wanted to be picked. I wanted Evrin to claim me, and I wanted to claim him right back.

I wanted everyone to know that *this one was mine.*

But like Evrin said, that wasn't what this was.

"I think we should stop doing... this." I was impressed with how calm and aloof I sounded, though, I had no doubt that my scent was giving me away.

Evrin nodded, resignation written all over his face.

A very large part of me wanted to scream *No! I take it back! Whisk me away into the darkness and make me come until I can't walk, and we can pretend this whole conversation never happened.*

But I was already in too deep for that. I'd been all but doodling *Mrs. Evrin* in my metaphorical notebook. If I didn't put an end to this now, I was only going to make myself miserable in the long run. *More* miserable.

"Maybe I was fine with what this was when we first started, but now... I'm just not sure this arrangement is fair on either of us anymore."

"I see." I suspected he didn't, not really, given how cautiously the words were delivered.

But that made sense, didn't it? Evrin didn't *see* why the arrangement wasn't fair, because Evrin wasn't emotionally invested in it the way I was.

I released my lower lip, not even realizing I'd been chewing on it, and gave him what I hoped was a convincing smile. "You're great, you know. You're funny and hot, and a really gentle, calming presence to be around. If you ever do decide to pursue a relationship someday, she'll be super lucky because you're such a catch. I hope you find what you're looking for."

"I hope you do too, Tallulah," Evrin murmured, his gaze lingering for a moment before he inclined his head respectfully and turned away.

Goodbye, I mouthed at his back as he left, my throat too tight to get the word out.

This was the right thing to do. I knew that. Evrin probably knew that—or he'd realize it soon enough. The Band-Aid had to be ripped off at some point, and it was better to do it now than to leave it any longer.

And maybe in a few hours—or days, maybe even weeks—I'd be grateful that I'd made this tough call and appreciate that I hadn't let these pesky feelings linger. But I sure as shit wasn't there yet.

CHAPTER 8

You seem... in low spirits," Caius observed, blowing out a ring of smoke and watching me critically. "You sure you don't want some?" he asked, holding out the pipe for me to take.

"You know I don't smoke before work."

"You also don't usually seem so miserable before work, though you probably should be, considering the circumstances. I can't think of anything more miserable than your job."

In the past, I might have disagreed with him, but the in-between was increasingly miserable by the day. Probably because the moment I stepped into the darkness, all I could think about was Tallulah and the memories we'd shared there.

What was she doing right now? Was she thinking about me?

It was pretty unlikely.

Until the missing ex-Hunter was found and returned to the realm, Tallulah's focus would undoubtedly be solely on her friend. It was selfish of me to even dream that she'd have spared me a thought since that day by the river when she'd ended... whatever it was that we'd had.

"Why'd you even come over?" Caius groused, glaring at me. "I didn't see you for weeks, and then you finally come back and you're terrible company today. It's not like you to be so... emotional."

"No, I suppose not," I agreed mildly. There was never space for me to have any emotions that inconvenienced him, but Caius didn't want to hear that. Long before Roan had sprung an underhanded challenge on Caius, I'd been the unwanted shame of the family, expected to stay out of sight and never complain about the life the goddesses had granted me.

Caius was fifteen years older than me. I doubted we'd exchanged more than a handful of words before his self-imposed exile. Only when he was alone and humiliated, then was I considered worthy of his company.

"It's really no wonder you're in a foul mood, lingering in the darkness for all of your waking hours. I don't know why you do it. It won't make them respect you, you know."

"I would never be so bold as to expect that."

I'd been putting this visit off, but I was glad I'd come here. For a brief moment when I'd woken up this morning, I'd entertained the notion that it was *unfair* that Tallulah wasn't mine. That I couldn't keep her. But Caius was the harsh dose of reality that I needed: I would never be anything more than I was now. That I'd even come as far as I had was solely because I was willing to subject myself to conditions that no other member of the Guard would accept.

If only I hadn't naively had hopes, if I hadn't foolishly gotten attached to her, I wouldn't feel so crushingly disappointed.

"I hear Roan is being primed for a junior position on the Council of Shades," Caius said bitterly. I blinked in surprise. I couldn't remember the last time I'd heard him speak Roan's name.

"How did you hear that?"

"One of my customers. I hear more than you think, you know."

I waited to see if that was a pointed remark and that he'd heard something about my life, but no follow-up was forthcoming.

"You're better qualified for a seat on the Council of Shades."

Caius shot me a look that could freeze shadows. "Obviously, I know that."

"Well, why not put yourself forward? Holding the family seat isn't the only criteria. Your education is better suited to it, as is your temperament."

Caius had his flaws, but Roan was both arrogant and lazy, and seemed to grow more so with each year that passed. His only redeeming feature was that, deep down, I suspected he knew how unqualified he was.

"It's pitiful how naïve you still are after all this time," Caius said with a heavy sigh, shaking his head before returning to his pipe.

I stood quietly, taking his words as a dismissal and silently excusing myself from his home. I'd tried. Someday I would learn not to bother.

Caius didn't run away from me. He didn't reject my presence outright like most Shades in the realm did. I should be grateful for it.

At least the visit with him had bridged the empty hours between waking and starting my shift—time I'd once spent with Tallulah. When the captain wasn't so busy with tracking down the missing ex-Hunter, I would request a meeting with him to discuss adding a couple of extra hours to the beginning of my shift. In the absence of having anything else going on, it seemed wasteful *not* to.

Today wasn't that day, though. I exchanged a nod with Captain Soren in the in-between as he and his mate headed for the human realm where they'd been monitoring the uncertain situation. At least, the captain's mate had more muted scents than the others who'd come here from the human realm. The scent of ex-Hunter—sad, happy, or otherwise—was playing havoc on my emotions lately.

I headed in the opposite direction from the duo, walking one of the several preplanned routes I had, though I selected one at random each day in case anyone was watching my movements. Unfortunately, this one took me past the spot I'd always brought Tallulah to, and I did my best to maintain my quick pace as I passed it, not allowing myself to linger in the suddenly oppressive darkness.

I'd never struggled with it before. In the past, I'd found the emptiness freeing. It was expansive, unlimited potential. It was space and time and possibility.

It was nothing. And nothing had been enough for me. It had been all I'd expected from my life. But I suspected that I'd met *everything,* and now I was struggling to find contentment in goddamn *anything*.

I shook my head, focusing on my surroundings. There was no point moping over Tallulah any more than I already had. She'd ended it. She'd wanted a safe way to explore intimacy between herself and a Shade, and I'd provided her with that.

It was enough.

The memories were enough. The in-between was enough. And for a Shade like me, enough was all I could hope for.

With the exception of a group of shithead kids I'd had to chase off, the in-between had been quiet. Almost eerily so, though it had been this way for days now. The realm seemed to be holding its shadows, waiting warily to see if the missing ex-Hunter would return or whether she'd stay in the human realm—whether by her choice or someone else's. For all the royal couple's apparent calm about the new way of filling the energy stores, the realm as a whole was less confident that we wouldn't imminently starve to death if King Allerick didn't allow us to travel to the human realm again soon.

But I couldn't think about that.

If I thought about feeding, I thought about Tallulah. Every path led me directly back to her.

I'd already hung around beyond the end of my shift, but I couldn't put reality off any longer. I made my way back to the portal, hoping there would be some warm food left at the barracks tonight and that no one would cower in horror at the sight of me, but an odd scent had me veering right. Something—*someone*—was in here. Someone who didn't belong, and who hadn't been here ten minutes ago when I'd passed this spot.

"Show yourself, by order of the Guard," I called out, calling my shadows to my palms, trying to place what the strange smell was. It almost smelled like a Hunter, but there was an astringent, sterile overtone to the scent that I'd never encountered before. With a muffled noise of surprise, I stumbled back, realizing I'd almost stepped on them.

Shit.

Shit.

Here was the missing ex-Hunter. Lying, seemingly half-dead, on the cold ground of the in-between. How could I have missed her earlier? No, it was impossible. Not with the strange scent clinging to her. Surely, I would have noticed that.

I scooped her up as gently as I could, alarmed by just how cold to the touch she was, before jogging through the portal, yelling for help before I'd even fully stepped foot on palace grounds. How had she gotten there? The portals were still closed on the human realm side, I'd have felt a disturbance if the Hunters had activated them again. Right now, the in-between was *only* accessible to a Hunter if a Shade was guiding them.

While I liked to *think* that no Shade would be so callous as to have dumped her in the in-between, alone and frail, I couldn't rule that scenario out. Nothing else made any sense.

The palace staff scattered to alert the necessary higher-ups while I brought her to the Healers' wing, following their guidance to deposit her on one of the empty beds before I was ushered out of the room so they could warm her up.

I regretted not bothering to learn her name, but I'd never paid attention to any of the Hunters who'd moved here except for Tallulah.

Were we even equipped to care for a sick Hunter? What did Shade healers know about healing humans?

For a brief moment, time itself seemed to stop as Tallulah rushed past me and into the room, the other ex-Hunter who lived in Elverston House following close behind. My chest felt tight at the sensation of being so close to Tallulah and yet so far away. She hadn't even seen me.

What if she forgot about me? It was only a matter of time, I supposed. The idea was agony.

"You did good," Verner said gruffly, startling me out of my reverie. I hadn't even noticed him arrive. "Where was she?"

"Right outside the portal. There was no movement from the portals on the human side, though, and no Shade with her. It was only luck that I found her," I added, slightly shamefaced. "She hadn't been there a few minutes earlier."

Verner frowned—an odd look on the usually peaceful Shade. He'd never been afraid to walk into my general vicinity and speak to me, though I wouldn't say we were friendly.

"The whole situation is strange. Are you up for relaying these developments to the king? He's at the trial..." Verner trailed off with a grimace.

"Of course," I agreed, taking Verner by surprise. It was pretty well known among the Guard that I didn't do anything outside of monitoring the in-between. I didn't usually have to.

But the idea that Tallulah would walk out of that room, look right at me and not acknowledge me at all was frankly terrifying. My already-fragile ego wouldn't be able to stand that blow.

I'd rather deal with the horrified looks and uncomfortable avoidance of every Shade at the realm who was attending the trial than that.

"Are you sure?"

"Absolutely." I was already jogging away. Even with my limited social interactions, I'd heard about this sham of a trial, and it would definitely need to go on pause now.

Unfortunately, it seemed that the Elders didn't agree. My message was passed on by the guard at the door, but I wasn't even allowed to set foot in the room. The Curia was off-limits to a Shade like myself.

I wandered back through the empty halls, feeling oddly deflated. It wasn't like I *cared* about things like politics or the running of the realm, anyway. I just stayed in my self-imposed prison, doing my job, and ignoring the fact that I was a malformed pariah to the best of my ability.

The distressed scent of the ex-Hunters reached me in the halls, and I picked up my pace, jogging to meet them, to see if there was anything I could do to help.

It was a whole contingency of them, but I only had eyes for Tallulah. And this time, she was looking right back. In the muddle of smells and emotions, I couldn't tell what she was feeling, but her blue eyes were plenty expressive, even without a scent to draw on.

She was sad. Tallulah looked at me and felt *sad*.

That idea was intolerable.

How had this all gone so terribly wrong?

"This is Evrin," Tallulah murmured, making introductions for the benefit of the other ex-Hunters. They didn't respond to my name with any indication of familiarity, which was what I'd expected, but it still stung. "He was the one who found you in the in-between. You were right outside the portal, you know. So close."

Fuck me, her voice was as rich and decadent as the sweetest syrup. If I closed my eyes, I could have sworn that I felt it dripping down my throat.

But I doubted anyone would have appreciated me bringing that up right now. So instead, I filled them in on the situation at the Curia, and stood aside as they rushed in, unobstructed by even the Elders' most loyal guards, because here were people who *mattered*.

They were the voices who would mingle with the royal family's, and shape the shadow realm for decades, maybe even centuries, to come. Even the ones who didn't seem to relish the role of policy-shaping diplomats had the power to change everything, simply by virtue of *who* and *what* they were. I'd be lying to myself if I pretended I wasn't at least a little envious of having that much sway.

Rather than leaving, which would have been the sensible thing to do, I headed for the elegant lounge bar on the upper floors that overlooked the Pit—a popular drinking spot for sociopaths who enjoyed overseeing the suffering of others. It was a favorite haunt for the most morally depraved members of the Guard—the ones the captain hadn't weeded out yet—and I usually avoided it, but I couldn't quite face the idea of leaving yet. I wanted to at least be close to Tallulah physically, if nothing else.

"Evrin!" Roan called out the moment I stepped foot in the dimly lit, glossy bar. "What brings you here?"

I did my best to hide my grimace as I crossed the room to meet my brother, carefully keeping my distance as I greeted him. He knew that my lack of horns wasn't some type of contagion, but the few other Shades sprinkled around the bar might not, and Roan had a reputation to protect. I was surprised he was speaking to me at all—perhaps he was deeper in his cups than I'd initially thought.

"I was nearby. Thought I'd get a drink. It's been a long day."

"I'm not surprised," Roan said with a booming laugh. "Given where you choose to work. Unless you've changed stations?" he added hopefully.

"Still in the in-between."

"Ah. Well, come. Sit. Let me buy you a drink."

I thought about objecting, but Roan had inherited the entire family estate and all the wealth that had come with it. He could buy me a drink.

"What brings *you* here?" I asked, wondering if Roan's Council training was further along than Caius's words had led me to believe.

"They're training me up for a junior position on the Council of Shades," Roan replied dismissively, confirming my theory. "Or rather, I'm competing for one. I have to attend these things now—you know, put in an appearance, do my part. I find it all very tiresome."

"How terrible," I deadpanned, though the sarcasm was entirely lost on

Roan. "Shouldn't you be in there, then? Watching the trial?"

"Nobody will miss me if I take a few minutes to myself, will they? It's not like I'm the one on trial," he laughed.

To Roan, that he was treated with such deference and given jobs and titles he didn't deserve was simply to be expected. He'd challenged for the role of heir—after weakening Caius with a goblet of wine laced with liquid silver—and he'd won. And Roan treated his privilege with all the respect that someone who'd never had to honestly work for anything was capable of.

"How is Caius?" Roan asked, his casualness seeming slightly more forced now. "Have you seen him?"

"No," I lied. Caius went out of his way *not* to be seen by anyone from his old life, and I would respect that choice. Given where I chose to spend the majority of my time, I could hardly judge him for it.

"An unfortunate business," Roan mumbled. It was so like him to awkwardly brush off anything that made him uncomfortable that, for a brief moment, I actually felt like we were brothers again.

That feeling quickly disappeared as Roan began recounting all of his many blessings and successes in life, as he was wont to do whenever anyone gave him the opportunity to speak. At least he was easy company—Roan was so content to hear himself talk that I wasn't obligated to add anything to the conversation. It was a good distraction from my own unsettled thoughts.

Though, the sadness in Tallulah's eyes and scent when she'd looked at me continued to haunt me. Why was she sad if she'd been the one to end it? Perhaps she was worried she'd hurt my feelings. Tallulah was a compassionate person—she would hate the idea of upsetting someone. I should have reassured her more that I was okay, but I'd been in too much pain to give her those words at the time.

"I really don't have any desire to work with the Council of Shades," Roan sighed as I reminded myself to pay attention to the conversation—as one-sided and dull as it was. "But it's the right thing to do. Respectful, you know. Of the family name. You have no idea the pressure that comes with the role."

Roan wouldn't cope for a moment being in my position, but it would be a waste of time pointing that out to him. Then again, Roan had never *had* to adapt to adversity. Maybe he would have coped just fine in my position if life had been a little less kind to him.

"I have a daughter. Did I mention that?"

I startled, blinking at him in surprise. "Since when?"

"She's a few years old," Roan replied with a dismissive flick of his hand. "Three or four, perhaps? She lives with her mother for now. Undoubtedly, she'll move in with me when she's older as the heir to the estate."

I took back all the compassionate thoughts I'd just had. With every year that passed, I understood Roan less and less.

"You don't feel as though you're... oh, I don't know. Missing out on her childhood?"

Roan laughed, looking at me as though I'd said the most outrageous thing he'd ever heard. "What's there to miss out on? She doesn't *do* anything yet. I'd forgotten how dire your company was when you were very young, always following me around, begging for attention. It annoyed me then and it annoys me now when Vivia does it. Best that I not have anything to do with her until she's more interesting."

I would do anything—*anything*—to be a father. It would never happen for me. Shade females only slept with me if they weren't superstitious, and they *were* very desperate. It was an infrequent event, and the chances of conception were already low between us. And Tallulah was done with me, though frankly, she deserved a better prospect for the father of her children than me.

Roan had been given everything—and what he hadn't been given, he'd betrayed his own brother to get—and yet it wasn't enough for him to feel any kind of happiness.

It made me look back on my experience with Tallulah in a less devastated, more grateful light. I didn't want to be filled with resentment over the one part of my life that had ever brought me joy.

CHAPTER 9

The following few days were a blur of activity as things got back to normal with Verity. They didn't *have* to be a blur of activity—no one was asking all that much of me. But I was going out of my way to keep busy, anyway. My denial had been ticking over pretty nicely when I hadn't had to *see* Evrin. But looking into his glowing navy eyes, seeing him right in front of me and not being able to reach for him...

I needed to get over this Shade or I was going to drive myself insane.

"There you are!" Ophelia said, greeting me with a beaming smile and a hug as I headed back inside Elverston House. Meera shot me a brief smile before scurrying back out to the quiet of the garden, apparently content to off-load socializing duties now that I was back. "Meera said you'd gone out."

"I was talking to Astrid about some extra supplies for Verity. Were you looking for me? I'm sorry to keep you waiting."

"Not at all. Shall we sit in the drawing room? I raided the palace kitchen for treats. Calix is in a particularly cheerful mood this morning—he's been so much nicer now he's all loved up."

I did my best not to feel outrageously bitter that other people were just out here, falling in love and living their best lives. I really tried.

But also... how dare they?

"Is everything okay?" I asked, leading Ophelia to the drawing room, hoping she didn't question the puddle of curtains that were still sitting abandoned on the floor. She must have already been in here since a shiny silver tray of charcoal-colored cakes was sitting on the coffee table, waiting for us.

"Of course. Why do you ask?"

I raised an eyebrow at her as we took our seats on either side of the table. It absolutely wasn't the norm for Ophelia to seek me out for one-on-one time. We got along well, but she was too busy to really spend time with any of us ex-Hunters aside from Astrid.

"Okay, there was something I wanted to talk to you about," she admitted sheepishly. "But we don't need to get into it right away. How have you been? What's new? I feel like it's been forever since we talked."

Oh, not much, just wallowing in heartbreak, missing mozzarella sticks and all my favorite comfort movies from home. "Nothing really."

"You've obviously been busy," Ophelia laughed, gesturing at the mass grave of curtains on the floor.

I snorted. "If I'd been busy, they'd be finished. The suspense is killing me, what did you really come here to talk about? It's got to be big if you're bribing me with pastry."

"They're not a bribe, I swear." She laughed nervously before clapping her hands together, an overbright smile on her face. "Right. Here goes. Allerick and I have been traveling around the realm, meeting a lot more Shades than just the usual ones we associate with at court. Away from here, there are some, uh, rumbles of discontent at the current ad hoc system of Hunters and Shades getting to know each other."

"Is this because of Austin and Selene?" I asked. Ophelia's face went as red as her hair, which was an answer in itself. Austin had mentioned that some of the more elitist Shades didn't feel like Selene fit the bill as far as mates went, which was one of the most ridiculous things I'd ever heard. Then again, I'd probably been a little naïve in assuming that Shades wouldn't have an unjust class system of their own, especially considering they had a semiconstitutional monarchy.

Ophelia exhaled heavily. "Look, there's no way around it—this is an awkward request. And I feel like I can only approach you with it because you're so confident and assertive, and I believe you could handle it. Not that Meera *couldn't* handle it. Agh, I'm making such a mess of this."

"No, you're fine. I get it."

Privately, I thought Ophelia—and everyone else—was underestimating Meera. She wasn't as loud as me or Verity, but she didn't appear to be riddled with self-doubt the way I was. Her confidence was quiet, but it was genuine.

"It's just… I don't suppose you'd be willing to go on a few prearranged dates? Just to meet them, nothing else. Of course," Ophelia added hastily. "There are a few Shades who feel they're not getting a fair shot because they aren't based at court, or they're quieter personalities. That kind of thing."

I didn't mind a shy boy, but a dude who ran to the king and queen whining for a date was a slightly less-sexy visual.

And I did need to get over Evrin. While I doubted I would be doing that by getting under someone else—my personality absolutely wouldn't let me move that quickly—meeting other Shades might not be the worst idea.

Maybe there was someone out there who was exactly like Evrin in every way, but actually wanted a relationship and to be seen with me in public.

"I mean, I guess it would be fine." I shrugged. I had free room and board, all my meals were provided, and no one expected me to work. If nothing else, I definitely wasn't opposed to giving back a little. "They're not all whiny complainers, are they?"

Ophelia let out a startled laugh. "I'll be honest, I don't know any of them particularly well, but I certainly hope not. The Council of Shades has been on our case about this—they never liked Allerick's laissez-faire approach to integrating the Hunters who moved here into life in the shadow realm." Ophelia cleared her throat. "Selene definitely made me realize that we were keeping the pool quite limited by not venturing outside of court."

The more I mulled over the idea, the less absurd it became. Allerick and Ophelia were happy together, and the first time they'd met had been at the altar. I didn't intend on being quite that extreme, but maybe some kind of speed dating arrangement would be helpful in finding my person. My Shade.

Since the one I wanted wasn't available to me.

"If there's anyone you think I *should* meet—someone who is looking to settle down, mating bite, all that jazz—that I haven't met yet, maybe mix them in too?" I suggested, hoping I sounded more casual than desperate. My own picker was clearly busted. I didn't want to rely on it anymore.

"Oh." Ophelia blinked before tilting her head to the side. "I didn't think you were having any trouble meeting Shades? Maybe I should have been paying closer attention..."

"No, no," I replied hastily, not wanting her to think she'd done anything wrong or missed something she should have seen. "I haven't had trouble *meeting* them. I've *met* plenty."

"But not the right one?"

"No." The lie tasted like bile on my tongue. But how could Evrin be the right one if I couldn't keep him? No, I didn't believe that. The *right* one would want me back. He'd want everything, and he'd never let me go. I wasn't going to settle for less than that.

Ophelia played with the ends of her hair, looking contemplative before straightening, a determined expression on her face. "I'll make some discreet enquiries. Whoever you end up with will be so lucky to have you, Tallulah. You've got so much love to give."

I hoped that my smile looked less wobbly than it felt. "I think so too. Now I just need to find someone deserving of it."

Ophelia returned my smile, though it looked a lot more genuine than mine felt. "You will, I'll make sure of it. Okay, if you're certain about all of this, I'll start making plans."

I nodded twice—once to convince her, once to convince myself. "Let's make it happen."

 TALLULAH

CHAPTER 10

"Hey," Astrid said, striding over to where Meera and I were having breakfast in the dining hall. "You two need to come with me today."

I'd mostly gotten accustomed to Astrid's blunt way of speaking, but there were still times when I couldn't help but be irked that she never said please.

Astrid softened her tone at whatever expression she saw on my face. "A Hunter has defected, they left a note where Soren and I had stationed ourselves in the human realm. It could be a trap, of course," she added, not sounding particularly concerned either way. Astrid was a weapon all on her own, I doubted she was afraid of anything. "But if it's not… Well, she sounded like she really needed help, and I'm not going to let her down."

"Do you want us to accompany you to the human realm?" Meera asked, immediately straightening.

Astrid looked horrified. "Fuck no. You two need to stay here where it's safe. The last thing we need is another Verity situation. I'll bring her to you. I just need you two to be on standby to help me get her settled in." Astrid shifted uncomfortably on the balls of her feet. "You know I don't excel at being, you know, welcoming or whatever."

"I'm sure we can fill in those gaps," I said with what I hoped was a reassuring smile. If it wasn't a trap, if more Hunters really were defecting and coming to the shadow realm, that could only be a good thing. I had a responsibility to do my part to help them acclimatize to life here, the way Ophelia had helped us.

Astrid gave me a curt nod. "Great. Finish up then come with me—Soren is setting up a temporary entry room closer to Elverston House so she can get onto the grounds more discreetly. The note made her seem kind of frail. We thought parading her through the palace grounds to get there was a tall ask."

"Very thoughtful of you," Meera said softly. "I do hope that life here won't be too much for her."

Astrid smiled grimly. "Only one way to find out."

Andrus, a particularly smug member of the Guard who I loathed making small talk with, stood watch at the makeshift entry room as we waited for Soren and Astrid to return. I'd expected a larger contingency of both guards and a welcoming party, but Astrid had really meant it when she said she didn't want to overwhelm the new arrival.

"So," Meera began. "What was it that Ophelia wanted to talk to you about yesterday? Not that you have to tell me, of course. I'm just being nosy."

"She, uh, asked if I would go on some prearranged dates," I admitted.

"With some Shades who don't feel like they've had a fair shot at getting to know us."

Meera wrinkled her nose slightly, the only outward sign of her disapproval. "How do you feel about that?"

"I mean, I don't have anything else going on."

"Except some unresolved feelings from your fling at the ball."

"Ouch," I gasped, twisting to look at her. "Meera! Right in the heart."

She shot me a brief, unapologetic half smile. "It's true, though. Isn't it?"

I was pleading the Fifth on that one.

"I support you, of course," Meera continued. "And you're not making any promises by meeting with Shades who just want to meet you. Just... be careful, okay? With your heart."

"I will," I promised, my voice slightly strained. "You need to stop being so great, or I'll stink up the place with my feelings."

That earned me a slightly more confident smile.

"Andrus is quiet today," she whispered conspiratorially, leaning in close to speak in my ear. "Usually, he's always trying to get your attention."

"There's fresh meat coming through that door," I replied wryly. Andrus's attentions were fickle. Even if I had been able to overlook his Trust Fund Baby energy, he just seemed immensely unreliable.

Meera wrinkled her nose at the description, but it was only the truth. Andrus saw us as power sources first, romantic interests second. He was exactly the kind of Shade I wanted to avoid. Hopefully, Ophelia's vetting process would weed those ones out.

He straightened as the door opened, Astrid emerging first and holding it wide.

The first thing I saw was a dog.

A golden lab, to be specific. In a red vest with "Service Dog" printed in bold white text along the harness.

Followed by a pale, wan woman with patchy brown hair—her face tilted up toward the sky as she walked, gaze unfocused.

Shit. Elverston House was basically the least accessible building I'd ever encountered. There were stairs *everywhere,* and no handrails. The layout was entirely illogical. The stone floors were cracked and uneven. The bathroom facilities were all in the basement. None of the bedrooms were on the first floor.

Frankly, it was hazardous for *anyone* to live there. It was an ADA nightmare.

"Maybe we could convert one of the sitting rooms downstairs into a bedroom?" Meera suggested, chewing nervously on her lower lip, her thoughts clearly running along the same lines as my own.

"Tallulah, Meera, this is Iris Nash," Astrid said, gesturing at the newcomer. "And Tilly," she added, nodding at the dog.

"It's a pleasure to meet you," I said faintly.

Wait, *Nash*?

As a member of the Thibaut family, I was well acquainted with the higher-ups in the Hunter world, and the Nash family was definitely part of that. Though, I couldn't recall ever hearing about an Iris, and we looked to be similar enough in age.

"It's so nice to meet you too," Iris replied, her voice as calm as a lake.

Astrid looked at Meera and I before glancing expectantly at Elverston House as though waiting for us to take the lead. Astrid was great at looking at the bigger picture, but individual nuances were sometimes lost on her.

I widened my eyes meaningfully, giving my head a small shake. It would be entirely unfair to Iris to set her up in Elverston House on top of all the other adjustments that moving to the shadow realm required.

"What is this?" a voice asked, making everyone jump—even the usually observant captain. Damen appeared on the path behind us, all glowing purple eyes and charming smiles as always. He immediately crouched down, admiring the labrador. "What a magnificent creature."

"He means Tilly," I said hastily, not wanting Iris to get creeped out thinking she was being ogled by Shades. Which she undoubtedly would be, but they usually waited until dinner at least.

"Thank you," she said, her head turning toward my voice.

"They don't have dogs in the shadow realm," I added. "Prince Damen, this is Iris Nash and her dog, Tilly."

"My service dog," Iris added, her voice sweet and angelic. "I'm blind. Tilly is my eyes."

Damen startled, but made a gracious recovery. "Well, you and Tilly are both most welcome here. I hope you will find the shadow realm a happy home for both of you." He hesitated, shooting a wary look at Elverston House. *Finally.* At least someone was paying attention. "Tallulah and Meera stay in the accommodation that has been set aside for ex-Hunters, but perhaps you would be more comfortable in the palace, Iris? I believe it would better suit you and Tilly."

Who was *this* gentleman? Damen was usually the most relaxed, mischievous Shade at court. I'd never heard him be so *formal* before.

Iris's soft, closed-mouth smile was incredibly comforting somehow. I'd only met her five minutes ago, and yet I was more confident than I'd ever been in anything in my life that this woman was *kind* all the way down to her bones. "Well, I've never been inside a palace before, just heard about them in fairytales.

It certainly sounds like the kind of place where anyone could be comfortable."

Oh, she was sugary sweet. I half expected little hearts to start floating around Damen's head as he stared at her.

"We'll accompany you over there," Meera said, visibly relieved that Damen had come up with a solution. The palace had resources that Elverston House had not, simply by virtue of being filled with *staff*. It also wasn't crumbling to the ground, which was a massive bonus. And Ophelia and Astrid both lived in the palace, so Iris wouldn't be totally without non-Shade company.

Damen strode off, muttering a quiet stream of orders to Andrus before sending him to run ahead. It was a level of authoritative I'd never seen from him.

"Um, we'll just start walking straight ahead," I said for Iris's benefit, unsure how to proceed, and not wanting to offend her. "It's about two hundred feet away. The path curves a little on the way, but it's flat."

Iris's smile could have stopped traffic. "Thank you."

Meera and I moved to walk either side of her, leaving Damen to walk ahead, and Astrid and Soren to take up the rear.

"What made you decide to come to the shadow realm?" Meera asked softly.

Iris frowned thoughtfully. "Well, my parents kept me hidden away because they were ashamed of me," she began with startling bluntness. "And my nana who raised me, recently passed away, so the options of what they were going to do with me were looking quite bleak. Bleak enough that one of the Hunters decided that this would be a better option for me."

"One of the Hunters decided that?" I asked in disbelief. Maybe the tides were turning? I liked to think that the cold war we were engaged in would eventually thaw out, and we could have some kind of dialogue with the Hunters again, but it had felt like a pipe dream recently.

"I suspect what my parents had planned for me was very grim indeed for him to make that decision," Iris said serenely, making all of us do a double take. "But it was very kind of him to help me. I owe him a great debt."

The palace descended into chaos as soon as we arrived, with everyone rushing around to accommodate the shadow realm's latest resident, seemingly with no real sense of direction.

I looked expectantly at Damen while the staff debated room choices with one another.

"I should get my brother," he mumbled.

"Why? I mean, I get that he has *more* authority than you, but surely it's within your power to sort this out?" I suggested tentatively. Or I did my best to sound tentative. My patience was growing a little thin.

"That's not... I don't really do that."

My smile was more of a grimace by that point. There was no good reason he *couldn't*—Damen had just demonstrated outside that he was perfectly capable of jumping in and taking the lead. He just chose not to.

"Damen, you handled things really well out there," I said softly, maintaining eye contact and doing my best nonconfrontational corporate face. "It isn't realistic for King Allerick to personally address every logistical issue that the ex-Hunters face in moving here. You could really help us in this area."

I wanted to tell him off a little bit, because he was being a spoiled little princeling, but I didn't want to let my mouth run away from me and get banished back to the human realm.

He nodded once, gesturing for one of the staff to come over. "You're right. Okay. Yes. There's a ground floor guest apartment with a small garden area out front, near where Captain Soren and Astrid stay.

Please ready that room."

"Have you eaten, Iris?" I asked.

"No, but I'll be fine."

"I'll send for food," Damen said with a decisive nod.

"And some water for Tilly. Perhaps we could eat in the dining hall?" I suggested to Damen before turning my attention back to Iris, lightly touching her forearm. "We'll give you a tour of the place now while it's empty."

"I would appreciate that. Thank you."

"Great, let's go. We're going to make you feel so welcome here, Iris. Anything you need, just let us know," I said, giving her arm a squeeze.

Selfishly, I was glad for the opportunity to be useful in a way that wasn't going on random filler dates for Ophelia, hoping I would meet The One, or fussing with curtains that nobody but me cared about. I *liked* being helpful.

No, I needed it. I needed to feel needed, because what was I bringing to the table otherwise?

EVRIN

CHAPTER 11

Evrin!" Captain Soren called, striding over and tilting his head in greeting. "I never thanked you for what you did the other day."

It took me a moment to realize that he was talking about me "rescuing" Verity.

"Please don't. I basically tripped over her. There were no heroics involved."

He almost smiled. "Thank you, regardless. I noticed you've been staying on longer and longer after your shifts recently. Is there anything you wanted to... discuss?"

I almost shuddered. This kind of conversation didn't come naturally to either of us. But I appreciated that the captain was at least not standing several feet away from me like his horns might disintegrate if he got too close. It had taken a few months after I'd first joined the Guard for any of them to feel comfortable standing even somewhat close to me.

"No, nothing."

Soren shifted his weight awkwardly. "Well, don't overdo it. Selene suggested that you go to dinner tonight in the dining hall. Join in. There's something of a celebration going on with the new Hunter joining us."

Selene *would* suggest that. She was an outsider too, among the Guard, though in a very different way from me. Others weren't actively repulsed by her presence.

"Is that an order?" I asked. Soren gave me a pointed look and I sighed in resignation. "Fine."

"Good. I'll be checking that you're there."

Delightful.

I waited until the vast majority of the court had entered the dining hall, intending to slip in discreetly and sit at the back of the room, drawing as little attention to myself as possible—from both my fellow Shades who would be disturbed by my presence, and from Tallulah, who would undoubtedly be sitting at her usual spot near the front.

But I hadn't reckoned with what it would feel like to see her. And not in the distressed condition she'd been in the last time we'd bumped into each other either.

Tallulah's presence was so magnetic, so energizing, that even I—who was conditioned to avoid any and all socialization—was drawn in by it. It was the reason I'd approached her in the first place. Of course, that magic hadn't lessened any with time.

She was sitting with Meera, and the latest Hunter to defect to the shadow realm, Iris. Interestingly, Damen had condescended to sit with the masses rather than make a grand entrance with the king and queen before sitting at the high table as he usually did.

I found myself drifting toward Tallulah, despite my best intentions, following the path around the outer ring of the dining hall that the guards who patrolled this area used. The look on her face wasn't helping in my attempts to resist the pull. She looked… lost, somehow. Which was absurd, because Tallulah was one of the most sought-after beings in this room, and should theoretically feel at home anywhere in the shadow realm simply by virtue of *what* she was.

But I knew that wasn't how Tallulah thought. Tallulah didn't feel like she belonged. She felt anxious, and worried about what other people were thinking, and whether or not she was living up to their expectations.

And that bothered me. When it had been just the two of us, she'd been able to get out of her own head, and a happy, radiant Tallulah was a fucking *sight* to behold, and I wanted her to feel that confidence all of the time, even in a crowded room.

Tallulah looked up as I approached her already full table, as if she could sense my presence. There was a brief flash of surprise on her face before she schooled her expression into something perfectly neutral and gave me a polite nod. It was like a blow to the chest with a silver blade.

"Evrin!" Damen called out, waving me over. "What are you doing out in the light? I haven't seen you in years."

He stood, clapping me hard on the back—the physical affection making me startle—and gesturing for a courtly-looking Shade to move down and make room for me. He practically fell off the bench in his rush to get away from me, which in this instance, was an advantage of my condition.

What was I *doing*? Tallulah didn't want me here. That brilliant, beautiful confidence wasn't mine to give. That came from within her. I'd just had the privilege of witnessing it from time to time.

"I thought I'd try spending more time outside. It's nice out here."

Damen laughed loudly before turning his attention to the three ex-Hunters at the table. "Ladies, I'm guessing you haven't met Evrin—he patrols in the in-between. Evrin, this is Iris, Meera, and Tallulah."

"We've met," Meera volunteered. "At the Curia."

She glanced at Tallulah, the one who'd introduced us, but Tallulah pressed her mouth into a thin line and said nothing.

It was possible that she wasn't best pleased to see me.

"Patrolling the in-between sounds like a difficult job?" Meera ventured tentatively, shooting Tallulah a questioning look. Probably because Tallulah was *always* polite and charming, everyone knew that. She was well known for her conversational skills.

"It's not difficult so much as tedious," I replied, hoping my relaxed tone smoothed over the obvious awkwardness. Even Damen, who could be rather self-absorbed, seemed to have picked up on the tension.

"Why would it be difficult?" Iris asked, tilting her head toward me.

"It's just darkness as far as the eye can see," I explained. "It's considered somewhat oppressive."

Suddenly, everyone was silent—eerily so. Even Tallulah had swapped her haughty expression for something more akin to horrified.

Had I said something wrong? This is why I didn't socialize. It felt as though I was constantly balancing on a precipice with every word I said.

"Endless darkness can be very tedious," Iris agreed serenely. "I hope they're not all glaring at you for pointing that out. Just because I'm always in the dark doesn't mean others aren't allowed to express their discomfort. It's not a competition."

Iris had the calmest manner of speaking I'd ever heard, but the censure in her voice was clear, though not directed at me.

Oh. *Oh.* She couldn't see.

Perhaps I should just leave now. The captain was busy, with far more important things on his mind than my whereabouts. He probably wouldn't notice.

"Of course not," Damen said hurriedly, more contrite than I'd ever seen him. In fact, I wasn't sure I'd *ever* seen him contrite.

"Are you two old friends?" Tallulah asked politely, looking between Damen and me. I hated the indifference in her voice, but it at least moved the subject along after my misstep.

Tallulah's irritation with me also seemed to have replaced the worry she'd appeared to be feeling before I'd interrupted, which I was choosing to interpret as a positive side effect of my presence, though it was probably an arrogant assumption to make.

"Something like that." Damen grinned, though I detected a hint of uneasiness in it as he glanced at Iris.

"We were comrades in hedonism when we were young and stupid," I added dryly, because I wasn't about to cover for him. There were always members of the Guard who joined for the escapism, and Prince Damen had been plenty wayward and eager to indulge them in his youth.

Damen had never held my lack of horns against me. He'd barely even acknowledged it.

"Very young," Damen agreed hastily, still watching Iris's reactions. "And we weren't *that* stupid."

"How lovely that you're still friends after all this time," Iris said simply. "My nana used to say that old friends were precious as jewels. I didn't have any old friends, but she had lots that she liked to talk about."

"You have new friends now," Meera offered, swooping in to rescue the conversation as the rest of us faltered.

Iris sighed happily, perfuming the air with a bright, pleasant scent that could only be joy.

I'd never smelled anything quite like it from Tallulah. I'd smelled her arousal, and it had been fucking *mouthwatering*. And there had been moments of sweet happiness when we were talking—a scent I missed desperately now—but it had never been as pure and uncomplicated as what Iris was clearly feeling.

Tallulah's happiness had always smelled a little more precarious.

"So," Damen began, leaning forward on his elbows to speak to Tallulah across the table. Were they friends? Of course they were. Tallulah would be well acquainted with all the highest Shades in the realm by now. "What's this I hear about some arranged dates for you?"

I knocked my still-empty goblet over at the same time as Meera started loudly coughing. Iris startled, and Damen hurried to reassure her while I pulled myself together, quickly setting the goblet upright.

"Arranged dates? What arranged dates?" I asked roughly. Whose fucking idea was this? None of the other ex-Hunters were doing that shit. Were they? Maybe I needed to spend more time outside.

Tallulah gave me a flat stare across the table, and I marveled for a moment at just how much she was able to convey with her eyes alone.

"The queen asked me to meet with some Shades who don't spend time at court. As a favor."

"That is *quite* the favor," I replied—a little too sharply, if the looks Damen and Meera were giving me were any indication.

"Of course, you won't be pushed to do anything you don't want to do," Damen said cheerfully, glossing over my outburst. "And I am personally looking over the list Ophelia has, making sure they're all good prospects. Most of them are just shy and less comfortable approaching in a crowded room."

I exhaled heavily, dragging my shadows inwards around my body as they moved of their own accord, wanting to lash out in frustration.

This was always going to happen, remember?

No one wanted a Shade without horns. My work hours were terrible, and I didn't have a home of my own, or even a private room. I had nothing to offer anyone but myself, which seemed like something of a raw deal.

Or it had in the past. Because with Tallulah, *myself* felt more valuable. She'd been happy with me. Calm. I'd been able to offer her that sense of groundedness, and she didn't appear to be getting it from anywhere else.

Maybe.... Maybe I should have fought for that.

But that wouldn't have been fair on Tallulah. She clearly hadn't understood the extent to which being born without horns was a curse in the shadow realm.

The right thing to do would be to silently and supportively stand aside while Tallulah searched for that sense of calm I had given her with someone who wouldn't destroy her reputation.

That would be the *right* thing to do.

But I was wrestling with the urge to do the wrong thing. The thing I actually *wanted* to do, which was to be a thorn in her side until Tallulah realized that I would do anything to make her happy, reputation be damned.

Tallulah glared at me across the table as though she could hear my thoughts, and it sparked a possessive need in me that I'd never allowed myself to have.

Stop it, she mouthed, narrowing her eyes at whatever she saw on my face.

My lips tilted up in spite of myself, because I was selfish and at least she was talking to me. But that was where my selfishness had to end. I knew that.

I had to let Tallulah find the happiness she deserved.

But there was no fucking chance that I was leaving those decisions up to the queen and Damen. They didn't know Tallulah like I did.

No one on that list would be meeting Tallulah until I'd vetted them first.

CHAPTER 12

Despite it being a first date, and despite me being vaguely aware that I should try to make a good impression, I didn't spend nearly as much time getting ready as I usually would.

Partly because I didn't know anything about the dude I was meeting, which made it hard to work up any kind of excitement over it, but I was pretty sure I'd be feeling flat about the whole situation, regardless.

It's just a favor for Ophelia and Allerick, I reminded myself. Maybe I'd get lucky and it would turn out well, but in truth, I didn't think anyone was particularly expecting something to develop out of this.

I was putting on my best Networking Event face and keeping my expectations firmly at basement level.

Ophelia was waiting for me in the foyer as I came downstairs, and I knew her guard, Levana, would probably be at the outside border of Elverston house, ready to escort us wherever it was we were going.

"You look beautiful!" Ophelia said with a beaming smile, which I appreciated because my compliment jar had been running low since Evrin and

I ended things.

"Thank you. Where are we going, by the way?"

"Just the garden. The palace staff set up a little date spot for you there—I thought you might be more comfortable sticking close to home?"

"Definitely. Thank you." I pulled her in for a quick hug before we made our way outside. "Who am I meeting?"

"Oh, right. Tavaris. He's, um, very rich. From a fancy family."

"But doesn't come to court?" I asked, not recognizing the name.

Ophelia winced. "I get the impression he finds it a little beneath him. But he hosted us when we were traveling around the realm, and he has a beautiful home, with the most luscious gardens I've ever seen."

I already didn't like him, but I didn't tell Ophelia that when she was trying so hard to make him sound like an even somewhat viable option. If there was one thing I really couldn't abide after my upbringing, it was elitism.

"I'm going to stay discreetly nearby the whole time," Ophelia said as we made our way through the winding gardens. "And you can leave whenever you want. Just give the signal, and I'll be right over. Tug your ear or something."

"I really feel like someone less important than *the queen* should be doing date monitoring duty," I replied with a laugh, smoothing down my plum-colored pencil dress as we walked, grateful I'd opted for the comfy heels rather than the stylish ones.

"Don't be ridiculous, there's nowhere I would rather be. Okay, here we are." She squealed a little in excitement as she gestured at the small round table and two chairs that had been set up in a corner of the garden, beneath a canopy of flowers. It was incredible to see the faint pops of color starting to thread their way through the foliage in the shadow realm since we'd arrived here. While none of the flowers were bright, bold hues, there were subtle, beautiful hints of pink, gold, and red in them, and the leaves were the darkest shade of green they could be without being black.

There was a small silvery orb glowing in the center of the table, framed by yet more flowers, and two goblets, a bottle of wine, and an assortment of elegant canapes on the table.

It looked like something out of a fantasy-inspired reality TV dating show. I half expected a slowed down, acoustic cover of a pop song to start softly playing in the background as I left Ophelia behind and took my seat at the table, the lid on my emotional pot barely staying in place once I was on my own.

This was stupid.

I felt stupid.

Why had I thought this was a good idea? I was basically three seconds away from a full-blown anxiety attack, and the dude hadn't even arrived yet.

Keep it together, I chided, forcing myself to take a few deep, calming breaths. *You've been doing so well at tricking everyone into thinking you're not a walking, talking ball of panic. Don't screw up now.*

My chair scraped loudly on the stones as I pushed back, ready to bolt, but I froze as my date casually sauntered into the clearing, giving me a charming smile.

No, *not* my date. Evrin was not my date.

But it annoyed me that I'd felt a bubble of hope and relief at the idea that he was.

"Hello Tallulah," he said easily, taking the seat opposite me. "Going somewhere?"

"No," I lied. "But you are. That seat is reserved for someone else."

"Sadly, Tavaris can't make it. He asked if I wouldn't mind stopping by to let you know."

Ophelia's head popped out from behind a bush, the frown on her face clear as she stared at the back of Evrin's head, mouthing furiously at Levana.

I could have given her the signal.

I didn't, though.

"I don't believe that. What actually happened?" I narrowed my eyes as Evrin smoothly popped the cork from the wine bottle, pulling my goblet toward him to fill first before pouring his own.

It was... *smooth*. We'd never done anything like this. Our trysts had been secret and the barest of barebones—we'd basically had the ground, some shadows, and whatever cleanup supplies Evrin had shoved in his bag that day.

And I'd loved it.

Evrin flicked his floppy hair out of his eyes, and the motion made my heart do something stupid. Intellectually, I was over him. I'd decided to be. I was a strong, independent woman, and I didn't want to be hung up on him any longer. Unfortunately, my heart rudely wasn't playing ball with the prescribed timeline I'd given it.

"I don't know what to tell you," Evrin said lightly. "He finds himself indisposed on account of him being a massive prick."

"Evrin! Did you do something to him?"

"That would be most unlike me."

"That doesn't answer my question."

"I merely had a conversation with him, in which I ascertained that he was a massive prick, and his intentions toward you were dishonorable, and I suggested he find somewhere else to be tonight."

I narrowed my eyes, taking a sip of my wine. Though, in all honesty, if that was what had happened, then I couldn't find it in myself to be mad.

"How did you even find out about it?"

Evrin took a sip of his own drink, apparently choosing not to answer that question. It had to be Damen—the two of them had been friendly at dinner.

"I guess, if Tavaris's intentions *were* dishonorable, that I'm glad you're here and not him," I mumbled into my goblet.

"It's not my intention to make you uncomfortable, Tallulah," Evrin said solemnly. "If you'd prefer that I leave now, I absolutely will."

Did I want that?

The battle between my head and my heart continued to rage on, but when Evrin was sitting right there in front of me—looking *outrageously* good— my head didn't stand a chance.

"Stay."

CHAPTER 13

Stay.

I did my best not to read into it, but it was a struggle. Even if it was only because I was a better—or at least, *safer*—option than Tavaris. I would be having words with Damen after this about how these candidates were being determined, because I strongly felt that a greater level of discernment was required.

"How much did you know about Tavaris prior to sitting down at this table?" I asked, suspecting I already knew the answer.

"His name." Tallulah's cheeks went pink. "And that he has a nice house? Not that I care about that," she added quickly. "That information was just made available to me."

I grunted in irritation. Not that Tavaris was rich—he was. He'd recently inherited an impressive estate and was presumably in the market for heirs, which was undoubtedly why he'd insisted on being on this ridiculous list in the first place. But that simply wasn't enough information for Tallulah to be provided with.

Unfortunately, I was a nobody and my opinion was worth less than nothing, so I doubted the queen would take it well if I voiced that.

"What did you say to him to get him to stay away?"

"Merely that I would be here." My presence was usually plenty of a deterrent to keep Shades away.

Tallulah looked at me warily over the rim of her goblet, as if trying to figure out what it was about me that was terrifying. It was wrong of me not to explain it, not to lay out in detail that I wasn't scary, I was *repulsive*—but my ego wouldn't let me say the words out loud.

"Is that something you intend to keep doing?" Tallulah asked mildly.

"Yes. If these suitors of yours have got any sort of spine to speak of, they shouldn't have a problem telling me where to go," I groused, immediately squashing the desperate, primal instinct to pull Tallulah into my arms and remind her who she belonged to.

I didn't have that right.

But it was made exponentially harder when Tallulah's scent sweetened, a hint of desire mingled in with her pleasure at that answer.

Outwardly, she scoffed, giving nothing of her feelings away. "Yes, I'm sure they'll all feel perfectly comfortable telling the giant, brooding Guardian of Darkness to get stuffed."

Judging by her tone, she hadn't meant the description as a compliment, but I took it as one anyway. Guardian of Darkness had quite the mysterious ring to it.

"Do you really want to settle for a mate who isn't brave enough to stand up to me?"

She mumbled something into her goblet, something that sounded like, "I don't want to settle at all."

"What was that?"

"Nothing." She shook her head. "This is just a favor for the king and queen. I'm meeting Shades for them."

"And no part of you is hoping that you might meet someone you actually like?"

I picked up the top plate, filling it with a selection of delicacies from the tray in the middle and passing it to Tallulah before repeating the process for myself. She nibbled daintily at the edge of a cake, watching me through narrowed eyes.

"I don't know. Maybe I *did* think that. Now, I'm thinking of focusing more on healing my inner child and loving myself."

"Those sound like good uses of your time, too."

Tallulah laughed, though she did her valiant best to suppress it. "You know we're on a date right now."

"It does appear that way."

"That's something new and different for us."

I hummed in agreement, trying to make sense of her tone. It almost sounded like that was something she'd wanted. That I'd been the one denying it to her.

"This is someone else's date. If it were my date, I would have waited for you at Elverston House, told you how magnificent you look—you do, by the way—and brought you somewhere far less... on show than this."

A faint blush stole across Tallulah's cheeks, and her scent sweetened again in spite of the irritated glare she was trying to maintain. On reflection, I had never complimented her as much as I should have. I'd been physically attracted to her—to the point of madness—and I'd lazily relied on that to demonstrate that I found her beautiful.

I wished I knew what I was doing. I had almost no experience in anything that even resembled flirting. And yet... would it have been so hard to just say the words too? Why hadn't I done that? I could have given Tallulah that.

"What have you been doing today?" I asked, knowing that once I happened upon the right topic, Tallulah would lose herself in the conversation.

"Spending time with Iris, mostly. Getting her set up."

"Is she settling in comfortably at the palace?"

I fancied Tallulah looked a little gratified at the question and cursed myself silently again for not taking more of an interest in her life and friends in the past. I hadn't even known the name of that ex-Hunter when I'd found her half dead in the in-between.

"Yes, I think so. She didn't really have a lot of the stuff she needed, so I went through it with her today, making lists of what we had on hand and could provide, as well as a list for Astrid to take with her on her next supply run."

"I'm sure Iris appreciates all your help." My chest was tight, the overwhelming *affection* I felt for Tallulah coming back in full force at the reminder of her kindness.

She was just so very *good,* right down to her soul.

"It's nothing, really. Damen has really taken it upon himself to help her get settled in at the palace."

"Damen?" I repeated doubtfully. I knew him well enough to know Damen had it in him to be decent and helpful and generous. Usually, he just... didn't bother. I supposed he had no need to—his life was going to be comfortable and easy either way.

"I was surprised too," Tallulah admitted. "He needed a little encouragement, but he's really stepped up."

"And who provided him with that encouragement?" I teased.

Tallulah groaned, hiding her face in her hands, and peering out at me between her fingers—impossibly endearing, as always.

"I don't *mean* to insert myself into the middle of everything, I swear. It just keeps happening to me."

I hummed. "Or perhaps you struggle to walk away from a problem if you think you can fix it."

Whether that problem was old curtains or broken Shades.

"Maybe," Tallulah agreed softly, finishing her wine before setting the goblet down. "I should go. Ophelia is probably losing her mind over there, wanting to know what's going on."

I nodded. "Until your next unsuitable date, I suppose."

Tallulah's laugh was a little shaky as she stood. "Until then."

As dangerous as it had been for my peace of mind, the "date" with Tallulah last night had settled something inside me. Perhaps it was just that the way things had ended between us still felt so unfinished that I'd needed that one last time to sit down with her, and see her face, and hear her voice.

It had to be the last time, though. If I had to interrupt a date again, I'd do it from afar.

There was a faint vibration in the air, a reminder of the loud buzz that had once filled the in-between back when all of the portals had been active. I followed the pull toward it immediately, pushing past Shades who had been passing through the in-between, and paused at the sudden change in the air.

It was only one portal. It was probably the same situation as when Austin had arrived in the in-between, before I'd started my shift and the other guards had been slacking. But it could be something else, too. Perhaps Iris was one of the ex-Hunters that their council would take up arms to steal back.

Three Hunters walked through the now-active portal—two men and a woman. The woman appeared to be significantly younger than the other ex-Hunters who'd moved here, and she was the only one I didn't distrust on sight. Her scent was tinged with a slightly sour nervousness, but there was a layer of bright excitement beneath it, and her smile was open and friendly.

The men were more... shifty.

"I'm Sebastian," one said, pushing his blond hair out of his face as he stepped forward with his chest puffed out. It was a look of self-importance I recognized well from my brothers. "Sebastian Taylor. Perhaps you've heard of me?"

I stared at him in silence for a long moment. His eyes wouldn't be able to make out much, but they'd certainly see the glow of my eyes. "No."

"Never mind," the woman said hastily, stepping forward with a nervous giggle. "I'm Cora. This is my brother, Lochan. We're so happy to be here."

"Are you?" I murmured. I could see the resemblance between them—they had the same dark hair, brown eyes, and similar features. But Cora's expression was open and honest, and Lochan's was anything but.

My stalling had paid off. The hum of the now-functioning portal had attracted the attention of everyone passing through the in-between, including some members of the Guard. "I will take you to the king. Remove your bags and jackets, and empty your pockets," I ordered, watching them closely. It wasn't a foolproof defense strategy, but the darkness worked to my advantage and likely gave them a sense of security they hadn't earned. If there was even a flicker of hesitation on their faces, I would see it.

They were either honest or skilled, all three of them instantly following my instructions and handing over their possessions to the waiting members of the Guard who'd moved in to assist.

"Tell them to hide Iris," I murmured, only barely getting close enough to say the words quietly, since the guard was busy trying to get away from me.

He nodded, sprinting ahead, and the other members of the Guard formed a loose formation around us—with a wide berth for me—as I led the trio to the portal in front of the palace, taking my time to allow the news to circulate.

All of the key decision makers in the realm had already gathered on the palace steps by the time we emerged, looking down at the newcomers.

"Absolutely not," Astrid said as I stood off to one side, alert and ready to intervene in case of an attack. "Send them back."

"Do you know them?" Captain Soren asked his mate.

"That one is Verity's ex-boyfriend," she said flatly, staring down a pink-cheeked Sebastian. "*That* one is a Council bootlicker, and the biggest narc I've ever met," she added, more derisive this time as she glared at Lochan, who narrowed his eyes right back. "And I don't know her."

"I'm Cora, the narc's little sister," Cora supplied cheerfully.

"And what, precisely, are you doing here?" King Allerick asked, angling himself in front of his wife so she was obscured from view.

"We're a peace offering," Sebastian said, spreading out his arms wide as though it was obvious.

"I think we should kill them, to be safe," Astrid suggested, turning to speak to the royal couple, though not troubling to lower her voice.

Queen Ophelia laughed a little too loudly. "She's joking. We don't kill peace offerings."

"The Astrid I remember didn't joke," Lochan replied with a frankly astounding amount of smugness, considering who he was talking to. Then again, he and Astrid had always been on the same team. He'd never had a reason to be afraid of her before.

He probably should be now. Astrid was a fierce warrior, and thus far, didn't appear to be afraid of anything.

"Speak about me like we're long-lost buddies again, and I'll cut out your tongue," Astrid said calmly. Lochan smirked at her, but wisely kept his mouth shut.

"Why don't you elaborate on the peace offering thing a little more?" Ophelia suggested, looking to Sebastian for an answer.

"Sure. I'd love to do that. It's just... Where's Verity?"

To my surprise, it was Damen who answered. "I strongly suggest for your own safety that you don't ask that question again. My brother is a possessive mate, and ill inclined to control his temper."

Sebastian paled before attempting a relaxed smile. I wondered if he knew that his acrid scent gave him away.

"It's pretty clear that the Hunters' plan wasn't working. As Ophelia—Queen Ophelia—pointed out, fear is part of the balance. She said removing the Shade presence would be shortsighted in the extreme and, well, she was right. Things have been..."

"Wrong," Cora volunteered when Sebastian's silence extended. "Just wrong. There's been a general air of wrongness since the portals closed—like the very air itself tastes strange."

"Can you see why we might have reservations about believing you?" the king drawled.

"Absolutely." Sebastian nodded enthusiastically. "That's why we're here. We are at your mercy, all but helpless in your realm, ready to prove our intentions are honorable."

"And those intentions are?" Damen laughed. "Find Shade mates of your own and make a home here? Make your own personal contributions to our power stores?"

"Yes," Cora said with a decisive nod of her head.

Her brother shot her an appalled look. "If that's what it takes. But we're here first and foremost as a delegation on behalf of the Hunters Council. We want to work together, to find long-lasting solutions that benefit everyone—Shades, Hunters, and humans. Sebastian and I have been given considerable decision-making power in this regard so that we are able to negotiate without constant delays to get feedback."

"I might be more optimistic if they hadn't sent a lawyer and a PR manager," Astrid muttered. "Why are you here, Cora?"

"Because I wanted to come, and my brother isn't good at saying no to me."

Lochan's expression, and his scent, soured at this—I suspected because Cora was speaking the truth. It certainly seemed as though she'd talked him into allowing her to tag along, and he was frustrated with his decision.

At that moment, Tallulah and Meera edged to the front of the crowd, and my focus shifted from the new arrivals entirely to Tallulah. She looked so beautiful in her dark green dress and her hair elaborately tied up with a ribbon, as she hesitantly glanced between the new Hunters, the royal contingency, and me.

"You're here to... negotiate?" Meera asked warily. "On behalf of the Hunters Council?"

"We are." Sebastian nodded earnestly. If he was an actor, he was a good one. "This probably won't surprise you, but there have been plenty of mixed reactions to the Council's edicts, and those who felt that their strategy was… short-sighted and ill-advised have become the loudest voices."

Tallulah and Meera exchanged guarded looks, and I desperately wished I could climb inside her head and see what was going on in there.

The king and queen made their way over to where Tallulah and Meera were standing, speaking in low voices. I shifted around the edge of the crowd, hoping it looked like I was just circling the new arrivals for security purposes and not so I could eavesdrop.

"…not mention Iris. Would you be comfortable with them staying at Elverston House?" Queen Ophelia asked them. "Or you two could move into the palace for the time being? We're not sure it's a good idea to have *them* in the palace, though. Obviously, we need to be careful what information they are exposed to until we know if their intentions are genuine."

"I'm more inclined to keep our enemies closer," Tallulah said, though she looked cautious. "If they're in Elverston House with us, we're in a better spot to assess their intentions."

Meera nodded. "It would probably be wiser than leaving them to their own devices."

"That's irrelevant if you two don't feel safe and comfortable," the king interjected. "We can easily set you both up in the palace and assign guards who *are* allowed on the grounds of Elverston House."

Tallulah shook her head, looking more determined this time. "No, it's better if we do it. They're more likely to slip up around us, and we'll have a better idea of what to look out for."

"If you're sure," Queen Ophelia said sternly. Why wasn't anyone asking me if *I* was sure? Because I was not. I didn't want Tallulah around this at all.

It physically hurt to hold back my opinion, but I wasn't entitled to give it. If only my head would get the message it was over, because it certainly didn't *feel* over. It felt like there was an invisible string connecting us, and while the edges had frayed a little, it hadn't snapped yet.

For the briefest of moments, Tallulah spared me a glance that was entirely honest, and just for me. A wide-eyed hint of the worry that plagued her, despite her best efforts to hide it. But then she pulled herself together as though it had never been, straightening her spine and smiling determinedly at the royal couple.

Of all the cruelty I'd experienced over the years because of my lack of horns and the disappointment I'd caused my family, not being able to walk up to her and pull her into my arms at that moment might have been the most agonizing blow.

And she'd allow it, which almost made it worse. The Shades closest to me shuffled away with as much discretion as they could manage, a reminder of why this connection between us—as amazing and right and *perfect* as it felt—could never be.

I'd ruin her.

TALLULAH

CHAPTER 14

There was an inconvenient fluttering feeling in my throat when I looked at Evrin, standing tall and proud in the daylight, having taken charge of the new Hunters and delivered them here. As much as I desperately wanted to be over him, last night had made it pretty obvious that I wasn't.

I'd woken up *jittery* from how horny my dreams had made me. Taking care of myself had been such a time-consuming ordeal that I'd missed breakfast, because one orgasm absolutely hadn't cut it. My vagina had developed a Pavlovian response to Evrin's presence, and I wasn't sure how long it would take to train myself out of it.

But at least I now had a really good distraction to keep me occupied.

"Come on," I told Sebastian, Lochan, and Cora. "I'll show you to Elverston House where you'll be staying."

"What about our stuff?" Lochan asked.

"I'm sure it'll be brought along shortly," Meera said appeasingly. *After it had been searched for weapons.* Something about Lochan's smile made me feel uneasy, but it might have just been the borderline *blinding* veneers. Those things could have lit the way through the in-between like a beacon.

On the other hand, Cora seemed so genuinely happy to be here that I felt bad for being suspicious of Lochan's intentions. Surely, he wouldn't have brought his bright-eyed and bushy-tailed little sister here if his motives were malicious.

Sebastian, with his false charm and somehow smug walk, I could definitely do without. But the duke wasn't my cup of tea, either. Verity had strange taste in men.

"So," Cora began, bouncing slightly with each step as we made our way through the gardens toward Elverston House. While we weren't being obviously followed, I had no doubt there was someone shadowing us. "What's it like here? Are you happy? Do you have a significant other? What do you eat? Do you miss your phone?"

I'd gotten so used to comfortable silence living with just Meera, that it took my brain a moment to process the bombardment of words.

"Definitely not to the last one," I laughed. I'd never been a fan of my phone even in the human realm, and I'd been living as off-grid as I could manage before I'd made the move here, so the adjustment hadn't been too difficult for me to make. "I'm happy. I'm dating, still finding my feet. There are plenty of food options, though, they are mostly meat-based. Meera is working on a vegetable garden. It's coming along really well."

Meera shot me a small, grateful smile, though I could see that she had shrunk in on herself slightly with the new arrivals. I had no doubt she was going to vanish into the garden the moment it was socially acceptable for her to leave, and that would be the last I'd see of her for hours.

"Wow," Cora whispered, staring up at Elverston House as we turned off the main path, heading up the smaller one that led to the front doors. "This is where we're staying?"

"*This* is where we're staying?" her brother repeated, far less enthusiastically. "I thought that Hunters were supposed to be all special and valued here. This place is a ruin."

"Come now, Lochan," Sebastian laughed, though it was in a very inauthentic, salesman-on-the-golf-course kind of way. "It might be nicer on the inside."

"It's not," I replied cheerfully. "But it's a private residence within walking distance of the palace—regular walking, not shadow walking, so we can get here without assistance. That's not usual in the shadow realm. Geographically, things are often pretty spread out, since distance isn't an obstacle for Shades. No Shades are permitted to enter the grounds of Elverston House, so this area is a safe haven of sorts—just for us." I shrugged. "It needs a little love, but we've been working on making it more comfortable."

I'd gotten more defensive about it than I'd intended to, but I think something about the grand, dilapidated building sort of spoke to me.

It just needed some love.

Ten out of ten, could relate.

"I, er, don't suppose Verity lives here?" Sebastian asked hopefully.

"No," I said flatly. "Prince Damen wasn't joking—don't let Verity's mate hear you so much as speak her name, or he will turn you into shadows. Whatever you thought you saw of Verity in the human realm, you didn't. Not the real her. She has a life here, she's happy here, and she did what she had to do to get back here. Do you understand?"

He swallowed loudly. "I understand."

Meera coughed lightly, probably a little shocked at my bluntness, while I side-eyed Sebastian for a little longer so he knew I was serious. If I was being gracious, I would accept that he didn't know how permanent and unbreakable a mating bond was. That he didn't fully realize that he had no shot with Verity, if that's what he was even hoping for. But I wasn't feeling gracious. Honestly, I'd been in a weirdly foul mood all day, even with the orgasms, and I couldn't seem to snap out of it. PMS, probably.

"We gathered as much," Lochan said evenly. "That Verity had perhaps misled us," he clarified.

"Outwitted, more like," Cora laughed, nudging her brother out of the way so she could head inside right after me. She looked at the high, arched ceilings and stone floor with the same awe that I'd felt when I first came here. Like she was seeing something magical and filled with potential, and it sparked the memory of that feeling within me as well. The weight of uncertainty and heartbreak and disappointment had been weighing on me, making me second-guess my decisions. But moving to the shadow realm had been a *good* one. And the pain I'd felt recently was kind of better than not feeling anything. In a weird way, it was kind of reassuring to know that I *could* get out of my own head long enough to feel so strongly about someone else that their absence could hurt me.

"Two of the rooms upstairs—Astrid's and Verity's old ones—are cleared out and ready for new occupants," I said, mostly thinking out loud. "We'll have to open up another one."

"I'll get the cleaning supplies," Meera volunteered, veering off at the base of the stairs while I led the trio up, vaguely giving them a guided tour, though there wasn't that much to say. Most of the rooms were still closed off to minimize the amount of maintenance we had to do.

Cora took Astrid's old room, and Lochan went into Verity's. The afternoon passed quickly as all five of us worked to make up beds and clear a dust-coated bedroom for Sebastian's use. The luggage was deposited at the boundary line at some point, and if anything was missing from their bags, none of them mentioned it while they unpacked. I liked to hope that if they'd been carrying weapons, one of the Guard would have let Meera and I know for our own safety, so I assumed that hadn't been the case.

"I'm going to wash up," I announced, smoothing over the quilt on the freshly made bed. "Dinner is a couple of hours away in the palace dining hall, but the bathing room downstairs is a communal space, so we're going to have to be... courteous of each other."

Maybe I should have taken Ophelia up on the whole move-to-the-palace idea, if only for the private bathroom. But living in the palace would be like living under a microscope. I need the seclusion of Elverston House to have my freakouts in peace.

I bathed quickly before heading back up to my room and picking out a dress for tonight, selecting a dark red one that I perhaps wouldn't have chosen if I hadn't seen Evrin earlier, standing around looking unfairly attractive.

That asshole.

I'd made the dress myself, tailored perfectly to my size, but it wasn't fitting well at all as I tugged it into place, fussing with the side zipper to try to get it up. Had I been stress eating? Probably. Still, it hadn't gotten stuck over the middle where I'd expect it to. It was the *top* I was having trouble with.

I knew my measurements. I'd known them for years, and I knew which parts of me were prone to gaining and losing inches. My bust, historically, was not one of those places. And yet, this dress was constrictingly tight around my breasts, there was no doubt about it.

Ugh, was I having another growth spurt at thirty? That would be incredibly unreasonable, since I finally had a collection of bras that actually fit me, and there were no lingerie stores in the shadow realm.

By the time I made it downstairs—in a far less form-fitting blue dress—everyone else was gathered and ready. Sebastian and Lochan looked vaguely uncomfortable in their business casual outfits, while Cora was dolled up to the nines in a slinky black dress and strappy gold heels, though it was definitely the blood-red lipstick that would catch everyone's attention.

I wondered if Lochan realized the same thing, since he was scowling so heavily. "Can we make some kind of announcement at dinner that Cora is only eighteen since she insists on dressing like a twenty-five-year-old?"

"Misogyny isn't a good look on you," Cora said with a sugary-sweet smile. "I can dress however I want."

"You look lovely," I told her, though she *was* young, and I was absolutely going to be making sure that no Shades got pushy with her. "You're in control here, okay? Always. And we're here to help if you want support or a hand to hold or an exit strategy," I added, gesturing between Meera and myself. "Deal?"

Cora squealed, throwing her arms around my shoulders to give me a quick hug. "Deal. You're the best."

Meera had discreetly taken a step back, and I was glad to see Cora read her body language in real time and only offered her a smile.

Unsurprisingly, the dining hall was even more packed than usual. The news of fresh Hunters must have spread, and while our usual spot at the front of the room was free, it looked a lot more cramped than usual—especially considering there were three more of us now.

It felt a bit like my very first meal in the dining hall all over again, with Shades craning their necks to try to catch a glimpse. I knew no one was looking at me, but the general attention in my direction made my face heat anyway.

"Wow," Sebastian breathed. "This is incredible."

He was looking around constantly, scanning the room, and I wondered if he was trying to spot Verity in the crowd. He wouldn't find her, though. She'd be tucked up in her mansion right now, in a nest of fluffy pink blankets, living her best life.

"Yes," Lochan agreed, his response far more muted. "It's much bigger and more organized than I expected."

I eyed him warily, hoping the captain had set a member of the Guard on Lochan's ass. We were from similarly high-ranking families and had run in the same circles, though I'd never interacted with him directly since he was a good decade older than I was. At least with Sebastian, there was the Verity factor working in his favor. *Maybe* he had good, albeit misguided, intentions.

But Lochan had everything to gain by participating in the Hunters Council's corrupt system, and nothing to gain by leaving it.

I was glad that the call had been made to keep Iris hidden away. Her mother was powerful, and I wouldn't have been surprised at all to discover that Lochan's angle in coming here was just recon on behalf of Moriah Nash.

I'd been so distracted by my musings that, for once, I hadn't automatically scanned the dining hall for Evrin the moment I walked in, but suddenly he was there, right in front of me.

Meera was ushering the others onward, eager to get to the table, and my good manners wouldn't allow me to just march off and ignore him.

Okay, maybe it was a little more than just manners keeping me in place.

"I didn't realize you were so fond of eating in the dining hall."

"Neither did I. I've been learning a lot of new things about myself recently." He leaned against the wall, serene as could be. Everyone gave us a wide berth, and I wondered what it would be like to just walk around, not being jostled constantly. "How are you feeling about your new housemates?"

"Fine."

I may as well have "not fine" tattooed on my forehead because that tone wasn't convincing anyone.

Evrin grinned, like my petulance was amusing to him. "You don't sound fine."

"What would you know about how I sound?"

I wished I could take the words back the moment I'd said them. There was an extra glint of teeth as Evrin's smile widened, his shadows seeming to curl toward me of their own volition.

Evrin knew a little something about how I sounded at least *some* of the time, but he politely didn't call me out on that. Not with words, at least. His expression was impressively loud, though.

"Well, great chat. I'm hungry," I announced, flipping my hair over my shoulder as I stepped around him, half stomping to my usual table. Evrin didn't quite dog my footsteps, but he did follow me.

And annoyingly, I kind of liked it. In the human realm, at 5'5, I was solidly average height for a woman. *Here*, I was dwarfed by even the smallest Shades, and moving around the packed dining hall was always a stressful experience.

Maybe Evrin was a fiercer fighter than his gentle giant disposition let on, because the crowd parted like the Red Sea when he appeared. It was bewildering and intimidating and *nice* all at once. The fear that I was going to be knocked into a table had all but vanished, but the fact that everyone responded to him this way was kind of weird. Like there was a bright, glittery red flag that was apparently obvious to everyone else but that I'd missed entirely.

I was being paranoid, right? Right. That was the intrusive thoughts talking. I liked to think that I knew Evrin... Okay, not that well. He actually had said very little about his personal life. But I was a good judge of character, wasn't I? And Damen liked him, which was a vote of confidence. Except for the fact that they used to be party buddies back in the day, and that was how they knew each other.

Shoot, I didn't really know this guy at all.

"Your table is a little more crowded tonight," Evrin observed.

"Very astute of you to notice."

Evrin laughed quietly, though it sounded loud to me. It echoed in my head and wrapped around my bones, encasing me in a feeling of false safety. How frustrating that I'd so easily given him the power to make me feel this way, and yet it was such a fight to get it back.

It wasn't until I was standing behind the group of *new* Hunters that I realized there really wasn't any room for me. Maybe there would be if I spoke up and asked them to squeeze up for me, but just the thought of doing that made my throat feel fluttery with panic. What if they said no? What if they were annoyed by my request? I could just find somewhere else to sit. It wasn't worth putting someone else out—

"Is there room for one more?" Evrin asked smoothly, leaning around me to speak to Sebastian. Judging by the way Sebastian startled, I was almost positive he exploded with some kind of unpleasant fear response scent, but Evrin didn't let on. He simply stood back and waited for them to move before lightly touching the base of my spine, encouraging me forward.

Goose bumps broke out along my arms as he leaned in to speak in my ear. "How is it that you're so good at speaking up for everyone else, hm? Enjoy your dinner, Tallulah."

And then he was gone as if he'd never been there. I sat down on shaky legs, ignoring Meera's probing look from the other side of the table, as I mentally reset my "getting over Evrin" scale back to zero.

CHAPTER 15

The captain had clearly made an effort to assign more members of the Guard to the in-between today, filling my peaceful sanctuary with loud, obnoxious assholes who didn't want to be here. It was likely only a temporary measure—the portal that had come back to life yesterday continued to hum away quietly, and it did require some additional monitoring.

It wouldn't last though. The others would get too antsy being in the dark for so long, and would eventually find an excuse to be somewhere else.

"This seems excessive," Galen muttered, pacing in front of the portal. I'd walked for miles today, checking all of the other ones, and finding them all still quiet as I expected—I'd have felt it if more had flared back to life.

That this one was still on didn't have to mean anything nefarious. It made sense that the negotiating party would have an exit strategy in place, one that wasn't dependent on Shades to help them return to the human realm. They were meant to be relaying messages between the various governing bodies, if nothing else.

Nothing about any of it felt particularly in good faith to me, though.

"How do you do this all day?" Galen muttered, watching me warily as I lingered perhaps a little too close to him for his comfort, mulling it all over. My presence clearly made him uncomfortable, but he wouldn't say as much while he was in what was widely considered to be my domain.

"Practice."

"Do you think any more Hunters will come through?"

I gave Galen an assessing look, trying to figure out why he was talking to me. Usually, no one bothered. Perhaps he was just out of his mind with boredom being in here for so long.

"No, I don't think so."

"Me neither," he agreed hurriedly, like he was worried I was going to end the conversation. He really *must* be bored. "I don't think these are actually peace negotiations, anyway. I think they've just come here to try to convince the ex-Hunters here to leave so we'll starve."

I stilled, not having considered that angle. Perhaps because the idea of the ex-Hunters who'd made their homes here leaving seemed too remote to be a real possibility.

Tallulah wouldn't leave. Right?

"Why do you think that?"

"Well, one of them was in love with Verity, right? So maybe they thought he could convince her. And I heard the young woman talking at dinner about Austin and how she used to watch him sing or something, so maybe she's here for him? Presumably, they wouldn't even bother trying to get the queen or Astrid back—they might have conceded defeat on that front. So then perhaps the other man knows Tallulah or Meera, or both? Or they think one will follow the other." He lowered his voice. "And we don't know if they know about Iris. None of *us* have mentioned her, but they haven't either. Maybe they know, you know?"

"It was a Hunter who directed Iris here," I murmured distractedly, having at least some information on that front. "But we have no idea if that Hunter told anyone else about it. There's a very good chance that they know, and the reason they're here is for her."

I shifted my weight uncomfortably, wishing my shift was over. Tallulah hadn't looked *overly* familiar with the new Hunters when I'd seen her interacting with them, but that didn't mean she'd never met them before. Fuck. What if that weaselly little Lochan had been in love with her, the way Sebastian had been with Verity? I should have just killed him the first time he'd irritated me.

"I don't think they'll leave," Galen said with unearned confidence, since the only ex-Hunter he'd probably had any interaction with was Astrid, as she was part of the Guard now. From what I'd heard, she *couldn't* go back. She was the Hunters Council's greatest enemy. "They're happy here, right? Why would they go back? The human realm seems terrible. It's so *loud*."

"Depends where you go, I guess," I pointed out. It was easier to feed in big cities, so Shades usually opted to go there when we went through, but that didn't mean humans had to live there.

I was desperate to speak to Tallulah.

The idea that she might someday leave had never occurred to me. She seemed to be such a permanent fixture at court, so popular with everyone, so depended upon by the other ex-Hunters, including the queen. But if the Hunters Council were willing to entirely forgive her for coming here in the first place, if she was allowed to return home without consequences...

By the time I exited the in-between after my shift, I'd worked myself up into a state of near panic. I wasn't even sure what I wanted to do first, though logically, I knew that I should go straight to Captain Soren and provide him with an update—namely that there were no updates. But logic wasn't ruling my mind at that precise moment.

"Evrin!"

I stopped instantly at the sound of Tallulah's voice, the relief I felt immediately energizing me after what had been a long and exhausting day.

"Hi," I said, embarrassingly breathless just to be speaking to her. "How are you? How was your day?"

"It was good." She shifted on her feet, pulling her pale pink coat a little tighter around her. The Herst winds were blowing today from the mountains, sending a chill through the usually temperate palace grounds. "I don't really know why I'm here."

Tallulah laughed nervously, and it broke my heart a little. She'd laughed like that when we'd first met, but over time she'd grown more comfortable with me, and it had changed into something throatier, and more authentic.

At least she hadn't used the bright, confident laugh that she used on everyone else, but it wasn't much of an improvement.

It was like what we had never existed.

"You're cold. Here, let's get out of the wind." I ushered her toward the palace where the smooth stone columns next to the stone outer wall would shelter her a little. "You should really stay inside today until the Herst wind dies down. It blows through every year."

I'd intended to bring up Galen's theory, to casually discover whether Tallulah knew Lochan, and if she was intending on leaving if he suggested it, but I was distracted by the sight of her overbright eyes and flushed pink cheeks. Even the tip of her nose had turned an adorable shade of red.

Tallulah shifted restlessly. I'd been staring too long.

"Oh! That's why I came to find you." Another nervous laugh. "I, um, just wanted to say thank you for yesterday."

"Okay." I couldn't think of a single thing I'd done that would warrant her gratitude. Unless she was thankful I'd led Lochan to her, in which case I didn't want to know.

"When you asked the others to make space for me at the table," she clarified.

Ah. "I thought you may be having trouble asking for what you wanted."

"That does seem to be a recurring issue of mine," Tallulah muttered. "How was your day? Anything exciting happen in the in-between?"

"No new arrivals, if that's what you mean. The captain has assigned me an abundance of colleagues. I suppose that's exciting."

Her smile looked a little more genuine this time. A little less brittle. "You sound thrilled about that."

"None of them want to be there. It doesn't make for the most relaxing work environment. How have you spent your day?"

"Sewing. Almost everything in Cora's room needs to be replaced. I thought I'd make a start on it."

"That seems very practical, especially since there are more of you living there. Perhaps more still to come, if some kind of agreement can be made. Did any discussions happen today?"

Tallulah's thoughtful expression was almost as delightful as her smile. "I wouldn't call them discussions. Introductions were made to the Council of Shades, apparently."

I wondered if Roan had been part of those conversations, or maybe his position wasn't quite secure enough to be included in that yet.

Tallulah shivered again, and I ushered out from next to the column. "Come on, we should get you inside before you freeze. Are you going to the palace, or shall I escort you to Elverston House?"

For the first time in many years, I wished I had my own residence. It wasn't something that particularly bothered me in the past—the barracks were clean, comfortable, and convenient—but if I had my own apartment...

Would I have invited Tallulah back there? Would she have said yes? Probably not.

"I wasn't really going anywhere," Tallulah hedged, her teeth chattering slightly.

That was all the opening I needed. "Come on. I know a spot in the palace where you can warm up."

I wouldn't have risked it if I thought we'd run into anyone, but there was always a lull in the afternoon, before the dinner rush started, from my memories of spending time in the palace with Damen. Tallulah followed me down the quiet corridors and spiral staircases with a gratifying level of trust. That, at least, hadn't disappeared. On the bottom level were the kitchens, but I led Tallulah through to a spacious room behind them, heated by a shared wall that housed the kitchen's enormous fire on the other side.

"Oh," Tallulah breathed, drifting toward the warm bricks, already unbuttoning her coat before crossing the room to sit in one of the mismatched chairs that had accumulated in this space over the years. "This is wonderful. I had no idea this place existed."

I leaned against the wall next to the door, ready to slip out and preserve Tallulah's reputation if anyone came in here to warm up.

"Damen and I would sometimes raid the kitchens after a night of drinking. This was many years ago. Before the current cook took up the post."

I wasn't sure I'd risk Calix's wrath in order to steal a few cakes. Old Jethro had never noticed.

"How come you drifted apart?" Tallulah asked, a soft smile playing around her mouth.

"We grew older. Grew apart. There's no real reason."

Privately, I suspected my presence had made Damen's other friends uncomfortable, and they'd encouraged him to avoid me. It had been a little unfortunate—for a few months, I'd experienced an almost regular version of friendship—but also not surprising.

"I hear you have a date tonight," I said casually. I could thank Damen for that, at least. I wasn't even sure why he'd told me, unless he'd heard about me intercepting Tallulah's last unworthy suitor, and thought Vicus deserved the same treatment.

Which he did.

Tallulah raised an eyebrow at me. "Did you now? Nothing is going to mysteriously happen to Vicus, is it?"

"I don't think it's mysterious that Vicus has been summoned back to his family estate to deal with an urgent flooding issue on his property."

Tallulah spluttered in outrage, and I thickened the shadows I was cloaked in, making sure my entirely inappropriate reaction wasn't on display. "You didn't... flood his house somehow, did you?"

I laughed. "No, of course not. I'm not risking being thrown into the Pit."

I really wouldn't be able to watch over Tallulah from there.

Besides, I hadn't needed to. Vicus's estate was built on reclaimed wetlands, and it flooded all the time. It had been something of a source of amusement to my father, who'd maintained a not-so-friendly rivalry with Vicus's father since adolescence.

Most of the time, I forgot entirely that I was from the same social class as those assholes, but it did come in useful from time to time. Personally, a flood wouldn't have kept *me* away from Tallulah, but Vicus had always been of a more fickle temperament.

"I assumed the queen would have informed you about the change in suitor for the evening," I added, feeling slightly guilty that I'd been the one to break that news to her.

"I haven't seen her today," Tallulah admitted. "Is it you?"

Dare I imagine there was a note of hopefulness in her voice? I was probably reading too much into it.

"No," I said slowly. "It's Aither. He was also on your list."

"It's not *my* list," Tallulah shot back, a little defensively. "I haven't even seen the list."

"Right. I don't think you would have put Aither on it if you knew him."

I was beginning to suspect that the queen—and whoever else was setting up these dates—didn't actually know Tallulah very well. They didn't know the Tallulah who snuck away from social events to find a small, dark space to collect her thoughts in. The Tallulah who was being courted by the finest Shades in the realm, but had only sought out the one who'd made her feel safe until I'd let what we'd had slip away by not holding on to it tightly enough. Well, that, and being with me would ruin her life.

Regardless, if someone was going to be choosing prospective mates for Tallulah, it seemed crucial to me that they knew those parts of her. But they couldn't, if she didn't tell them.

"Why do you say that?"

I shrugged. "Just a guess. I'm not concerned for your safety or anything—he's very honorable. He just doesn't seem like... you."

Tallulah swallowed loudly, dropping her gaze to the floor.

"What have you advised your committee of experts to look for in a prospective mate?" I asked, silently demanding her attention once more. Needing to see those beautiful eyes staring back at me.

"Committee of experts?" she repeated, spluttering slightly. "It's nothing so formal as you're imagining. I'm just... helping the king and queen out. Taking some of the pressure off of them that they're facing from the Council of Shades, and the other fancy Shades around the realm who feel like they aren't getting enough attention. Or I'm *trying* to, but my dates keep mysteriously vanishing."

"I know you're fond of putting other people's wishes before your own, but surely, you're a little curious about them for your own benefit, too? Hoping that they'll be a good fit for you?"

"I want to find love. Is that so outrageous? I know I'm not perfect, but I think I am worthy of that. And I have a lot of love to give."

I softened my tone, the defensiveness in hers making my chest ache. "You are more than worthy of love, Tallulah. You're incredible, and I have no doubt that whoever you choose to bestow your affections on will be the luckiest Shade in the realm. And that is why I will keep interfering—to make sure you don't have entirely unsuitable Shades like Tavaris sitting across the table from you, salivating over your neck as though they are even remotely worthy of placing their bite there."

Tallulah's face was carefully blank, but her scent wasn't. It sweetened instantly, filling the warm air with the smell of her need.

I swallowed thickly, pressing myself as far back against the wall as I could go without leaving the room entirely. Perhaps leaving would have been the smarter thing to do, but I was too fucking obsessed with her to go through with it, even if I was trying to do the right thing and let her move on.

"Don't say stuff like that," Tallulah whispered, breathing heavily. "I can't... I can't keep a lid on how I'm feeling when you say stuff like that."

"I'm sorry you feel like you have to," I rasped. *Desire,* I reminded myself. *It's just desire.* I wanted to say more, wanted to beg to get inside her head and find out what she was thinking and whether there was any affection there for me or if I'd squandered even the potential of it, leaving only sexual attraction in its wake.

But I couldn't do that. She clearly didn't place the same importance on horns as everyone else in the realm did, but it would come up eventually. It would ruin her life here, her social standing, her friendships. Undoubtedly, if she wore my bite, Tallulah would be treated with the same revulsion I was, and that idea was untenable.

"Can you find your way out of here?" I asked. "Or shall I walk you up...?"

Her scent soured instantly. "I know my way back from the kitchens. Thanks, though. I guess I'll see you around."

I nodded once, backing out of the room so I could keep her in my sights until the last possible moment, memorizing her pouty, down-turned mouth and glistening blue eyes.

The goddesses were cruel indeed to put Tallulah in my path but make me too damaged to keep her, and I cursed them every step of the way to see Captain Soren and report on my shift.

"There you are!" Damen huffed, intercepting me on my way back to the barracks after I'd debriefed Soren. "I've been looking everywhere for you."

I glanced behind me, though I was certain I hadn't heard anyone else on the path.

"*You*, Evrin."

"What is it? Has something happened?"

"Tallulah's date is going terribly. This is a great opportunity for you, come on." He grabbed my arm with an impatient huff—the physical contact startling me—and tugged me toward the palace, only releasing me when he was satisfied that I was keeping pace with him.

I watched surreptitiously to see if he would try to wipe the hand that had touched me on something, but he didn't.

"Damen... This isn't a good idea. I need to stop getting in her way. I want Tallulah to be happy."

Damen shot me a dismissive look over his shoulder. "And you think she's going to be happy with *Aither*?"

I came to a stop, forcing him to do the same. "Obviously not, but that doesn't mean that I should interfere. I can't keep interfering. Everyone is going to start noticing how much I speak to her if I keep doing this, how much she speaks to *me*. You know that would be disastrous for Tallulah."

Damen scowled as though this personally offended him, which wasn't the reaction I'd expected. While he'd never been as bothered about my condition as, well, everyone else in the realm, he'd never voiced any opinion to indicate that the treatment of me had bothered him.

"I'm not saying it will be easy, but times are changing. Don't you think she's worth it?"

It was easy for him to say, and yet the words were still a blow to my chest. "*Of course,* Tallulah is worth it. That's why I have to stay away. Damen, she doesn't understand. She doesn't get why everyone treats me the way they do. I'm not even sure she's noticed how bad it is. And I can live with it, but I'd fucking *kill* someone who spoke to her as if she was less than because of me."

Damen's shadows rippled in irritation, but he didn't argue with me. He couldn't. We both knew that I was telling the truth.

"At least if you explain it, explain the... *risks*, Tallulah would be able to make that decision for herself."

I was shaking my head before he even finished speaking. "She'd choose me out of pity, Damen. Just to make me happy. Tallulah puts everyone's happiness before her own."

He made a sound of frustration, but nodded in understanding. This wasn't some unsolvable riddle. The answer was as glaring as orb light.

I couldn't tell her.

I couldn't have her.

"Okay. Fine. I'll let it drop. But if you care for her at all, you'll join her on her date."

"I'm sure Tallulah would appreciate that," I replied dryly, ready to walk away. To return to my small room in the barracks and speak to no one until tomorrow's shift started.

"She would. She's presently outnumbered, and she looks extremely uncomfortable."

"Why didn't you say that earlier?" I demanded, storming toward the palace. *Fucking Damen.* Why didn't he lead with the most important information first?

He overtook me when we entered the palace, leading me to one of the private drawing rooms on the first floor. I inhaled the air constantly, trying to catch a glimmer of Tallulah's unhappiness in the air, and finding nothing. Then again, she was good at hiding it when she wanted to.

"This one," Damen whispered, nudging me forward before backing away. "Good luck."

It was not a room designed for privacy, which I appreciated. There was a decorative glass panel in the center of the door, perfectly framing the sitting area in the middle of the room and its occupants.

Its many, *many* occupants.

I'd categorized Aither as an *okay* prospective candidate because at least he had a close relationship with his family, which would provide Tallulah with a support network here. That was certainly something I'd never be able to offer her.

Though perhaps it was a little *too* close if he'd brought the whole lot of them on a first date.

Aither and Tallulah were sitting in the very center, closest to one another, and they spotted me at the same time. He frowned, and before I could come up with some half-cocked excuse for why I was here, Tallulah stood, eyes lighting up as she beckoned for me to come in. As far as I was concerned, if she wanted me there, that was all the excuse I needed.

"Good evening," I said, opening the door as though the plan had been for me to join them all along. It only seemed fair that Tallulah have some guests if Aither was going to bring so many.

The silence that greeted my entrance was deafening. If space had allowed, I had no doubt that everyone would have backed up, eager to get away from my grotesque form.

"Hi," Tallulah said shakily, glancing around the room with a slight frown. Her scent wasn't one of distress, but it certainly wasn't one of joy, either.

"Aither, how are you?" I asked, keeping my voice pleasant and mild. Internally, I was a little more conflicted after a lifetime of being told to stay out of everyone's way, to not make them uncomfortable with my presence. "I'm sorry to say I haven't been acquainted with your family yet."

The looks of revulsion at the empty space where my horns should be were impossible not to notice. Tallulah's frown had grown increasingly pronounced as she took in each guest one by one.

There had been plenty of similar looks when I'd joined her table at dinner, but Damen had clearly been enough of a buffer for Tallulah not to notice. What she was seeing now was how regular Shades reacted to it. Perhaps I owed Damen a thank-you for ensuring I was here. I couldn't *tell* Tallulah about why everyone hated me without her pitying me, but I could *show* her.

This is what your life would be like with me. See how awful it is? I would never do this to you.

I care about you too much to inflict this existence on you.

After an uncomfortably long pause, Aither finally made the introductions. "Evrin, this is my mother, Gratiana. My younger sister, Eydis. My grandfather, Bard. And my cousin, Drustan. This is Evrin. He guards the in-between."

"Ah, that makes sense," his grandfather muttered. Tallulah's smile remained fixed in place, but her gaze took on a sharp edge. I should have expected that fiery defensive side to appear—it only ever did for anyone other than herself.

"Did you need something, Evrin?" Aither asked, polite but pointed.

"He's here for me," Tallulah interjected with a beaming smile. "Just like you said you wanted your nearest and dearest to meet me, I wanted the same."

I almost wished she'd said anything else. There were too many Shades in this room. Those words would get out. The court would start their whispers.

"*Evrin* is your nearest and dearest?" Aither repeated derisively.

"Evrin knows me better than anyone in the shadow realm," Tallulah said confidently, patting the chair next to her and giving me a pointed look, telling me with her eyes to sit down.

I walked over stiffly, acutely aware of the scrape of seats as everyone except for Tallulah moved back.

"How is it that you two came to meet?" Aither asked uncomfortably. "You're not usually a fixture around court, Evrin."

I'd only interacted with Aither because of his friendship with Hamlin, the Shade whose room was directly opposite mine in the barracks, and even then, "interact" was probably a generous term for it. He mostly glanced at me in revulsion and went about his day.

"He is if you know where to look," Tallulah replied airily.

My intentions had been to be of genuine support to Tallulah, but there was a small part of me that was petty enough to take joy in Aither's obvious irritation at her answer.

"Yes, well, I suppose Evrin knows better than anyone that not all Shades are created equal. Did you advise Tallulah to seek out assistance from the royal family in weeding out... less desirable options? That was wisely done of you." Aither inclined his head at me begrudgingly, and his family made murmuring sounds of agreement.

"I can't take any credit for that," I said while Tallulah looked outraged. I lounged back in my seat to show her that Aither's words hadn't bothered me. "What were you discussing before I interrupted you?"

"This, actually. The advantages of Tallulah meeting Shades this way," Aither replied. "Of having a curated selection for her to talk to. I was suggesting a similar method be set up for that new Hunter who arrived. Cora, isn't it?"

"Perhaps we should let Cora settle in a little before thinking about that, hm?" Tallulah suggested, the coolness in her voice unmistakable.

Given how undesirable I was, I'd never done this formal dating thing—with the exception of the one I'd stolen with Tallulah—but I assumed they usually went better than this. Otherwise, what was the point? Surely no one would bother with this slow torture.

A trolley of refreshments arrived from the kitchens, which I politely declined to partake in, knowing Aither's family wouldn't touch the food if I'd gotten near it. For the most part, I was content to sit back and say nothing. While *I* didn't think Aither was worthy of being in Tallulah's presence after showing up with his entire family, it wasn't my decision.

If she decided that he was the one she wanted, I would support her. Probably.

"Did you know that your brother and I are competing for the same junior position on the Council of Shades?" Aither asked, forcing me back into the conversation.

Tallulah narrowed her eyes at me, redirecting a little of that irritation she was feeling my way. "Brother, hm?"

In hindsight, I wish I'd shared a little more of my life with her. I didn't like that she was hearing about it from someone else.

"I didn't know he was competing against you."

"Quite the honor for your family to be in the running, considering." *Considering your lack of horns, and therefore polluted bloodline. Considering the challenge between your brothers.*

"Indeed."

"You should have said," Tallulah said, voice tight. "I would have congratulated you."

Shit. She was hurt. That hadn't been my intention at all.

"Probably best he didn't," Aither told her, his voice filled with false compassion. "It's not a nice story. Sometimes those are better left untold, wouldn't you agree? Now, next time we do this, you simply must visit my home, Tallulah. Of course, the palace is very nice, but my estate is in a far more desirable location..."

This was going to be the longest evening of my life.

TALLULAH

CHAPTER 16

God, that had been a shit show.

It had been pretty bad from the moment Aither had shown up with half of his family tree in tow, but it had definitely gotten more complicated once Evrin had entered the picture. I could only blame myself for that—I'd been begging him with my eyes to come in and rescue me from the dire date situation I'd found myself in.

It was only once he'd entered the room, that I'd seen how Shades reacted to him in confined quarters with no other distractions around, that I realized they weren't *afraid* of him.

They were repulsed by him.

It hadn't escaped my notice that they had been looking at the empty spot just above his head almost the entire time.

Things that hadn't made sense, that had been sending my insecurities into a tailspin, were falling into place now. Like the fact that Evrin seemed *so* into me, and yet totally unwilling to do anything about it.

Almost as though he was trying to protect me.

Stop, I chided. This was how false hope began. My heart couldn't handle doing this dance again.

Elverston House seemed oddly loud when I got back, with the new contingent of Hunters chattering away happily in one of the drawing rooms. Sebastian waved me over as I passed the arched doorway, but I shook my head with a smile, pointing toward the kitchen. My social battery had been sending me warning beeps for hours now, and I couldn't face the idea of going in there and making small talk with the others.

Even though I didn't trust them, I still felt like I had a responsibility to them to be cheerful and positive about life in the shadow realm, and while I *was*, there were a few black thoughts hanging around that I didn't want to slip out in their presence.

The kitchen wasn't empty either, but Meera looked to be hiding, too. She shot me a sheepish look while sitting at the hearth, adding another log to the fire.

"Needed a break?" I asked sympathetically.

"Is that awful of me?"

"Never."

She hummed, gesturing for me to join her. "How did it go? Shall I make tea?"

"Tea would be amazing."

"I'm assuming it didn't go well, then," she said, climbing to her feet and pumping water into the kettle before hanging it in the hook over the fire. "That sounded more like a request for commiseration tea than celebration tea."

The weight of all the secrets I'd been keeping was feeling suffocating. It had been fine when I'd had Evrin to talk to, to rely on. But without him, it was just me and the loud self-recriminations that played in my head all day, and the bitter aftertaste of my bad decisions.

"Tonight was just the next episode in an ongoing saga that started the night of the ball," I sighed, kicking off my shoes and climbing up on the wide ledge below the fireplace, tucking my legs to my chest and pulling my dress down over them.

Meera glanced at me out of the corner of her eye, filling a teapot with loose leaves. "The saga of the mystery Shade?"

"The very one."

"Does it have anything to do with those long midmorning walks you would always come back smiling from, and why they stopped?"

"The two may be interlinked."

Meera hummed. "Well, if you're ready to talk, I'm ready to listen."

"Are you going to judge me?"

She suppressed a smile. "Did you do anything I should judge you for?"

I exhaled heavily. "God, yes."

"So," Meera said, setting the kettle back over the fire for the third time. "He stayed for your whole date, then? Didn't Aither have something to say about that?"

"Did you miss the part where I said he brought his *entire family* along? It's not like he had room to complain. Ophelia looked like she was about to pop a blood vessel when they rocked up, but I didn't want to make it awkward by asking them to leave, so I told her it was fine."

She'd left very reluctantly, insisting Damen stay in her place since she had to attend dinner.

"I don't have room to judge because I also dislike confrontation, but Ophelia would have been more than happy to be the bad guy there if you'd let her," Meera pointed out, giving me a slightly exasperated look as she washed out the teapot.

I opened my mouth to object, to make excuses and justify my actions under the guise of not wanting to upset anyone. But I probably *had* upset Ophelia by not speaking up when she'd gone to all that effort to set the date up in the first place. And I'd upset *myself* by staying in an avoidable situation I wasn't comfortable in purely for the sake of not ruffling feathers.

Maybe... maybe I needed to advocate a little harder for myself. Not just tonight, but in all things.

"I want to preface this by saying that I am Team Tallulah, always. I've only met Evrin a couple of times, and while he seems nice, my loyalty lies with you," Meera said gently, looking at me like she was about to tell me some home truths that I might not want to hear. "Did you ever actually *tell* Evrin that you like him?"

"*Liked* him," I corrected hastily. "Past tense."

"Okay. Sure. For argument's sake, let's pretend that's true."

I snorted. "I mean, not in so many words. But I feel like I *showed* it a lot. And he never said he liked me either," I added a little defensively. "I don't even *know* for sure that he does. I mean, did. Whatever."

"That's strange," Meera mused. "Because *I* know that, and I've only spent perhaps an hour in the guy's company."

"I came here for emotional support, not helpful feedback," I laughed, accepting the fresh cup of tea Meera slid toward me.

"Well, you're getting both." She gave me another ghost of a smile that almost reached her eyes. Not for the first time, I wondered what it would take to make Meera really smile. "Just... I don't know. Maybe neither of you have been as wholly honest as you should be."

"No, maybe not," I agreed, holding my cup up so the steam warmed my face. "It seems like we should be having bigger problems than that though, right? He's not human. Shouldn't *that* be what I'm struggling with?"

She raised an eyebrow at me. "You didn't seem to mind that in the courtyard that night. Or on any of those long walks—"

"Okay, okay," I laughed. "Point taken."

"I'm half asleep, I'm going to head up to bed. I'll leave you to reflect on all that helpful feedback," Meera added, mouth twitching with amusement as she blew me a kiss over her shoulder before leaving me next to the glowing embers of the fire.

I didn't want to reflect, because reflection meant acknowledging my own mistakes, and my head was a more pleasant place to be when I ignored those.

But at the same time, I *hadn't* told Evrin I liked him. I'd assumed that he'd known, then gotten mad when he hadn't. I downed half my tea like it was whiskey, admitting at least to myself that it wasn't the only unfair burden of expectation I'd placed on Evrin.

He had been such a calming presence from the moment I'd met him, and I'd leaned hard on that. But Evrin wasn't my emotional support Shade. It wasn't his responsibility to handle my raging insecurities. It was mine. And perhaps a lot of those insecurities would have been mitigated if I'd understood why he was so reticent to pursue anything more with me.

And perhaps they would have been mitigated if I'd just had the courage to have the conversation.

It was a scary prospect, but if anyone was worth being brave for, it was Evrin.

EVRIN

CHAPTER 17

I was *such* an even-tempered Shade. Everyone said so. The only things the realm knew about me was that I was calm, cursed without horns, and I guarded the in-between.

The latter two still held true, but I felt anything but calm this morning. From the moment I'd gotten back to my room after the end of Tallulah's "date" last night, I'd been in a restless, frustrated *rage*. The kind of rage I hadn't felt since I was a child, and I'd realized just how different I was and how inferior that made me in the eyes of everyone else.

It wasn't fair that Tallulah looked at me like she needed me when she didn't. It wasn't fair that if I wasn't who I was, I'd be perfect for her. It wasn't fair that I knew how she tasted on my tongue and felt against my body, and I'd just have to live with those torturous memories for the rest of my life, watching from the darkness as she moved on.

I groaned as someone knocked on my door, tentatively calling my name. No one ever knocked on my door or spoke to me, I didn't see why that had to change now.

On the off chance that it was an emergency, I forced myself to get up and open the door.

"Hey," Cavan said, immediately taking several steps backward. "Tallulah is at the barracks asking for you."

"Tallulah is *here*?" I asked, stumbling out into the corridor and slamming the door shut behind me. "Who is accompanying her?"

"No one—"

I pushed past him, sprinting down the long corridor to the small stone entrance to the building where we received guests—in the very loosest sense of the word, since no one would ever choose to entertain here.

Of course, by the time I got there, Tallulah was surrounded by curious members of the Guard who were eager to impress. And while I wanted to stay strong, and keep some emotional distance between us, I couldn't hold myself back when Tallulah's pleading eyes found mine, the hints of overwhelm already present in her tight smile and the way she kept smoothing down her hair.

"Move," I barked, grateful for a change, that so many Shades jumped out of my way, worried their horns would vanish by proximity. "Can't you see that you're crowding her?"

Tallulah's smile turned into something far more genuine, but I couldn't let it get to me, or this obsession would never run out of fuel.

Now that the initial panic to get to her was over, the realization of why she was probably here set in. I hadn't given her a chance to address the awkward response to me last night—I'd excused myself and asked Verner to walk Tallulah back to Elverston House.

I should have known I couldn't put it off forever. This was the reckoning I'd been trying to avoid.

"Hi," Tallulah said slightly sheepishly, glancing at the crowd who'd taken a few steps back but were still filling the entryway. "I was hoping we could talk?"

"Sure," I agreed tightly. Why was she saying this in front of everyone? The other members of the Guard were going to get the wrong impression. "Did you want to discuss the security of the in-between?" I asked awkwardly, attempting to provide her with a plausible excuse for talking to me.

"No, I want to talk about us."

Never mind then.

Our small audience broke out into a chorus of muttered speculation, and I ushered Tallulah outside, striding toward the entry room. This was a disaster enough already. The very least I could do was give her the privacy of the darkness so as not to add to the whispers.

"Wait!" Tallulah said, her small, soft hand coming to rest on my forearm, stopping me instantly. "Can we stay out here? Maybe walk through the gardens?"

"Tallulah," I began slowly. "I'm not sure you understand the damage you are doing to your reputation by being seen with me."

"Is this what the weirdness has been about the whole time? *My* reputation?" she repeated, her fingers tightening slightly on my arm, a frown marring her expression.

I gritted my teeth, my fangs pricking uncomfortably at my gums. "I am a pariah here, Tallulah. Surely, you've noticed that. You shouldn't be touching me," I added, forcing myself to move my arm away despite the burning need to feel her hands on my skin. "It will bring you shame."

"You're going to need to explain this to me more, because I don't understand. But I also don't care—they can say whatever they want about me." Her voice grew more insistent and frustrated with each word, her shoulders straightening and everything about her body language confrontational. Like this tiny, soft delight of a woman was willing to go to war for me.

It was that righteous anger that had me softening my tone, a little of the desperate longing I felt for her slipping through.

"I was born without horns." Shame coated my throat, making it hard to get the words out, but I pushed on. I'd been cowardly in not explaining properly earlier. When Tallulah had first touched the stumps where my horns should have been and hadn't screamed in horror, that was when I should have told her what the appropriate reaction to my malformed head was. "It happens sometimes, but it's very, *very* rare, and it's a great source of shame both to the hornless Shade and their family, who may be seen as less-desirable breeding prospects."

Breeding prospects, Tallulah mouthed, her scowl growing increasingly fierce. Perhaps I wasn't explaining it well.

"For more superstitious Shades"—*like Aither's grandfather*—"it's seen as a curse. A sign of the goddesses' disfavor. I've been selfish, Tallulah. I should have stayed away from you. I realized after our first time in the in-between that you didn't understand the gravity of what it meant, and I kept seeking you out anyway."

"So, you're saying that you *do* want me—you've wanted me this whole time—but you feel like you should stay away from me because you don't have horns? Have I got that right?"

"Yes."

"Evrin, that is some bullshit. We literally could have been together this whole time. What the hell."

I must not have explained it properly.

I opened my mouth to try again, but Tallulah continued speaking before I had a chance. "No, stop. You're going to tell me the exact same thing again in more dire tones, I can tell, and frankly, I don't want to hear it. I do not give a single, solitary fuck that you don't have horns. I just wanted you. I still just want you."

"You don't… you don't care? I'm malformed. I will always be this way. I may pass these defective genes on to my children someday. I will constantly be shunned by the realm at large—"

"If anyone tries to shun you ever again, I'll tell them where to shove their stupidity," Tallulah snapped, pacing in agitation in front of the entry room. "I should have done that last night with Aither's family, but I wasn't one hundred percent sure that was what was going on."

"Are you… are you saying you want to be with me, Tallulah?"

She shot me a frankly scathing look that shouldn't have been nearly as comforting as it was. "I am with you. We're together now. I mean, I guess tell me if that's not something you want, but I'll probably keep coming back. I think I could wear you down."

I let out a startled laugh. "You don't have to. Of course you don't. I will happily, willingly, gratefully follow you anywhere. I still have concerns about how this will affect your standing in the rest of the realm—"

"I don't care about that."

"You might," I pointed out gently. "When your friends are all in positions of influence, attending every grand ball in the realm, living in elegant estates. I can purchase a home for us, but it will be small and simple—"

"So long as you're there, I'm happy." Tallulah ceased pacing, coming to stand before me and sliding her hands into mine, easily avoiding my claws as though the action was second nature. "I don't need a big, fancy house. I need you to hold me tight and wrap me in shadows when I'm freaking out. I need you to make me laugh. I need you to keep being patient with me when I'm a neurotic mess. And I need to fight anyone who has ever made you feel less than—"

"Well, we can talk about that later—"

"—and I need you to let me keep you. Let me care about you." Her smile grew a little shaky. "If you could just need me the way I need you, that would be perfect."

"I already do." I pulled her into me, wrapping my arms around her shoulders and breathing in the *glorious* scent she was perfuming the air with. It wasn't her syrupy sweet desire, it was something brighter yet just as intoxicating.

It was joy.

"How soon can you arrange that cozy little house for us because I'm really wishing we had somewhere private we could go right now," Tallulah mumbled against my chest.

I laughed, squeezing her a little tighter. "So do I."

"The in-between?" she suggested hopefully, looking up at me.

I grimaced. "Not with that portal open. Besides... I want to do this right this time. I want to lay you down on a mattress and worship you properly."

The idea of doing that in my tiny single bed in the barracks was appalling. If nothing else, there was nowhere near enough privacy.

If anyone else smelled the scent of her desire, I might go on a rampage which wouldn't do wonders for my career.

I'd been worried that Tallulah would take my words as a rejection, but her scent was the happiest it had ever been. "Okay. We can do that. I can be patient. Maybe."

"Can you?"

She grinned mischievously. "I guess we'll find out. But I want a kiss first."

I immediately cloaked us in shadows, lifting Tallulah off the ground as she pressed her lips to mine, her hands gripping my shoulders. Her blunt teeth bit teasingly at my lower lip before she ran her tongue across it, and my knot ached in anticipation of being inside her again.

"You're a tease," I growled, the sound mingling in oddly with the purr that had rumbled out of my chest.

Tallulah laughed, shimmying down my body before pressing a kiss to my chest. "I can't really stay, anyway. I wish I could, but Meera and I have been summoned to a meeting this morning."

"With?" I asked, straightening.

"I don't even know really—I'm guessing the king and queen, and a bunch of Shades. It's for the negotiations with Sebastian and Lochan." She sighed wistfully. "I really don't want to go now."

I checked that I wasn't squeezing her too tight, desperate to hold on to her, to this moment, for as long as I could.

"Do you have time to walk me up to the palace? Or do you need to start your shift?"

My instinctual reaction was to say no. To protect Tallulah's reputation as much as I could. But she'd said she wanted this, and this wasn't going to work if I didn't put my trust in her the way she had repeatedly put it in me.

"I've got time."

I didn't think I could deny Tallulah anything when she was looking at me like that.

TALLULAH

CHAPTER 18

While I was playing it cool on the outside, walking arm in arm with Evrin up to the palace, I wasn't totally naïve.

This was a big deal for him, and he was trying for *me*. I was extremely conscious of not pushing him past his comfort level with each gasp or stare we received.

The brazenness of the Shades we passed was blowing my mind a little, though. Had Evrin always had to deal with this kind of thing? His entire life?

I exhaled heavily before I start rage perfuming the air around us.

"Good?" I asked, glancing up at him through my lashes.

"I'm not worried about me, Tallulah. I'm worried about you."

"And I'm worried about you. Look at us, being all cute and thoughtful."

He almost succeeded in suppressing his smile.

"There you are," Meera said, giving me a serene smile as she waited on the front steps. "I didn't see you this morning."

"Sorry—I had to go have a long overdue conversation."

"I can see that. Hello again, Evrin."

"Meera." Evrin inclined his head before gently disentangling his arm from mine. "I should start my shift. Will you be okay from here?"

"Of course. Maybe I'll see you later?" I asked, embarrassed at how hopeful I sounded.

Evrin's expression softened. "You will."

He hesitated for a moment, like he wasn't quite sure how to say goodbye, before leaning in to brush a light kiss to my temple. "Have a good day, Tallulah."

"You too," I managed to get out, fake swooning against Meera the moment he turned his back.

She shook with laughter—*real*, actual, genuine laughter—as she dragged me inside.

"Tallulah!" she whisper-shouted.

"I know, I know! But be cool because I'm trying to manage my expectations."

"How is that going for you?"

I snorted. "Poorly. Do you know where we need to go?"

"I think so." She led the way, though, we did have to stop and ask for help from a member of staff when the spiraling corridors that led into the center of the circular palace all started to look the same.

"I think this is it," Meera said, moving to lean against the wall opposite a grand-looking door. "How are you feeling about this? Are you nervous? I'm nervous."

I grabbed her hand, giving it a reassuring squeeze. Oddly, I didn't feel nervous. But this meeting wasn't about me, it was about the general relationship between Hunters and Shades, and creating a vision for our shared future.

It was a lot less nerve-racking to speak in abstracts rather than specifics.

"I feel okay. I'm not really expecting much to come from this," I added wryly. "I used to work in HR. I know how this goes."

"It does feel very corporate vision board."

We fell silent as the door opened and Damen poked his head around the corner, his horns sticking out first. "Ready?"

I nodded, linking arms with Meera as we walked in together. The packed room was dominated by a large circular table, and Damen led us to the two empty seats next to his. I recognized most of the attendees—Allerick and Ophelia, Soren and Astrid, Damen, Sebastian and Lochan—but there were a lot of Shades I didn't know, who I suspected made up the Council of Elders.

I did a double take as I noticed the one Shade lurking on his own in the corner, arms crossed and a scowl on his face directed squarely at Sebastian. Verity wasn't here, but her mate had apparently decided to make a rare appearance at court.

"Shall I do the introductions?" Ophelia asked brightly, not waiting for a response before listing off every Shade in the room.

"Do you two want to introduce yourselves?" she suggested, giving us her most encouraging smile. She was so sweet and endearing, I could almost overlook the corporate retreat energy of this whole thing.

"Sure. I'm Tallulah. Ex-Hunter. Currently jobless, though I do sew from time to time. Embarrassment to my high-ranking family back in the human realm." I gave an uncomfortable Lochan and Sebastian my most charming smile.

Meera was a little more reticent. "I'm Meera."

She didn't bother expanding on that, and I kind of loved her for it.

"Great," Sebastian said weakly. "Well, Lochan and I are really interested in hearing about your experiences, and anything that you feel would improve relations between Hunters and Shades, and make for a more cooperative, collaborative relationship going forward."

"I feel like not bombarding them with silver daggers the moment they materialize in the human realm would be a good start," I suggested.

Lochan's lips thinned while Ophelia hid a smile behind her hands.

"I think that goes without saying," he clipped.

"Doesn't hurt to make sure," I replied sweetly. "Ultimately, things aren't going to improve until some level of trust has been rebuilt, so this is all moot. The ideal situation for us—" I gestured at Meera and myself, then nodded at Ophelia to include her too "—is probably a world where we have the freedom to move between realms without punishment. Where we could go and get the things we need from the human world, and return home—*here*—at the end of the day. I know that's probably an ambitious ask, but I figure we're in the blue-sky-thinking phase, so I may as well go all out."

Apparently, I'd stunned them into silence, though I failed to see why. Obviously, having the best of both worlds would be my ideal solution. Maybe no one had dared to dream of a setup where we weren't kept rigidly separate.

"That wouldn't work for Austin," Lochan said eventually. "Not with the notoriety he has now."

I shrugged. "I doubt Austin cares about that. His life is here."

Quietly, I suspected that Austin enjoyed how mysterious he now was in the human realm, because he was a shit-stirrer first and foremost. I didn't think that would go down well, though, so I kept that observation to myself.

"It couldn't be unrestricted movement," Sebastian said slowly. "At least not right away. And Austin absolutely couldn't go. But... I don't know. There's something to it, isn't there? I'm really enjoying my time here, but I won't pretend I'm cut out for life without technology full time."

Theon made a derisive noise in the corner, and the king shot him a warning look.

"But what will happen to the Shades who visit the human realm?" Meera asked softly. "Can they feed safely?"

"Our preferred outcome is that the energy stores are filled primarily by the relationships between Shades and Hunters," Allerick put in with only a minimal amount of awkwardness, considering the topic. "It's far safer and more efficient for us."

Everyone was watching the king's face, but I was watching Lochan's. Whatever he *said*, he obviously wasn't a fan of the idea, if the vaguely repulsed expression he quickly wiped away was anything to go by.

"What do you think, Lochan?" Sebastian prompted.

"That's certainly something to consider. It would make life easier for the seven Hunters who have already made a permanent move here. Well, six, excluding Austin."

"Five, excluding Austin," I corrected sharply.

There was a long silence, and out of the corner of my eye, Ophelia paled.

"My mistake," Lochan agreed smoothly. "Five, excluding Austin. What else would you suggest going forward?"

Meera's leg was jittering next to mine under the table. Was that a genuine slip of the tongue? Or did he know about Iris?

"Some reassurance that this is, in fact, a genuine attempt at outreach, though, I don't know how you could provide that in a way we'd believe," I mused, before going off on a rambling tangent about the last time the Hunters had broken a good faith agreement. I flicked Damen under the table, and he got the hint, quietly slipping away to check on Iris.

It had to be her, right? That had to be the reason why they were here.

Sebastian seemed enthusiastic enough that there may have been a thread of truth in what he was saying, but ultimately, returning Iris to the Nash family had to be their end goal.

They had no idea what they were up against.

Meera and I went our separate ways once we got back to Elverston House, both needing a little recovery time in our rooms after an intense morning, but we'd perked up by the time we headed to the palace for dinner.

I think we both felt like we had to after Lochan's comment. We both had to prove that there was no weirdness here. We weren't hiding a whole person. Nothing to see here.

As much as I wanted to see Evrin, I figured his shift wouldn't end until well after dinner. Maybe I'd meet him at the entry room again like I had one night before.

Sebastian and Lochan were making small talk with some Shades at a different table, and I relished the opportunity to have our spot back to ourselves.

"Where's Cora?" Meera asked.

I peered through the sea of horns and tall bodies, finally spotting her on the other side of the hall with a younger female Shade I didn't recognize, with glowing pink eyes just like Verity's mad duke.

"Over there, see?"

Meera followed my gaze, eyebrows lifting. "I have a good feeling about her. What about you?"

I hummed in agreement. "Her brother, not so much."

"Agreed," Meera said quietly as we took our seats, jumping in surprise when Astrid dropped down on the bench opposite us, scowling at nothing.

"How do you *do* that?" I asked, clutching my chest. "You're like a ghost."

"Most people—and Shades—are remarkably unobservant," Astrid deadpanned, a ray of sunshine as always. "How'd the meeting go? Ophelia said I wasn't allowed to come."

"Why not?" Meera asked.

"Something, something, pessimism. I don't know. I've been in the human realm all day, scoping out the portal on their side. How did it go?"

"I mean, it was mostly just talk. Idealism. You'd have hated it," I added with a laugh as she wrinkled her nose. I glanced around, making sure no one was listening in. "There was one weird comment from Lochan, though."

I leaned across the table and Astrid did the same while I mumbled out an explanation, my eyes occasionally flicking to where Lochan and Sebastian were sitting.

"Damen went to check on her?" Astrid confirmed, her lips barely moving. I nodded. "Alright."

She lightly slapped the table as she stood. "I'm going to find Soren. I'll see you around."

I was so distracted that it wasn't until the meal had started that I realized how quiet our table was. No suitors. No crowd of Shades squeezing onto the benches next to us.

In fact, we were getting some kind of weird looks.

No, *I* was.

I blew out a long breath, recognition setting in. "Meera, you might not want to be sitting with me. The Shades think I've caught hornless cooties."

Meera raised an eyebrow at me, breaking her piece of hard bread with both hands. "Hornless cooties?"

"It's a long story."

"No, it's not. Evrin doesn't have horns. It's pretty self-explanatory."

I choked a little on the piece of meat I'd been swallowing. I loved that she was opening up more, feeling a little more confident showing off what turned out to be a very sharp sense of humor.

"I'm quite enjoying being able to eat my bread and vegetables in peace," she added with a shrug, returning to her meal.

Well, okay then.

"Is it bothering you?" she pressed.

I looked around, mulling it over. "I don't care that no one is sitting with us. And I don't care if they shun me, but I'm mad on Evrin's behalf."

The moment I was finished eating, I pushed my plate away, ready to get out of here, before I started to rage perfume.

"He doesn't look mad," Meera said, nodding toward the door where Evrin had just walked in. Instantly, my mood lightened. This must be what drugs felt like.

"Do I have anything in my teeth?" I asked Meera frantically.

She shook her head, suppressing a smile. "You're good. You look beautiful. Go show that Shade some love in front of the whole court."

It couldn't have been a bad idea if Meera suggested it.

I headed down the side of the hall to meet Evrin halfway, keeping my shoulders back and walking with purpose. There was no shame, no shyness, here. That Shade was mine, and I didn't care what anyone thought about that.

"Everyone is staring," Evrin muttered, his shadows flicking around him in agitation.

"Good." I reached up, grabbing his jaw so I could pull his face to mine, and planted a firm kiss on his lips. "Hi, I missed you."

He blinked, seemingly in shock for a moment. "I missed you, too. I know it's getting late, but I was hoping to take you out while it's still light."

"Out?" I repeated in surprise. "Out where? Never mind, I don't care so long as you're there. Let's go."

I slid my hand into his, looking up expectantly for Evrin to lead the way out of the silent room. His mouth twitched as he squeezed my fingers, guiding us toward the door.

"You know," he began casually. "In this moment, with the most beautiful woman in the realm staring up at me, holding my hand, I feel like I have the biggest fucking horns in the realm."

I may not be able to smell emotions, but I could sense that those words hadn't come easy for Evrin. He was pushing himself to say them out loud for me.

"Good. I'm going to make you feel like that every day." I rested my head against his bicep, not trusting myself not to say anything else without crying. Fortunately, the crisp, fresh air outside helped me get my emotions back under control.

It was weird of me to feel so weepy in the first place. My emotions were always a rollercoaster, but they didn't normally include waterworks.

"Where are we going?" I asked, snuggling in close as Evrin led me to the portal.

"There's a cottage for sale that I thought I would show you, if you want—"

"Yes!" I squealed, barely resisting the urge to jump up and down. "Ooh, I'm so excited."

"Tell me about the meeting this morning."

I filled him in as we made our way through the in-between, keeping my voice low. *Really* low, which made me realize that Shade hearing was much better than I'd previously thought.

Evrin's responses were more muted than Astrid's, but his arm was tense beneath mine as I relayed Lochan's words.

"What do you think?" I asked.

"I think it's wise to be cautious around Lochan. And I hate that you are sleeping under the same roof as him."

"I don't love it either, but at least Iris isn't."

Evrin hummed, guiding me out of the in-between and into an entry room that seemed a lot smaller and lower than any of the others I'd been into.

"This is Carneath," Evrin said, pushing open the door, the sound of crashing waves and the smell of the ocean immediately greeting us.

"Wow," I breathed, stepping out and scanning the horizon. There was a meandering stone staircase that seemed to perfectly follow the curves and contours of the gray land, like it had formed as a natural part of the landscape. At the top of the stairs was a clifftop with small stone cottages scattered along it, though they were several hundred feet apart. "Evrin, this place is magical."

I tore my gaze away from the view to look up at him, finding him already staring down at me. "You like it?"

"I love it. It looks like a fairytale." I hesitated for a moment. "It looks expensive."

"Not at all," he replied, surprised. "Carneath is an ancient settlement. Shades used to be shorter than we are now—the internal beams in these homes are a hazard for anyone with horns."

"Which is conveniently not an issue for us," I said cheerfully, very much seeing the silver linings.

"No," he agreed wryly. "It's certainly an advantage I'd never considered before. Shall we? We're going to that one," he tilted his chin at the closest cottage, at the top of the stairs. "The owner has left it unlocked for us."

"Let's go!" I was already dragging him toward the steps, desperate to get a closer look.

"You don't think it would be too isolated for you out here?" Evrin asked.

I almost squealed at the *seriousness* of the question. The future it implied he was certain of. I'd been trying to keep my expectations at a firmly manageable level, but it was impossible when he talked like that.

"I don't think so."

There were other cottages, but they were so far away that they were barely noticeable along the cliff's edge. "You could just drop me at the palace or Elverston House before your shift if I want to see everyone, right? Selene and Austin don't live at court, but Austin still seems to pop up pretty regularly."

"I'd had the same thoughts. And my shifts in the in-between don't need to be as long as they are—I can reduce them, or take more frequent breaks should you wish to return home during the day," he said, seeming as though he was mostly thinking out loud to himself.

"Home," I sighed dreamily, one of my inside thoughts making its way out of my head. Evrin gave my waist a gentle squeeze, fussing over me as we climbed the stairs before promptly tripping over one himself.

"They were designed for shorter Shades," he pointed out, nudging me as I attempted to squash my smile. "As you'll see when we get up to the cottage. This area is very old."

I hummed, examining the rough-hewn stone steps with new eyes. My parents had once taken me to Greece to attend a Hunters gathering, and these stairs reminded me a lot of the ones we'd seen in Rhodes. They were *old* old.

"I wonder if the Hunters—back when they were the *Hunted*—ever lived here. Maybe Shades weren't so giant back when they were knocking up my kind on the regular?" I suggested. "You know, shrunken down by those human genes."

"You might be onto something there," Evrin murmured, absently touching his hair with his free hand. The lack of horns *did* give his head a far more human shape. Maybe it was more of a recessive gene than... curse, or whatever it was being attributed to?

He pushed open the heavy wooden front door, and I could have sworn my heart stopped for a moment. "Oh, Evrin, it's beautiful. The *ceiling*! Oh my god. That is incredible."

Right above the sitting area was a circular window in the roof, made up of glass panels in a decorative pattern. But what made it truly spectacular was the ledge below it, which housed shimmering pots of vines, with fine string crisscrossing beneath the glass for them to grow along. The swirling sky was only just visible through bright gaps in the leafy foliage, lending what could have felt like an overly exposed space a very cozy feel.

"It's so striking," I murmured, stepping away from Evrin's hold to explore the small but functional kitchen just off the entrance, with low beams that would have absolutely caused chaos for someone with horns.

There was a bathroom—with hot water from an underground spring—and three small bedrooms dotted around the outside of the central living area. The back of the cottage opened up to a stone patio that overlooked the churning black ocean at the base of the cliff. It was incredible. Like something out of a dream.

"It's not perfect," Evrin said worriedly. "But it is liveable. And has potential."

"Very liveable," I agreed, running my fingers over the disintegrating curtains. My days of sewing drapes apparently weren't over, but I was feeling a lot more confident in my skills now, at least.

"Do you like it?" Evrin asked, leaning against the doorway, looking fucking delicious. "It's okay if you don't. We can keep looking."

"I *love* it, but are you sure about this?" I felt my face heat. "I don't have a job. I should get a job."

"I can comfortably afford this," he assured me. "I've been living in the barracks for free for years, and the low beams make these cottages not particularly appealing for Shade buyers. They're very inexpensive."

"But they're perfect, magical, fairytale cottages!" I objected. If I had horns, I'd just crouch. Or wear squishy little horn toppers so I didn't impale myself on the beams. This house was worth the inconvenience.

Evrin laughed out loud at that. "Perfect for us, perhaps. Do you want to live here with me, Tallulah? You don't have to right away, of course," he added hastily. "Regardless, I am more than ready to get out of the barracks."

I bit my lip, trying to hide my smile, but Evrin didn't let me. He carefully gripped my chin, tugging my lip free of my teeth until he got the full, cheesy grin I'd been trying to disguise—with a side of borderline hysterical giggles to boot.

"Yes, I want that."

"Then I'm going to make that happen."

How was I meant to manage expectations when I was already falling in love with him?

TALLULAH

CHAPTER 19

I still felt like I was floating as Evrin dropped me back at Elverston House. There was a teeny little insecure part of me that was struggling to let myself believe that this was actually going to happen. It *seemed* like it was. Evrin had sounded genuinely enthusiastic, and not in a false-hope kind of way, but in a I'm-going-to-make-this-happen kind of way.

A fairytale home by the sea with someone I was genuinely catching feelings for was everything I'd ever wanted, and that was what made it so terrifying. It was in my grasp now. It would hurt so much more if it was taken away.

"Tallulah!" Sebastian yelled, spotting me in the entryway. "Come party with us. We're playing truth or dare!"

I stopped in surprise in front of the archway, finding almost the whole crew assembled in the living room. Verity held up a goblet in cheers from where she was perched on the couch next to a beaming Cora, while Ophelia was kneeling on the floor in front of the coffee table, slicing cheese. Sebastian and Lochan were side by side on the smaller chaise, looking far more relaxed than they usually did with full wine goblets in their hands. Only Austin wasn't here.

Astrid was overlooking the whole scene from a spot in the corner, arms crossed over her chest and expression impassive. I had absolutely no doubt that she'd been the one to organize this, perhaps hoping that a little social lubricant and a party atmosphere would loosen lips.

"Sit down, so I can dare you to tell us all about this new boyfriend of yours," Verity said with a mischievous grin.

"I will, but where's Meera?" I asked, scanning the room again.

"She wasn't feeling well," Ophelia replied, glancing sympathetically at the floor above us where the bedrooms were.

"Oh no! I'll be back soon. I just want to go make sure she's okay," I said, making a hasty exit. The wine had clearly been flowing, and I needed a few minutes to brace myself before even attempting to engage with that.

While it wasn't exactly unusual for Meera to not be in the thick of a larger crowd, she didn't usually avoid social gatherings entirely, so I assumed she really was feeling bad. I knocked lightly on her door, not wanting to disturb her if she was asleep.

"Meera? It's Tallulah."

"Come in."

I let myself in, finding Meera curled up in the fetal position in the middle of her bed, blankets pulled all the way up to her chin.

"Are you okay? What do you need? Tea?"

"I'm okay," she mumbled, eyes still closed. "My uterus is trying to kill me, and my clothes feel weird, and my hair is frizzy, and I want cinnamon donuts. But I'm fine."

I made a noise of sympathy. "Tea it is. And a heat pack."

She opened one eye hopefully. "It's not too much trouble? The fire isn't lit—"

"That won't take long," I assured her. Also, it gave me a convenient excuse to avoid truth or dare a little longer.

I headed for the kitchen downstairs, fantasizing about living in the cottage, which was all on one level. It had a beautiful fireplace in the kitchen, with a tile surround that I'd love to have gotten a better look at, but it needed a good scrub first.

It was only once I had the kindling burning in the grate, a log in my hand ready to feed the flames, that Meera's words truly sunk in.

My uterus is trying to kill me.

A cold sweat broke out on my forehead, despite my proximity to the fire.

When was the last time *my* uterus had tried to kill me?

I scrambled to figure out how long it had been since my last period, drawing a blank. But I had to be misremembering, right? I had a copper IUD. It couldn't be... that.

Ash spilled out of the fireplace as I clumsily shoved the log in. I glanced down, noticing not for the first time that my dresses weren't fitting well around the bust. Almost like my boobs had suddenly decided to grow after being reliably the same size for at least a decade. I swallowed thickly. There was probably a totally rational explanation for that, too.

And the brief, but intense mood swings I'd noticed recently. Definitely an easily explainable reason for those.

Right?

Right.

I went through the motions of making tea for Meera, pouring some of the boiling water from the kettle into the teapot, before tipping the rest into an earthenware warmer and screwing the lid tightly on top. There was a selection of sweets that had undoubtedly been brought over from the palace, and I arranged some of them on a plate before setting everything on a tray to carry upstairs. It wasn't until I was outside Meera's door that I registered that I'd even left the kitchen.

"You're amazing," Meera sighed, wincing as she sat up and wriggled up to sit back against the headboard. "Seriously, I owe you."

"Don't mention it."

She glanced at me sharply. "Are you okay? What's happened?"

I set the tray down carefully next to her, taking a step back from the bed.

"Nothing." I shook my head slightly. "I'm just in a weird mood. It's fine."

Meera patted the other side of the mattress, giving me a pointed look. And even though I didn't usually like imposing my problems on other people, the idea of going downstairs and acting fine at that moment made me want to weep. I rounded the bed, climbing under the blankets in the same curled up position Meera had been in earlier.

"What's going on, Tallulah?"

"My period is late."

She paused, cup halfway to her mouth. "How late?"

"A lot late."

"Okay." She took a sip of her tea. "How are you feeling about that?"

"Terrified."

"That's reasonable."

"I want kids," I clarified. "I always have. But Evrin and I have never talked about it. And we're *finally* in a good place, but it's brand-new and it's fragile. What if this ruins everything?"

"Don't spiral until you've had a chance to speak to him, Tallulah," Meera said firmly.

That was good advice. I mean, maybe he'd be happy? That was always an option. Even if the timing was terrible.

"I have a copper," I mumbled. "I don't understand how this happened. Unless it moved or something, maybe?"

I looked up at Meera slightly desperately, and she grimaced. "The copper acts as a spermicide. For *human* sperm. We don't know how effective it is against Shade sperm."

"We do now," I muttered, annoyed with myself that I hadn't considered that earlier.

But not totally annoyed. Because I was also quietly excited—in a having-heart-palpitations kind of way. Because if I was pregnant... I wanted this child *so* much, but Evrin had to want them too.

"There are pregnancy tests in the supply closet," Meera said softly.

I nodded, already crawling out of her bed. Part of me wanted to wait until the party downstairs was over, but I physically couldn't do it. I *had* to know.

Fortunately, they all seemed distracted enough with their game that no one noticed me sneaking down to the bathroom.

Meera was sitting up expectantly by the time I returned, giving her a simple nod in confirmation as I closed the door behind me and immediately climbed back in her bed.

"Is this what you want?" Meera asked quietly, looking at me with those oh-so-perceptive eyes.

"Of course."

The answer was rote. It was what she expected to hear, what she *wanted* to hear, and so that was what I gave her.

But I was trying to be a little more honest—both with myself and with everyone else. Life was too short to go through it catering to everyone else's whims and never prioritizing my own.

"It *is* what I want," I added. "It's everything I want, which is terrifying all on its own. But what if I'm a bad mother? I'm scared that I'll look at my not-human baby and not love it the way a mother should love their child. I'm scared that my body won't be able to handle this pregnancy, and I'll die in childbirth. I'm scared that a half-Hunter, half-Shade child won't fit in anywhere."

Meera hummed. "And what about the things that could go *right*? What are some of those? What are some of the things you're looking forward to?"

"Holding them for the first time," I replied instantly, smiling to myself. My hand had drifted protectively to my midsection without me even realizing it. "Seeing what they look like, what their eyes are like, what traits they'll inherit from each of us. Getting to know them, their smile, hearing their laugh." I swallowed, my throat suddenly thick. "Seeing Evrin as a father."

"Do you think he'll be good at it?" Meera asked, her tone entirely neutral.

I contemplated the question, forcing myself not to respond with empty platitudes. "Yes, I do. Though, I imagine it'll take him some time to build up his confidence. He'll probably be... He'll probably be scared, too."

"Probably," Meera agreed mildly. Were doulas trained as therapists, or was she just really good at encouraging me to process my feelings?

We stayed there in silence for a long time, with Meera stroking my hair the way my mom had when I was little. It was the first time since I'd come to the shadow realm—or even in the years before that—that I'd truly wanted my mom around. It was an emotional response though, not a logical one. She'd be disgusted that I was carrying a half-Shade child.

"Are you happy here?" I asked Meera, having wondered about it for a long time.

"I am. I probably don't look it," she added dryly. "But that's just my face. I promise, I'm a lot happier on the inside."

"We're total opposites that way," I laughed. "I usually look a lot happier on the outside than I am on the inside. Not that I'm super sad or anything," I added hurriedly, not wanting her to get the wrong idea.

"No, I know. You're just very smiley. We've never really talked about how you ended up here," Meera said tentatively. "How it was you came to be kicked out of the Hunters in the first place."

"No, we haven't," I agreed thoughtfully. Neither Meera nor I were the *type* to be booted out of the Hunters, not really. I was pretty confident she hadn't harbored secret monster fucking fantasies—I certainly hadn't. Meera was so reticent about sharing her life in general, I'd never asked.

"Not that we have to now," she added quickly, flushing. "I didn't mean to pry. I've never brought the subject up because... well, because I don't like telling my own story," she finished with a nervous laugh.

"And you don't have to. Mine isn't very interesting. I'm perfectly happy to tell you about it. But that doesn't mean you should feel any pressure to reciprocate." I gave Meera a wry smile. "I wasn't even kicked out, necessarily. Not really."

"You left?" she asked, eyebrows shooting up to her hairline.

"Well, no. Not really. Kind of?" I could already feel my face growing hot just talking about that stupid, embarrassing time in my life. "I'm a Thibaut, right? My family is old money among the Hunters. I hate mentioning that, but it's a fact, and it's relevant. I don't personally have any of that sweet, sweet generational wealth–Grandfather hoards it like a dragon–but it's there. A lot of those old school families—like Lochan's family—like to exclusively socialize with each other. Same private schools, lacrosse teams, rooftop parties, all that jazz. I'd never really fit in, but I was always pushed to hang out with that crowd anyway. My parents couldn't fathom why I wouldn't want to."

Meera nodded along understandingly, though I suspected we'd had very different experiences of the Hunters growing up. I was under no illusions about how the Hunters operated and the disparities within the organization.

"I'd done everything that I was meant to do. I lived in a beautiful apartment in the city—subsidized by my grandfather. I had a very respectable job in HR that I got right out of college—thanks to my grandfather, and certainly *not* thanks to my Fine Arts degree. Later, he gifted me my own small firm as a birthday present. I arrived early and finished late for every night patrol, no matter how exhausted I was the next day, and I worked my ass off to run my business when I could barely keep my eyes open. My morning alarm was a recording of myself saying 'rise and grind' on repeat," I added with a snort, wanting to paint the full picture of just how committed to the rat race I'd been.

I'd followed the rules. I'd done everything *right*.

"What happened?" Meera asked, all gentle curiosity and no judgment.

"I was put on patrol one night in a park with a few of those obnoxious rich kids—or obnoxious rich young adults—that I'd been forced to associate with in high school. It wasn't uncommon, but usually I wasn't put on with so many of them at once. None of them were taking the patrol seriously. They were lounging around in the park, smoking and drinking. Getting annoyed with me that I wouldn't sit down with them, that I was actually Shade hunting and taking my duties seriously."

God, it was still so humiliating to talk about this, even though it had been *years*, but the embarrassment was mostly directed at myself these days. *They* were in the wrong—I still felt strongly about that, even though I fundamentally disagreed with everything the Hunters stood for nowadays—but I'd been so silly and naïve to think that I could do anything about it. That doing the right thing mattered more than your last name when it came to the Hunters Council.

"I made a note of everything. Took pictures of that night, showing them lounging around, not contributing. A Shade did enter that park—I chased them off on my own. I didn't kill them," I added hastily, though I doubted Meera would judge me if I had. "I took it to the Council and filed a complaint."

"They didn't believe you?" Meera asked, almost a little too shrewdly. Like perhaps that was a phenomenon she'd experienced firsthand.

"They probably did—the pictures were pretty clear. But most of the people I'd reported were *related* to Council members. I was narking on them to their own parents in many cases. And those parents did not take my criticisms of their precious little flowers well at all."

Meera grimaced. "So they banished you for reporting on their lazy kids? I mean, in hindsight, I'm glad they were too unmotivated to slaughter Shades en masse, but it does seem awfully hypocritical of them."

"I wasn't banished, not really. I was more... shunned. My complaint was swept under the rug. People I'd considered close friends stopped replying to my messages. I wasn't rostered on for patrols anymore. Even my parents started acting strange—screening my calls and refusing dinner invitations, stuff like that."

"I'm so sorry, Tallulah. That must have been horrible."

"I don't know. It was so gradual that it almost *wasn't* horrible, not right away. I was still busy at work. By the time I *really* noticed how distant everyone was, months had gone by, and the grief started to set in. At that point, I contacted an old college friend who had a house they'd been building—an off-grid place in Idaho Springs. I asked if I could visit, and he offered to let me live there while he was working offshore, just to look after the place. I wanted a fresh start, so I sold the business, packed up and left. It was right as he came back and I was looking for somewhere new to go that Astrid got in touch with the offer to come here."

I still felt guilty about leaving Josh's so abruptly. I'd told him that I had a job opportunity on a yacht in the Caribbean and it'd be difficult to get in touch. Hopefully, he didn't think I'd died.

"You don't ever wish you'd got some kind of closure in that situation?" Meera asked.

I mulled it over for a moment. "No? I think, when there's a possibility of love—romantic, platonic, familial, whatever—I find myself grasping desperately to keep it. But when I'm cut off like that, my ego finally kicks into gear and allows me to let it go. You know?"

Meera tilted her head to the side, looking thoughtful. "No. I want closure. More specifically, I want revenge. Someday, I'll get it."

That she sounded so cool and calm about it was honestly more terrifying than if she'd sounded angry.

"I'll be there for you when you do."

Meera gave me another one of those mysterious half smiles. "I know. Want to sleep in here tonight?"

"Yes, please."

"Perfect. Let's get some rest. No stressing about tomorrow, okay?

You've got this."

I nodded decisively. "I've got this."

And, for once, I didn't feel like I was lying because it wasn't just my future at stake anymore.

CHAPTER 20

Tallulah's scent was all wrong today. My stomach flipped, a nervousness I wasn't accustomed to settling in. I'd thought that we were making progress, but maybe I'd moved too quickly by showing her the cottage.

Fuck. I'd probably terrified her. What was the usual order in which these things were done? I'd almost gone to my brothers yesterday and asked for guidance, but I suspected they knew as little about courting as I did.

And perhaps I'd been a little cowardly, too. I wasn't ready to hear the disbelief in their voices when I told them that a coveted ex-Hunter had chosen me.

"Everything okay?" I asked, aiming for cheerful as we wandered along the bank of the river opposite Elverston House. I was desperate to go ahead and purchase the cottage so we had somewhere we could be alone, but I'd hold off until I was sure Tallulah wasn't just going along with the idea to appease me.

"Yup. Everything is fine." Her smile was shaky, but it was nothing compared to the anxiousness in her scent.

"What's going on, Tallulah?"

She wrung her hands together in front of her as we walked instead of holding my arm like she usually would, and rejection lashed relentlessly at my skin, despite my attempts to tell myself to be patient and not jump to conclusions.

"I'm pregnant."

My mind went entirely blank. For a long moment, there were no thoughts, no feelings, not a whole lot of anything.

And then there was too much.

"Sit down, sit down." I could vaguely hear Tallulah, feel her hands on my body guiding me to the ground. "Lean forward, head between your knees, breathe. Does that work on Shades? Crap, I don't know. Maybe I should get a healer—"

I wrapped my hand around her wrist, pulling her down, stretching out my legs at the last moment so she was seated sideways on my thighs. She was pregnant. I couldn't let her sit on the hard ground.

"Evrin!" Tallulah squeaked, grabbing my shoulders to brace herself. She almost immediately settled though, giving me a gentle squeeze and an understanding look. "It's yours, by the way. In case that wasn't clear. I haven't been with anyone else. I know you might not believe me—"

"I believe you."

She gave me a shaky smile. "I'm sorry, Evrin. Well, I'm kind of sorry. I'm terrified, but I'm really excited too. But I know we didn't plan this, and this wasn't what you expected, and you can be as involved as you like—"

"What does that mean?" I asked, a little more sharply than I meant to. At some point, I'd wrapped my arms around her waist, holding her close as though she'd disappear at any moment. "I want to be as involved as possible. All the way involved."

I want you. I want to build a life with you. A family with you.

I love you already. I've loved you all along.

I want you to wear my bite.

I didn't say that, though. What if Tallulah thought I was only offering because of the child? No, there would be plenty of time for mating marks. It didn't need to be right this second.

Even if that would be preferable.

"I need to go talk to the owner of the cottage. We need our own home," I muttered, my shadows wrapping protectively around Tallulah while my mind ran through all of the things I would need to do.

My shifts would have to be shortened, that much was certain. More guards would be required to do regular patrols of the in-between, to take the pressure solely off me.

"You're taking this really well," Tallulah said, soothingly rubbing circles into the base of my neck with her thumb. I wondered if she even realized she was doing it.

"I've always wanted to be a father. This child is a gift beyond measure... One I never thought I'd be worthy of receiving."

"You are worthy, Evrin. You're going to be an amazing father."

But was I? I would give this child everything I had to give, but would it be enough to undo the stain of having me for a father? They would always be looked down upon. Always kept at a distance. Even Roan, who was being groomed for a spot on the Council of Shades, who mingled with the elite and by all accounts had an easy life, was marred by the blood association to me.

"Are you warm enough?" I asked Tallulah. "Have you eaten? You look tired."

"I am," she agreed, stifling a yawn. There were dark shadows under her eyes I wasn't accustomed to seeing. "I was a little stressed last night about telling you. I didn't sleep well."

I stood immediately, bringing her with me and setting her on her feet. "Come, I will walk you back to Elverston House so you can rest. You need your sleep. Is there anything I can have sent for you? I need to talk to the owner of the cottage before my shift starts. And the captain, to work out a more manageable schedule."

Tallulah rubbed my arms, looking up at me with tired eyes and a soft smile. "Don't stress, okay? We've got time. Though, I do wish we had a place of our own right now, so we could nap together," she added, yawning again.

"We will shortly, I'm going to make sure of it. Go and sleep now. I'll come back at the end of my shift and meet you here."

"That sounds good." At least now she snuggled into my side as we made the short walk back to the house. The lingering scent of her nervousness was still there, but it was vastly overwhelmed by the sweetness of her joy.

I pulled her in tight—though not as tightly as before, in case I squashed the baby—as we said our goodbyes, dropping a kiss to her temple.

For a long moment, Tallulah looked up at me as if there was something more she wanted to say, before shaking her head slightly and pulling away.

"Until tonight, Evrin."

"Until tonight, Tallulah."

TALLULAH

CHAPTER 21

After the best nap of my life, I headed to the palace with Meera to grab some food for lunch, updating her in hushed tones about how the conversation had gone before she slunk away to spend some time with Iris.

I felt guilty that I hadn't been doing the same, since Iris was cooped up in her apartment, unable to leave while Lochan, Sebastian, and Cora were hanging around.

Tomorrow, I resolved. *Tomorrow, I would go and spend the day with her.*

I'd almost joined Meera, but I didn't trust myself to be good company at that moment. I was too worried about Evrin to focus on anything else.

Had I ruined his life?

I genuinely couldn't tell. He'd been so caring and careful with me, but he seemed more worried than excited. Then again, I was worried too. There were a lot of unknowns with this pregnancy, and if I thought too hard about them, I'd rapidly start spiraling. I guess I'd been hoping that Evrin would bring his signature calming energy to the situation, which wasn't a fair expectation, considering it was his baby and his life too.

"Tallulah!" I turned at the sound of my cousin's voice, finding Austin jogging toward me, Selene following behind. I doubted she ever jogged anywhere—Selene was elegant. She never looked like she was rushing.

"Hi!" I pasted on my brightest smile for Austin's benefit, and took a calming breath in the hopes of tricking Selene's olfactory senses. "How are you guys?"

"What's happened?" Austin asked, immediately frowning. "It was that prick, Lochan, right? I've always hated that guy."

"No! Wait, do you? I didn't realize you even knew him."

"I don't. It's just the *vibes*, you know?"

In Lochan's case, I did kind of know. There was something just a little *off* there.

"I've barely spoken to him," I assured Austin.

"Then what's upsetting you?" Selene asked.

"I'm pregnant," I blurted out, immediately clapping my hands over my mouth. I hadn't intended to say that. I'd wanted to discuss sharing the news with Evrin first. But Selene was also pregnant. If anyone knew what I was going through, it was her.

"You're *what*?" Austin asked loudly.

Selene blinked at me. "I wish you hadn't told me this right before my shift was about to start. I can't get out of it—not with the Hunters' recent activity."

"I don't expect you to," I assured her quickly.

"Well, I'm not doing anything. Let's go back to Elverston House and have some girl talk," Austin suggested, already ushering me along the path.

"I'll come back here at the end of my shift," Selene said, and I turned away, giving them a private moment to say goodbye.

"Alright," Austin said, grabbing my hand and setting a pace that was just beyond comfortable for my short legs. "We have a lot to discuss. Who knocked you up?"

"Oh my god, Austin."

"I thought we'd just rip the Band-Aid off, you know what I mean? Oh shit, do you not know? Maybe I should have found a more tactful way to ask that—"

"Please stop talking. Evrin. It's Evrin. You haven't met him. He's stationed in the in-between."

"I haven't *met* him, but I've waved at him once or twice, on our way to Cartava. How did *you* meet him? Are you dating him? Is he going to make an honest woman out of you? Do I need to have a manly talk with him? I'll do it."

"He'd eat you alive, Austin."

"We both know that, but that should tell you how much I love you. Obviously, I'd bring my wife along to save my ass."

"You two are so cute, it's sickening." I nudged him with my shoulder before pulling my hand free so I could open the front door. "And I don't know about making an honest woman out of me, but we had been looking at a house to move into. You know, together."

"Oh. *Oh*. So, it's serious then. How am I just hearing about this now?"

Honestly, I was wondering that myself, considering how much of a stir Evrin and I had caused by greeting each other at dinner. Then again, Austin didn't live at court, and Selene didn't strike me as someone who would even notice gossip, let alone relay it.

"Well—" I cut myself off as Lochan appeared in the entryway, charming smile perfectly fixed in place.

"Ah, the Thibaut cousins, together at last! Austin, I was beginning to think your presence here was just a myth."

"Mm, I did think about stopping by and saying hello," Austin replied, not bothering to offer any explanation for why he hadn't. Why didn't I get those Thibaut genes? The I-don't-give-a-fuck-about-your-opinion genes?

I'd got Grandfather's everyone-is-out-to-get-you paranoia genes instead.

Lochan's eye twitched ever so slightly. "I really was hoping to chat with you both. I was just making tea. Do you guys want some?"

I was absolutely craving a cup, in all honesty. Was this what a pregnancy craving was? It was less aggressive than I expected. I didn't feel like I was going to murder someone if I didn't get a cup of tea soon.

Though, I *did* feel like I was going to *die* if I didn't get a cup of tea soon. Huh.

"Yes, please. Where are Sebastian and Cora?"

I did my best to give him a genuine smile. He was being nice. I could be nice. I'd passed Astrid in the palace and she hadn't given me any indication that last night's drinking games had gone badly. Maybe in her investigation of Lochan, there had simply been nothing to find.

"Apparently, Cora feels that I'm cramping her style," Lochan said, sounding unimpressed. "She requested that Sebastian be the one to accompany her to meet with her new friend today."

He shook his head slightly as he headed toward the kitchen, muttering something about baby sisters.

"Why did you agree?" Austin hissed as I led him into a drawing room. "We can't talk properly if he's around."

"I feel like I've given you the salient information!" I whisper-shouted.

"I'm pregnant. Evrin is the father. We were planning on moving in together. I think we still are? Obviously, he was pretty taken by surprise when I told him."

"What did he say?" Austin asked sharply.

"Nothing bad! I think he was just in shock. He mostly seemed worried about me and my comfort."

Austin cut me an alarmed look as we sat down on opposite ends of the chaise. "I'm also worried about your comfort. I'm not sure your insides are built to withstand infant Shade claws."

"Thanks for that," I deadpanned.

"I'm sure it'll be fine, though," he added hastily. "I mean, it's going to be great. Our kids will grow up together. How awesome is that?!"

The idea actually hadn't really occurred to me until Austin had said it. "They will, won't they? That's amazing. And if they're, you know, *different* from everyone else in the realm, they'll have each other."

Austin's usual bright and easy grin turned a little softer and more sentimental. "Yeah, they will. Kind of like us when we were growing up, right?"

I laughed. "I'm not sure we were ever that close, Austin. Though, it was sort of hard to get close to anyone, considering we were basically in a herd."

He snorted. The Thibauts were prolific breeders—our family was enormous. It was a great point of pride for Grandfather. I'd lost count of the number of cousins I had at this point.

"Do you ever miss it?" Austin asked. "Home?"

"I miss some things, sure. But the negatives vastly outweigh the positives. What about you? No regrets about choosing the nuclear option?"

I hadn't given it much thought before, but at least I *could* go back to the human realm if I wanted to, though I'd have to avoid all Hunters forever. Austin had publicly made a scene—he didn't have that luxury.

He grinned. "Not one. I'd do it all over again if I had the option."

We fell silent at the sound of Lochan's footsteps approaching the drawing room, and I did my best to stay positive. This was a good opportunity to get to know Lochan, with the benefit of having Austin here as a buffer.

And if there was something shifty going on with him, maybe being able to talk to him without Sebastian around would help me figure out what that was.

EVRIN

CHAPTER 22

The elderly Shade who'd owned the Carneath cottage had accepted a pittance for it, which I felt somewhat guilty about, even though I would have paid more had she asked for it. Much of the furniture would remain, but I wanted to tell Tallulah the news and ask what new pieces she'd like.

Especially for the nursery.

The thought was both a thrilling and a terrifying one. A child. *Our* child. I'd been so overwhelmed with emotion—and no small amount of panic, considering we had no home of our own, we weren't mated, and I was a blight on the realm—when Tallulah had told me, I couldn't even recall exactly what I'd said to her. Had I been supportive enough? She was prone to worrying, and I wasn't confident that I'd given her the reassurance she needed.

If I hadn't, I'd do it tonight, I resolved, sparing a nod of acknowledgment for one of the guards who was reluctantly taking a shift in here.

I'd shower Tallulah with affection, and do my best not to scare her off with the intensity of my feelings for her, and tell her that I'd secured the cottage. And perhaps, if I was very fortunate, we could discuss when it was she'd be looking to move in.

Unfortunately, I hadn't had a chance to speak to Captain Soren yet, but I didn't envision any obstacles there. He'd always been wary of the amount of time I spent in the in-between, and would probably happily encourage me to reduce my hours.

I'd half expected him to pull me aside after Tallulah and I had so publicly greeted each other at dinner. Perhaps it had been unfair of me, but I assumed that he would have some opinion on me getting involved with an ex-Hunter, and that opinion would be a negative one.

Not everyone held such narrow-minded views about my affliction. Most of them did, but not everyone.

I paused midstep, my shadows rippling with a sense of foreboding. A heaviness, like the very caspite that made up the in-between was holding its breath.

And then the air was vibrating, and I found myself trying to shield my ears from the overwhelm of noise, though it was impossible when it was coming up through the ground itself.

Once upon a time, the in-between had always sounded like this. The silence had only descended when the portals had gone dark.

They weren't dark now.

There was a group of Shades in the distance, who'd frozen at the sudden portal activity. They were too stunned to even move away from me when I started speaking to them.

"Alert the palace!" I shouted. "By order of the Guard. Tell them all the portals are open."

They began running in the right direction to get to the palace, which was a positive.

There were more of us in here, but I still wasn't abandoning my post. Not when I knew the layout of this place better than anyone.

I moved from portal to portal, inhaling constantly, searching for any trace of a Hunter nearby, and finding none. That didn't mean there weren't any, though. It just meant that they were moving sneakily.

While Sebastian and Lochan had been reporting back on negotiations to the Hunters Council, there was no way that this was some act of altruism on their part. We would have definitely been informed if a decision had been made to reopen the portals, which meant that either Sebastian and Lochan hadn't told the king, or they weren't involved in this decision either.

And I wasn't prone to giving them the benefit of the doubt.

"Evrin!" Soren called, running toward me with Astrid following close behind. "How long?"

"Minutes—"

We both fell silent, glancing around as the vibrations began to change, flickering and bouncing around.

"This is coordinated," Astrid said. "There are physical keystones that have to be inserted into place to activate the portal and removed again to deactivate them. They're messing with us."

She looked up at Soren, determination written all over her face. "Get me through there, back to Denver. I want visuals on that side. Then, you come back. You need to be here."

"You're out of your fucking mind if you think I'm leaving you there alone," Soren snarled.

"Where are Lochan and Sebastian?" I interjected, because the captain was never going to be rational when it came to his mate. "Has someone got eyes on them?"

Astrid made a sound of impatience. "Get me through, Soren, or I'm going to wait for the next time the Denver portal flickers on and run through myself—screw whatever is waiting on the other side. You are the captain. You need to be here."

Soren growled, scooping her up and taking off at a run toward the Denver portal, searching for a dark spot to walk her through to. "I'm sending someone in after you. Not you, Evrin," he called over his shoulder. "Stay here. Delegate areas to any members of the Guard you can find."

It was chaos.

I barked orders to anyone I could find, and in the absence of any other leadership, they seemed to listen to me. But they weren't actually *useful*. None of them had a good sense of direction in here unless they were walking toward a specific end point. The in-between itself had a good way of making one lose focus.

I fell silent as Selene, my superior, ran past me looking frantic, grabbing my arm on the way and dragging me with her.

"What is it?" I asked, alarmed by her frenetic demeanor. Selene was always calm under pressure.

"Austin. Austin has gone through to the human realm, I can feel it through the mating bond." She paused in what must have been the through point, but we could both sense that it was flooded with light on the other side. "He was visiting with Tallulah earlier."

My entire body went cold. "What did you say?"

"I didn't put it together until afterward. That you two were the couple everyone was talking about."

"Yes," I rasped, confident that everything that had been said was terrible.

"I can't pass through realms, I'm pregnant." Selene didn't give much away, but the despair in her voice was clear if you were paying close attention. "Even if I could, wherever he's being kept is flooded with light."

"We'll find some darkness, there has to be some. And once we do, I'll go through."

She nodded. "Thank you. But first, go to Elverston House and check if Tallulah is there. I suspect not, but..."

I suspected not, too. The persistent bad feeling that had been niggling at the back of my mind wasn't lessening.

"Does the king know?"

"He'll need an update. Elverston House, update the palace, then come back here," Selene instructed.

I nodded once before sprinting for the portal outside the palace, shouting instructions at a few members of the Guard as I went.

As much as I wanted to think there was no way Tallulah could have gotten past without me noticing, the chaos had been the perfect cover.

I sprinted for Elverston House as fast as my legs could carry me, conscious that it had been a while since I'd fed, and I wasn't at my strongest. In any other situation, it might have been disastrous, but my terror for Tallulah and the baby was more than enough to keep me moving.

Elverston House looked dark and imposing as I ran up the path, ignoring the boundary line that had been set for Shades.

"Tallulah!" I yelled the moment I was inside. I jogged straight up the stairs, inhaling deeply for any trace of negative emotions that may have lingered, and finding nothing.

There was an odd scent in the air though, something I couldn't quite place. Something... unpleasant. Unnatural.

I followed it to a cupboard upstairs and yanked open the door, stumbling backward in shock, when I realized I was staring into the in-between. Or at least, a path to it.

How could this be? There was no entry room built into Elverston House, or into *anyone's* house, for that matter.

As much as it didn't make sense, the evidence in front of my eyes was irrefutable. Though, even as I watched, the caspite seemed to be dissipating in the orb light that was coming through from the corridor behind me, which wasn't something that happened in regular entry rooms. This was... artificial, somehow.

Unnerved, I checked all the upstairs rooms for inhabitants, finding them empty, and lingering in Tallulah's room for a few extra moments until the aching pain in my chest subsided.

Austin was definitely in the human realm, and the fact that he was in a bright room surrounded by light on all sides suggested he was being held prisoner there. If Tallulah had been with him then, I was almost certain she still was now, but I did a sweep of the downstairs anyway before rushing to the palace, hoping against all hope that she was there.

Neither of them would just leave. Neither would go voluntarily. Perhaps, I might have assumed the worst once and thought Tallulah would do anything to get away from me, but not anymore.

The newcomers *had* to have something to do with this.

The palace was in uproar, with most of the court crowding into the dining hall, though it seemed more by chance than through organization.

"Evrin!" Meera said, grabbing my arm and looking up at me with panicked eyes. "I can't find Tallulah."

I nodded curtly, the reality of the situation settling in. Fortunately, the king and queen pushed through the crowd to get to me at that moment, so I didn't have to explain everything twice.

"Austin is in the human realm. Selene can follow the mating bond to his general location, but it's a brightly lit area with no obvious entry point. He was visiting Tallulah earlier today." Meera sucked in a shocked breath. "I went to Elverston House to verify it for myself, and there seems to be some kind of temporary entry room inside a supply closet, though the caspite was vanishing even as I stood there watching it."

I'd expected them to be as baffled by this phenomenon as I was, though of course, they had access to information that I didn't.

"My brother's creation," the king offered, not expanding any further than that. "I don't understand how it could have fallen into the wrong hands. Only a select few of us, plus the Council of Shades, have even seen it."

"Where are the new Hunters?" I asked sharply.

"Sebastian and Cora are here," Meera put in, frowning. "And their surprise and confusion does *appear* to be genuine."

"Their scents indicate as such," the king agreed. "But Lochan hasn't been seen for hours."

"Iris?" I prompted.

"Safe in her room with Damen," Ophelia replied. "Did you see Soren and Astrid in there?"

I filled them in as quickly as I could. "Can I speak to Sebastian and Cora? I need to get back out to the in-between as per the lieutenant's orders, but she would want me to do this first."

"Go ahead," the king said, stepping back and gesturing toward the bench where the two of them were sitting. There was no crowd of admirers surrounding them this time. They sat alone, looking convincingly confused.

"Do you have any news?" Cora asked hopefully the moment I

approached. "We have no idea what's going on, we don't know where my brother is—"

"We believe your brother has somehow taken Tallulah and Austin back to the human realm, and is keeping them captive in a bright room that no Shade can access."

Cora's jaw went slack as she stared at me. "No. No, that can't be right."

I looked to Sebastian to see his reaction. He wasn't stunned the way Cora was, but he was frowning. "I swear to you, as far as I'm aware, we all came here with the same good intentions. We were both handpicked for this role, given our remit by senior members of various Hunters Councils from around the *world*. There was a very genuine push to open a dialogue with you all, to try to find some semblance of normality before the Hunters started a revolt."

"Why Lochan?" Meera asked. "You, I understand. You had that connection to Verity, and perhaps they thought that would come in handy. Lochan doesn't have a pre-existing relationship with anyone."

"Well, no," Sebastian admitted, his cheeks flushing. "That was something I raised with a few of the higher-ups. But Lochan is Cal Thibaut's protegee. No one can really tell him no—Mr. Thibaut holds the purse strings."

Meera cursed softly. "You didn't think *that* was pertinent information to mention? That Lochan works closely with Austin and Tallulah's *grandfather*?"

Sebastian's blush darkened. "I had assumed that Lochan would bring it up himself in his conversations with Tallulah. And I certainly didn't have any reason to believe he had separate goals in mind."

He switched his attention to me, eyes narrowing slightly. "You're the one who guards the in-between, right? Shouldn't you have seen them leave?"

"The in-between is an expansive place," the king cut in sharply. "And there were deliberate obfuscation methods at play from the Hunters. I suppose you don't know anything about that either."

Sebastian's scent soured, but his words had done enough damage. The mood in the dining hall had shifted, the negative attention I usually found directed my way back in full force.

They could hate me all they wanted. I wasn't going to politely and silently stay out of the way like I had time and time again.

"I'm going to check in with Selene. I'll send a runner to report back if there are any new developments," I told the king, giving the royal couple each a brief bow.

Before I could leave, Meera tapped my arm, cautiously requesting my attention.

"Don't give up on her, okay?" she murmured, something a little harder and more vicious in those dark eyes than I expected. "Don't underestimate the Hunters either."

"I won't. I'll be bringing Tallulah home. You can be certain of that."

TALLULAH

CHAPTER 23

hy was my mouth so dry? My head was pounding, and my stomach was churning like there was a whirlpool forming in my gut, even though I didn't think there was any food in there to actually throw up.

"Tallulah! Wake up. Come on. Wake up, wake up, wake up."

Was that Austin? The words were such a low hiss, I was struggling to place the voice.

"'m awake," I slurred, annoyed that my tongue was being so uncooperative.

"Tallulah." Okay, that was definitely Austin's voice. Austin's serious voice. "I need you to wake all the way up, because we are in something of a predicament right now."

"Are we?" I mumbled, trying to make my eyelids cooperate with my brain. "I don't feel good."

"You were drugged. We were drugged."

We were? I blinked my scratchy, heavy eyes open, immediately blinded by the uncomfortably bright light filling the room. And it wasn't the soft, silvery orb light of the shadow realm either. It was a harsh, fluorescent white, complete with the faint buzz of electricity that I hadn't heard in months.

Fuck.

"How did we get here?" I rasped.

"I'm still trying to work that out. I'm guessing it has something to do with Lochan, though."

Right. Right! Lochan had been there. He'd brought us tea. Everything after that was a blur.

My eyes came into focus slowly, and I took in our surroundings, trying to work out where we were. It looked to be some kind of cell, but not a permanent one. Like someone had shoved the contents of their basement to the outer walls and erected a temporary cage in the middle. As the feeling came back to my limbs, I realized that I was bound on a chair, my ankles tied to the chair legs and wrists tied behind my back. Austin was in the same position, judging by the impatient huffs and grunts of exertion as he struggled against them, but I couldn't see him. We were back-to-back, not in touching distance.

"How are you feeling?" Austin asked worriedly. "Any, um, aches or pains?"

I swallowed thickly, trying not to think too hard about the baby or I was going to lose the tenuous grip on calm that I was maintaining.

"Nothing unusual," I managed, my voice sticking in my throat. I definitely felt dehydrated, and my head was pounding, but I imagined Austin was going through that too.

"Stay positive, okay? We're going to figure something out."

I really wished I could share his optimism, but I wasn't there yet. The bonds around my wrists and ankles were secured tightly, and as much as I struggled, all I seemed to succeed at doing was rubbing my skin raw.

We both fell silent and still for a long moment, and I fixed my gaze on a distant spot on the wood-paneled walls between the bars, waiting for the room to stop spinning.

The more I stared at it, the more I felt like I'd been here before. The seventies-style wood paneling was sparking something in my brain, and whatever memory I was scrambling to grab hold of didn't feel unpleasant, either. Everything about the situation was terrifying *now*, but it still felt like it hadn't always been this way somehow.

"Does this place look familiar to you?" I murmured, wondering if I was imagining things. Maybe it was just the drugs.

"Kind of," Austin replied cautiously. "Though there definitely wasn't a giant fucking cage in it, because I'd have remembered that."

"If you recognize it, then maybe we've been here as kids," I said slowly, looking around with fresh unease. Aunt Carol had a giant basement that we'd sometimes come down to when we were playing hide-and-seek. It had always been filled with assorted boxes and holiday decorations and abandoned exercise machines.

"Oh my god, is this Aunt Carol's house?" Austin whispered loudly, coming to the same realization I had. "Did our own fucking family kidnap us? This is insane. They are insane. We should have a reality show or something."

"We might end up on Dateline."

Austin made a choked sound. "That was bleak, Tallulah."

I winced. "Sorry. But also, you know... Maybe."

I didn't want to say it out loud and make Austin feel bad, but he was kind of public enemy number one, *maybe* number two, after Astrid. But Astrid wasn't recognizable to the general human population, and Austin was a full-blown internet conspiracy.

It was chilling to think about, but I couldn't imagine any scenario where Austin was allowed to walk free. And if they'd taken me as well... Presumably, Grandfather wished to dispose of both of the grandchildren who'd brought him shame.

"I'm sorry, Tallulah," Austin whispered. "I think you might be here because of what I did. And I was fine with making that choice when I thought it was just me that I was endangering. You shouldn't be suffering for it."

My heart ached for him. For us. For the loved ones we'd left behind in the shadow realm, who were undoubtedly frantic with worry. For all of it.

"It's not your fault, Austin. We should have seen this coming. Grandfather was never going to accept any of his family members defecting, publicly or otherwise."

There was a sort of squirmy guilty feeling in my gut that the idea hadn't occurred to me before. I'd been convinced that Iris, as a Nash, had a target on her back, yet it had never occurred to me that my family would do the same. I'd never considered that I might in any way be valuable enough to be worth getting back. And I *wasn't*, not really. I was just a miscellaneous Thibaut descendent who'd already shamed the family name once before.

"Do you think he'll come down and see us?" Austin asked.

"No." I shook my head before remembering he couldn't see me. "He won't want to deal with this ugliness firsthand."

Grandfather would consider such messiness beneath him. I fully expected that we'd only see Lochan and other minions firsthand, and that the family would be kept away from this entirely.

"I can't understand how he got us here," I muttered, my head thick and aching. If he'd gotten us to the in-between, I could see it being doable. After all, one of the portals had remained open and accessible from the human realm side. Yes, the in-between was guarded, but from what I gathered, Evrin was the only one who actually took it seriously and knew his way around, and he couldn't be everywhere at once.

But there was no way Lochan could have gotten us to the in-between without someone seeing us. He'd have had to traipse through the palace grounds, somehow transporting two unconscious bodies. Even if Sebastian had been helping—and Cora—that would have been an impossible feat.

"I don't think they could have done it without insider help."

"From a Shade?" I gasped, the idea not even crossing my mind once. Obviously, the shadow realm wasn't all sunshine and roses, but I'd always felt safe there.

"Maybe?" Austin hedged. It was such a grim thought, I didn't even want to entertain it.

I lost the battle to keep my eyes open, dozing in my chair for long enough that my neck and back were stiff and aching by the time I woke up.

"Someone's coming," Austin whispered, bringing me back to full alertness. I rolled my joints as much as I could, wishing I had some way of making myself at least *look* less defenseless.

Lochan pushed open the basement door first, holding it open for two of his minions to follow him inside, though I didn't recognize either of them.

"Thibaut cousins! Welcome home," Lochan said cheerfully, unlocking the cell door. A tall woman approached me, not making eye contact as she shoved a water bottle with a straw into my mouth.

As much as I wanted to object, my mouth felt like it was lined in sawdust, and my head was aching from thirst, so I drank and hoped for the best.

"What is the point of all this?" Austin drawled, far better at hiding the fear in his voice than I was. "Do you need us hydrated before you kill us?"

Lochan snorted. "The timeline is still being established, so I'm to keep you functional in the meantime. Unfortunately, the Council are being rather shortsighted about the whole thing, not appreciating your grandfather's vision."

"And what vision is that?" I demanded.

"Nothing you need to concern yourself with. Regardless of what they say, neither of you will ever be returning to the shadow realm. That's all that matters."

"I'd love to know how much Grandfather is paying you for this," Austin said mildly. "What is the going rate for sacrificing pieces of your soul these days?"

The words seemed to have struck a chord.

"*You're* the sacrifice, not me," Lochan snarled, ushering the others out of the cell.

"Sure," Austin agreed easily as Lochan secured the lock. "But you don't think you're going to walk away from this unchanged, do you? After taking two lives?"

"I've killed *dozens* of Shades!"

The words made me feel nauseous, but Austin managed to respond. "In their wraith, human-realm forms. Where they couldn't speak. Couldn't scream. Couldn't bleed. I fully intend on looking you in the eyes while I bleed out, just so you know. I hope the image haunts you for the rest of your life. You're going to leave my child without a father. How does that feel?"

Tears silently tracked down my face at the picture he was painting. At the future we'd miss out on. The lives we could have, that we were *supposed* to have.

"I'll be sure to remember the look in your eyes while I'm drinking cocktails on the beach in the Seychelles," Lochan snapped, though his hands shook slightly as he finished locking the door, the other two already heading up the stairs. With a final glare—though it was a wary one—Lochan followed, shutting the basement door behind him.

"You definitely rattled him," I whispered shakily.

"I wish I could have done more."

So did I, but our options were at a solid zero. If only we could knock out even *one* of the lights that was flooding this place with brightness. It wasn't some high-tech place with difficult-to-access LED lighting. It was Aunt Carol's straight-out-of-the-seventies basement. There was a dangling lightbulb in one corner that was practically begging to be used as target practice, except they'd been very careful not to give us anything that could be remotely used as a weapon.

CHAPTER 24

The portals continued to flicker for hours, keeping everyone in the in-between in a state of panic. Selene eventually had to leave, to corral members of the Guard and give them orders, but I stayed in the post where she'd left me, as close to Austin—and hopefully Tallulah—as I could be without being able to pass through to their world.

I did my best not to be angry at the king and the Council of Shades, but it was a struggle. Why did it feel like we were never ahead in this battle? We had a dependency on either human fear or Hunter desire, and that put us at a disadvantage, but we had to start being more proactive, or we were going to be wiped out.

There were some shouts of alarm deeper into the in-between, and I dragged myself away from my post long enough to investigate, since I appeared to be the highest-ranking member of the Guard in here right now. The Captain had followed Astrid to the human realm, trying to get a read on the situation from the other side.

I stumbled to a stop, finding a group of ten Hunters of all ages standing in front of a portal, *reeking* of nerves.

"Hello," one man said tentatively, glancing around and seeming to realize that none of his party were going to speak. He was older, with deep lines around his face and thick gray hair. "We're here to fulfill the Hunters' side of the agreement."

"We would love to hear what that agreement is," I replied evenly, for once not minding as members of the Guard jumped out of my way so I could get to the front.

The stench of the man's fear was so acrid that it took everything in me not to move away.

"The agreement for us to move here as replacements for the two Hunters returned...?" he said hesitantly. It wasn't lost on me that every single one of this group looked exhausted, and not entirely healthy. Some of them had threadbare clothes, and they barely carried any possessions.

And they all looked unwilling.

"We were told to ask for Aither if there was any confusion," one woman whispered, staring determinedly at her feet.

Aither.

I gritted my teeth. That fucking traitor.

Selene appeared at that moment, barking orders to round the newcomers up and keep them in a secure location. She wasn't interested in soothing their nerves, and I could understand why. Though, a small part of me felt slightly guilty as they huddled together, escorted out of the in-between by a large contingent of the Guard.

"Someone needs to find Aither," I grunted, trying to keep my anger at a productive level.

Selene nodded once. "I'm delegating that task to you. I'll stay as close to where Austin and Tallulah are as I can get. If there's any change, I will send for you. Time is of the essence, but I need you to go to the stores and feed first, Evrin. You are of no help to anyone if you can't function."

As much as I didn't want to waste a single second, I sprinted for the storeroom in the palace, feeding as efficiently as I could before heading to the dining hall.

The higher-ups must have already been briefed, which saved me a task, at least.

"You're going to find Aither?" King Allerick asked, looking frazzled. With Damen watching over Iris, Queen Ophelia seemingly focused on Cora, and Soren in the human realm, he appeared to be managing the nervous court single-handedly and it was clearly getting to him. "He's not here—I'd have already sent him to the Pit if he was."

If it came down to it, I'd cheerfully, willingly execute Aither for his betrayal. But there was always a good chance that it would come back to haunt me if I did. Far better that I got him securely locked away at the Pit to face a trial instead.

But Guard resources were thin, and I was only one Shade.

"I can send for Damen—or Theon—if you need more support," King Allerick said, watching me closely, offering two of his brothers.

But I had brothers of my own, discordant and dysfunctional as they were.

"No need. I have a plan. I'll have Aither at the Pit in a few hours."

The king nodded, seemingly having unquestioning faith in my ability, which I hadn't expected. I headed straight back out, quickly taking stock of the in-between before going home.

Home to Marseden, where I'd grown up. I'd left the moment I came of age and joined the Guard, and I'd never been back since. It was eerie how unchanged the whole place was, though it had been in the family for centuries, and that continuity had always been a point of pride.

Roan was asleep when I arrived, and I half expected him to turn away the staff member who went up to wake him at the news that I was here. Instead, he appeared on the sweeping staircase, rumpled and frowning, but there.

"What is it?"

"Do you want to see Caius?"

Roan straightened, the tiredness clearing from his expression. "Of course."

"Then come with me."

He didn't question it, just fell into step with me as we headed out of the house and to the entry room I'd just arrived via. The route didn't take me past where Selene was patrolling, and as tempted as I was to take the long way and look, I had a job to do here.

Roan was quiet as we emerged into the region where Caius had made his home—a cold, damp area at the base of a mountain. It was a good spot for growing flux moss, which was the sole reason Caius lived here. It certainly wasn't for the ambience.

"Caius!" I called, banging on the door. "Can I come in?"

He mumbled a disinterested answer in response, which was about as much as I expected, and I pushed open the cracked circular door, leaving it wide so some much-needed fresh air would circulate in the single room residence.

Caius blinked disinterestedly from the bed before realizing I wasn't alone.

"What is he doing here?" Caius snarled, jumping to his feet and glaring at Roan, who was hovering in the doorway, taking in Caius's living situation in horror.

"He's here because I asked him to be here. We can return to the bitterness tomorrow. Right now, I need help. I need my brothers."

In an instant, Caius straightened, a clear, sober look in his eyes that I hadn't seen in years. This was the authoritative oldest brother I remembered. The one who'd been raised to lead the family, to uphold our legacy, before Roan had slyly issued a challenge and usurped him.

"What happened?" Caius demanded.

"The Hunters have taken my—" I broke off with a strangled sound, the word *mate* getting stuck in my throat. Tallulah wasn't my mate. She should have been, but she wasn't.

"My Tallulah," I said eventually, my voice hoarse. "My love. My future mate. The mother of my child."

"What is being done to retrieve her? Where is the captain?" Caius demanded, looking horrified.

"As much as possible, considering the circumstances." I exhaled heavily. "A new contingent of Hunters has arrived, claiming they were an agreed-upon exchange for the loss of Tallulah and Austin. They were given instructions to seek out Aither if there was any confusion."

Roan cursed loudly in our mother tongue while Caius's shadows flared dangerously.

"Aither and I are competing for the same position on the Council of Shades. We were both tasked with undertaking projects for the greater good of the shadow realm, and expected to report back on them this week," Roan explained.

"And you think *this* was his version of the greater good?" Caius asked sharply.

"It's ten Hunters in exchange for two," I pointed out as Roan shifted uncomfortably. "I suspect Aither would not have been so eager to cooperate with Lochan—the Hunter traitor—if not for the fact that he'd failed to initiate a courtship with Tallulah. He was probably... *displeased* that she chose me. I imagine he's not alone in those views."

"Fuck all those idiots," Caius growled, as though he hadn't been the first to remind me of my lack of horns every time he suspected I had developed an iota of confidence. "You have my full and unwavering support in this, Evrin. Whatever you need, I will be at your side."

"As will I," Roan volunteered quietly. For a moment, I almost thought I saw approval in Caius's expression, but then it was gone again. "He'll be at the apartment he keeps in Cartava, I imagine, in an attempt to lay low. I should be the one to approach him—Aither won't expect me to be working with you."

Undoubtedly, because Roan had said so many terrible things about me in his company in order to distance himself from me. Whatever. It would work in my favor now.

"Then, let's go," Caius said, naturally falling into his old role as leader. "Aither can give his presentation to the Council of Shades from the Curia during his trial."

TALLULAH

CHAPTER 25

With no windows and constant, glaring light, the passage of time was impossible to track. I definitely had to pee, my eyelids were heavy, and my muscles burned, so I *assumed* that at least a few hours had passed since Lochan had left, but there was no way of knowing.

Austin had been snoring quietly for a while, and I hoped he stayed asleep and that his dreams were pleasant.

I was so exhausted that my brain mostly didn't have the energy to go into a panic spiral, so that was nice, at least. There was definitely plenty of fear at the forefront of my mind, but I was almost at peace with it, because right now, there was nothing I could do.

If there was so much as a minor chance that we could fight back, then I was going to. I would go down kicking and screaming, and causing as many headaches for as many people as I could.

But until then, I was conserving my energy.

The stairs creaked, and I hissed at Austin to wake up, though he didn't until the door flew open with a bang.

This time Lochan was alone, and he looked *furious* about it.

"How's it going?" I asked him cheerfully, emulating Austin's confidence from earlier. "All alone this time, I see. Not facing any fallout from your terrible choices, I hope?"

Austin snorted.

"People don't know what's good for them," Lochan muttered furiously. "They should be *grateful*. At least someone is taking decisive action. Until they realize that this is the right plan—the only plan—apparently, I'm on babysitting duty."

"I just want to know if Sebastian and Cora were part of this plan," I said, keeping my tone light and nonconfrontational as Lochan unlocked the cell door and let himself in, not making any effort to hide the dagger he held in one hand.

His body language wasn't screaming "I'm about to murder you," but I'd also never come face-to-face with death before, so maybe I was reading the signs wrong.

"No." Lochan narrowed his eyes at me. "Nothing we said was untrue. Sebastian and I *were* given a remit by the Hunters Council to open lines of communication. My sister really did want to come with me." He swallowed thickly, looking uncomfortable at that. "I tried to convince her not to, but... Well, it doesn't matter. I was given a separate remit by your grandfather, who disliked the Council's plan. Frankly, as one of their primary financial backers, I felt that his opinion held more weight."

"Unfortunately for you, the Hunters Council isn't a total oligarchy yet," Austin shot back. "So that was a weird choice to make. Of course, you were going to face some backlash."

There was a funny sort of irony in the fact that we were giving our kidnapper a pep talk about making better life choices.

"Could you two just stop fucking talking for five minutes?" Lochan growled. "I'm going to cut the ropes. Once I am out of the cell and it is secured again, you may approach the bars and I will release the cuffs. Until some level of consensus has been reached, apparently, I'm meant to keep you alive."

"Are we going to see our grandfather at any point?" I asked.

"He's in New York," Lochan replied, cutting through my binds first with a warning look that had me staying firmly seated while he switched his attention to Austin's ropes. "Everyone is in New York. Negotiating with small-minded morons who don't understand his vision."

That was interesting. New York was where the *big* Hunter headquarters was located. This plan of his was going very badly indeed if he'd been summoned there to answer for it.

That idea brought me great joy, as well as the tiniest inkling of hope.

If Grandfather had gone against the majority, then there was a sliver of a chance that someone might intercede on our behalf and let us go—if only to try to undo the damage he'd done to the negotiations Sebastian had been having in good faith.

"Did you work with any Shades to get us back here?" I asked.

Lochan snorted. "Yes—thanks for that, by the way. I was having some difficulty in finding someone to collaborate with, but you rejecting a perfectly nice rich boy in favor of an apparently mutilated one was a real ego blow. Aither was more than happy to provide assistance to have you removed from the shadow realm."

That fucking asshole. I was mad at myself all over again for not laying into him and his horrible family on that date for being so rude to Evrin.

Once Austin had been released from his binds, Lochan stood, backing toward the cell door and unlocking it with a beep. Austin and I both stared him down, but neither of us made a move. Our hands were still in cuffs behind our backs, and Lochan was armed. We had to be smart about this.

Lochan triple-checked the lock was in place before moving to stand at the bars. "Approach one at a time, turn around and present your hands to me so I can remove the cuffs. Don't do anything stupid."

Except, I had just had a very stupid idea. Or a genius one. Or perhaps it was a little of both.

"You first," I said to Austin, tipping my chin at Lochan and rolling my shoulders, trying to get the blood flowing to my arms. If Austin had any objection to this, he didn't show it. He just glared at Lochan as he stood, crossing the small space before turning around, obediently presenting his back to have the cuffs removed. I watched as discreetly as I could as they clicked open, while Lochan struggled for a moment to get a hold of the cuffs and pull them back through the bars.

My plan involved a level of hand-eye coordination that I wasn't entirely sure I possessed in that moment, but I'd been a people-pleasing Hunter who'd attended every training session, and a World Softball Champion in middle school. I could pull it off. Maybe.

Austin moved away, and I stood up on shaky legs, making my way over to take his place. Giving Lochan my back was a terrifying prospect, considering what he'd already done to me. But I needed these cuffs off.

I held my breath as the first one clicked off, my wrist instantly feeling a hundred times lighter. The moment I heard the second one go, I was twisting away from Lochan, snatching up the sharp metal in my hand.

"Hey!" he yelled, but I was already running—or stumbling, rather— to the outer corner of the cell. If there had been a light closer to us, I would have gone for that, but the only one I had a clear shot of was the lone, dangling bulb in the corner of the room, above a stack of archive boxes. I hurled the handcuffs through the bars, not quite hitting the bulb square on like I'd intended, but at least sending the glass crashing into the concrete block wall, which did the job for me.

Austin whooped as the bulb shattered, spraying glass all over the boxes and plunging that one corner of the room into darkness. It wasn't much—I wasn't even sure it would be dark enough for a Shade to get in, but it was… something. For a very brief moment, I felt somewhat powerful.

"For fuck's sake!" Lochan said, slamming the bars with his hand and making me jump. "Thanks for that. I hope you feel real good about it for the three minutes it's going to take me to get a replacement and come back downstairs," he snapped, already stomping away. "How very impressive of you. Fucking childish."

"Childish," Austin snorted as the basement door slammed shut behind Lochan. "Apparently, we're supposed to have a more mature response to kidnapping. Someone should put that in the manual. It's looking pretty dark over in that corner. Maybe it'll work?"

I was pretty sure the hopeful note in his tone was purely for my benefit, rather than coming from a place of actually believing it was going to do anything, but I chose to cling onto it, anyway.

I hoped to believe that Evrin would come. I didn't have a mating bond to feel him through, so there was no way of knowing, and my anxiety practically demanded that I *not* believe it. That I assume the worst, because there was a plenty big-enough part of me that felt that was what I deserved.

And I would have to work through that, no doubt. If not for me, then for my child, who deserved to have me as the best version of myself.

But for now, it was enough just to tell those persistent negative voices to shut the fuck up.

If that patch of darkness was enough, Evrin would come for me—for us. He was going to swoop in to save the day. And the moment we were free from this place, I was going to demand he bite me and claim me and keep me forever.

CHAPTER 26

As agreed, I waited in the in-between, trusting that Roan would emerge with Aither as he'd promised. He seemed convinced that he knew what to say to get Aither to follow him, and I'd alerted a few of the nearby guards just in case.

So long as we got Aither in here, we'd get him to the Pit.

Caius fidgeted next to me, his shadows weak from not feeding enough recently. "Do you trust him?"

"Roan?"

Caius grunted.

"Not particularly. That's why you're here."

He glanced at me. "Me?"

"Roan doesn't give a fuck about me." I shrugged. "But he always wanted to impress you. Sure, he betrayed you and stole your position, but I doubt that desire for your approval has ever truly left him."

"Evrin! Selene needs you!" one of the guards yelled, sprinting toward me.

I didn't even pause to say goodbye to my brother or issue any instructions. I'd made my wishes for Aither known, and if there had been any change in circumstances for Tallulah and Austin, that was my priority.

The moment I approached, I saw the small glimmer of darkness that definitely hadn't been there earlier. I didn't need any encouragement from Selene to dive through it, vaguely aware that I could be walking into a trap as I felt myself change, my physical body vanishing into my ephemeral human-realm form.

But I didn't care. So long as I got to see Tallulah, nothing else mattered.

I emerged in a dark corner of a packed room, the center of it brilliantly lit, illuminating the metal bars and the two ex-Hunters within them.

Tallulah!

She looked so distressed. Her skin was pallid, and the light in her eyes had all but gone out. I needed to get her out of here.

It had been instinctual to call for her, to communicate the way that Shades communicated when we were in this form. But she didn't respond. She didn't hear me. Without a mating bite, Tallulah had no way of communicating with me in this realm.

"Someone is here for you," Austin said, squinting into the darkness where I was waiting. Right, Austin *was* mated. He could hear me. "I'm guessing it's your baby daddy."

"Don't try to be funny right now, Austin. You know he's more than that."

"Sorry, I did know that," Austin said, sounding genuinely contrite. "Sorry, Evrin. I'm having a rough day. How's my wife?"

A little frantic. The sooner we get you both home, the better.

"What did he say?" Tallulah asked.

"That Selene is missing me." Austin's voice cracked slightly, and he cleared his throat.

Please tell Tallulah that I'm missing her. That we are going to get you both home, whatever it takes.

This time, Austin relayed my message word for word. Tallulah promptly burst into tears, and I panicked that I'd said the wrong thing.

"We don't have long. Lochan is coming back to replace the light in the corner," Austin rushed out. "Do you have a plan?"

Maybe. I'll be back.

It took all of the discipline I'd curated from years of patrolling the in-between to go back into it, to leave Tallulah behind, but I needed support. My human realm form wasn't enough.

The moment I solidified in the in-between, I came face-to-face with Meera.

"I need Astrid," I said, looking around. Where had Selene gone?

"Selene has gone to get Astrid and Soren, but you don't have them right now. You have me."

"And us," Andrus said, ushering over a few more members of the Guard. Ones who'd usually do anything to avoid getting so close to me.

"There's not enough darkness for all of us right now—"

"Get me in there," Meera demanded, grabbing my forearm. "I'll take out the light. Then more can follow."

"Where did you even come from?" I looked around somewhat desperately, hoping Astrid would materialize in front of me, but she was nowhere to be found.

"I thought I could help! I *can* help. Come on, Evrin." Meera tugged on my arm, eyes wide with worry.

"Fuck! Okay. Fine. Please don't get killed," I muttered, dragging Meera along with me. I didn't have complete confidence in this decision—Meera was no warrior, as far as I knew—but time wasn't on our side.

There was no subtlety to our entrance—Meera basically fell through the darkness into a stack of boxes, sending them tumbling, and only just catching herself before she landed on her face at the last minute.

"Meera!" Tallulah whisper shouted. "Oh my god, what are you doing here? Where's Astrid?"

"I also have a solid form and opposable thumbs," Meera snapped, kicking through the boxes of assorted junk and crossing the room, hitting little white things on the wall that made the room increasingly dark. She flicked off the one by the only door before turning it back on again, staying in place with her hand, ready to do it again.

I couldn't communicate with her, but we seemed to have landed on the same plan, regardless.

Andrus and Galen slipped in behind me the moment there was enough darkness for them to materialize in, floating through the cell bars with ease, though they had to stick close to the wall to stay out of the circle of light still cast by the one over the door.

Take Tallulah and Austin back to the shadow realm, I ordered.

"Wait!" Tallulah cried. "Evrin, what are you doing? Why aren't you leaving?"

"We're not leaving without Lochan," Meera said calmly.

"No!" Tallulah shouted as Austin dragged her back, Andrus and Galen guiding them into the darkness. "Just leave him! Come back with me!"

I will come back to you, I projected, hoping the message got through before they disappeared, and that either Austin or the others would pass it on.

We couldn't continue on the way we'd been going, constantly taking the high road, and merely reacting to the Hunters' attacks. And maybe I was no one, and it wasn't my decision to make.

But they'd taken *my* love, so I was going to be doing something about it anyway—consequences be damned.

There was the crashing of footsteps on the steps, and Meera exchanged a determined nod with me, her hand resting on the wall, ready to plunge us into darkness again.

That she was unarmed wasn't lost on me. The moment the door flew open, Meera doused the lights, all but tackling Lochan to the ground and wrestling him for control of the blade in his hand. She cried out as the dagger sliced into her forearm, but managed to wrap her uninjured arm around Lochan's neck, climbing onto his back to pin him to the ground, and yanking his head roughly upward until he was gasping for air.

"Drop the knife," she ordered, her voice as soft as it always was, though with a deadly edge to it that I'd never heard before.

The blade clattered noisily to the ground.

"Happy now?" Lochan snarled, trying and failing to buck free of her hold.

I had definitely underestimated Meera.

"There are more of us—"

"You'll be back in the shadow realm before they arrive to help," Meera said mildly.

"The fuck I will."

Soren and Astrid stepped through the darkness, materializing next to me. Astrid was so silent and light on her feet that Meera and Lochan didn't even notice her arrival.

"You're not really in a position to negotiate," Astrid said flatly, picking her way through the debris as she pulled two silver blades from the holsters at her thighs. "I did say we should have killed you on sight. I'll be sure to point out to Ophelia that I was right."

"Don't hurt my sister," Lochan said suddenly, the acrid scent of his fear filling the room. "She wasn't in on it. She didn't know. Cal Thibaut insisted that I bring her with me when she expressed an interest in going. He thought she would be a good... distraction."

"You're such a disgusting little man," Meera said, smooth and damning all at once. Between her and Astrid, they kept him solidly pinned between them as Soren and I guided the three of them back to the shadow realm, where a struggling Lochan was promptly grabbed by the guards.

The moment my form solidified, Tallulah was crashing into me, and I scooped her up off the ground, her legs wrapping tightly around my waist.

"You came back," she whispered against my neck, the scent of her tears mingling with her lingering fear and her overwhelming relief.

"Of course. I'll always come back for you, Tallulah. I love you."

I held her a little tighter as her tears got noisier, but for once, I was confident that I hadn't said the wrong thing.

"I love you too. I was so scared, Evrin."

"You're safe now. I'm going to take you home and keep you safe." I gently set her back down on her feet. "But I need to finish dealing with this first."

I looked to Selene, who had a tight grip on a smiling Austin. "What now?"

"I have to go update the king and get medical attention for Meera," Soren said, already heading away, giving me a pointed look.

"Your brothers returned with Aither," Selene said, tugging Austin away. "I'll be taking a contingent of the Guard with me to supervise his journey to the Pit."

Austin grinned. "We're not citizens of your realm. No need to bother with trials for us."

I nodded in understanding as the crowd cleared out, my shadows coming to wrap around Lochan, holding him in place.

"Are you going to kill me?" Lochan rasped.

"Were you going to kill her?" I countered, not needing a verbal response since his scent so thoroughly gave his answer away.

"Don't look, my love," I told Tallulah calmly, not taking my eyes off Lochan for a second. I'd do far worse than this to keep her safe, but I didn't want her to have to *witness* it. I didn't want to risk that she wouldn't be able to see me the same way afterward.

"Okay," Tallulah agreed, turning away.

Unfortunately, it didn't protect her from the fleshy, bloody sound my claws made as they pierced Lochan's chest, punching through bone to get to his still-beating heart. I held it in my fist for a moment, watching as he gurgled, mouth open in a silent scream, eyes unseeing.

It only seemed fair. He'd held *my* heart in his hands when he'd snatched my love and my child away from me. Now we were even.

Red blood soaked my hand and forearm, dripping down my claws as I pulled away, leaving his body to collapse to the ground.

Tallulah sighed, not in disgust as I expected, but almost in relief. "I don't know if it's over forever, but at least it's over for now."

I wrapped my nonbloody arm around her shoulders, leading her out of the in-between and back toward the palace.

"You're not afraid of me?" I checked, horrified by the prospect.

"No. Feel free to do that to anyone who kidnaps me."

I smiled in spite of myself, squeezing her shoulders. "Come on. Let's get you out of here and get cleaned up. Do you need food? Water? Medical attention? I'll arrange it. Just tell me what you need, Tallulah."

"I don't think I need medical attention, but I'm not going back to Elverston House by myself right now, so you need to find somewhere we can stay together."

"Done."

CHAPTER 27

In the end, I didn't have to make any demands.

Damen met us at the palace steps, ushering us in and leading us to one of the grand, empty apartments in the palace, leaving us at the door with the promise of delivering food and supplies later. I barely heard him. The moment Tallulah was inside, I did a sweep of the four small, elegant rooms before securing the front lock with my shadows.

She followed me quietly as I strode into the bathroom, using the pump to fill the small wash basin first and submerging my bloody arm to the elbow. Tallulah stepped up beside me, unwrapping a bar of gray soap streaked with silver from the thin paper it was packaged in, and holding it out of my reach when I went to grab it.

"Let me," she murmured.

"Tallulah..." I warned. "This is the blood of one of your kind. You don't need to do this."

"You're only covered in his blood because you were protecting me. Us." Her hand briefly touched her stomach before she lowered the bar into the muddy-looking water. She gently tugged my arm toward her and methodically scrubbed every inch of my skin. I didn't so much as blink as she cleaned around my claws, worried I'd twitch and slice her fragile skin.

Once I was clean, I emptied the basin and dried off while Tallulah brushed her teeth, rinsing her mouth several times, and I began the laborious process of pumping water into the bath.

Tallulah didn't have any blood on her, but the stench of her terror was clinging to her skin, making me fucking crazy. I never wanted to smell fear on her again. She should never feel it for as long as I lived.

How could I make sure that happened? The mating bite would help. I'd at least be able to feel if she left the realm.

Maybe she should start carrying around weapons, too. I would suggest to Astrid that she source some appropriate ones.

And no more dates with Aither, or anyone else, for that matter. I intended to be every date Tallulah ever had from now on.

She didn't say a word as I shredded her clothes to ribbons, gently pulling the strands of ruined fabric away from her body, pausing for a moment to smooth my hand over her belly.

Usually, I wouldn't be so cavalier with her clothing, knowing how much effort she put into making it, but I never wanted to see these things on her again. I wouldn't be able to look at them without seeing her in that cage, her fear coating the air around us. No. I couldn't bear it.

I guided Tallulah into the bath, nearly falling over the edge when she grabbed my arm, insisting I go with her.

"Stay," she pleaded. "I swear, I am strong and independent ninety-nine percent of the time, but right now, I need you."

"You have me," I assured her, sitting on the bench that ran around the edge of the bath and pulling her onto my lap, cradling her in my arms.

We were both restless, our hands traveling over each other's bodies, checking that we were still there. That we were safe, and whole, and together.

"I love you," Tallulah mumbled against my shoulder, brushing soft kisses over my skin. "I hope they let us stay here awhile. I'm not ready to sleep apart from you."

"I bought the cottage."

"You did?" She sat back, smiling up at me with shining eyes. "Really?"

I hummed in agreement, giving her hip a gentle squeeze. "I did. But we're going to spend a few days so you can properly rest. There are a thousand things that need doing at that place, and I suspect you'll try to do all of them immediately."

She hid her laugh against my throat, the gentle scrape of her blunt teeth making my cock stir beneath her thigh.

"You've got me all figured out." Tallulah's scent bloomed—her joy mingling in with the heady smell of desire.

"Not entirely," I admitted. "But I intend to."

"Can you take me to bed now, please?"

I had us out of the water instantly. Tallulah laughed as I attempted to roughly dry her off, swatting my hand away so she could do it herself before wrapping the towel around her body and sauntering into the adjoining bedroom.

"Tell me now if you don't want my bite," I told Tallulah, guiding her onto her back on the bed. The towel fell open instantly, and I guided her legs the same way.

"I want it more than anything. I want you. I want to build a life with you, a family with you," Tallulah breathed, looking up at me with shining eyes.

Finally, *finally,* the look in her eyes from the night of the ball, from our very *first* night together, was back. It was trust, and hope, and adoration, and I felt like a fool that I'd ever squandered it.

I kissed my way down her body, occasionally taking a moment to taste her skin, and inhale her glorious scent.

"Legs up, Tallulah. It's been too long since I tasted this sweet cunt."

She made a somewhat desperate sound of agreement as she pulled her knees up to her chest, pinning them perfectly in place while I swiped my tongue through her sweet, glistening pussy.

A purr rumbled out of my chest, and I did nothing to hold it back as I licked up every drop of slick I could reach, greedily demanding more from her body.

I moved my hands to the back of her thighs as she came, squirming away instinctually, but I wasn't done with her yet.

"Again, on my tongue," I ordered. "I want you nice and wet for me, Tallulah. You're going to be spending most of tonight on my knot."

She made a dazed noise of agreement, briefly looking down at me between her thighs before head flopped back on the pillow.

I wrung two more orgasms out of her before I was satisfied that she was ready. The blankets were soaked with slick where Tallulah was lying, and there was definitely precum where I'd been grinding my cock into the bed, desperate to be inside my future mate.

Tallulah moved to touch my hair, hesitating at the last moment and grabbing my shoulders instead, encouraging me up the bed. I climbed over her, settling between her thighs, and wrapped my fingers around her wrist, guiding her up to the top of my head.

"You can touch me."

"Are you sure?" she asked softly, lightly running her fingers over my hair.

"Of course, Tallulah. It's you."

The smile she gave me was *everything*. She tangled her hands in my hair, thumbs resting at the base of my stumps, as I slowly sank into her warm, wet pussy.

Instantly, my knot was throbbing, desperate to be lodged inside her, but I had to take it slow. Gentle. Tallulah had been through a lot. She was pregnant. I couldn't get carried away. But I'd missed her so much, and the imminent promise of finally seeing my bite on her skin was setting off an instinct I didn't know I had that could only be described as feral.

"I won't break," Tallulah huffed, hooking a delicate ankle around the back of my thigh and attempting to tug me forward.

"You might," I replied gruffly, carefully keeping my weight off her as I lowered myself over her body. "You're very fucking breakable, my love. I could crush you with one hand. Rip you apart with a casual swipe of my claws. Tear your throat out with my teeth."

Tallulah grinned up at me, showing off blunt little fangs of her own. Her thumbs started massaging the stumps beneath my hair, and while I knew horns could be erogenous zones for others, I'd assumed that wouldn't apply to me. I'd never let anyone touch them before to find out.

No one had ever wanted to.

But *fuck*. If she kept that up, this was going to be over far quicker than I anticipated.

"You won't, though. You think I don't know how fragile I am compared to you? I'm perfectly aware. But I have complete faith that you'll do everything within your power to keep me—and our child—safe from harm, at your hand or any other. I don't just love you, Evrin. I *trust* you."

"Your sweet, beautiful words aren't calming me down," I gritted out, though it was an unnecessary observation since I was already starting to rut her like a beast.

"I'm not trying to calm you down. I've been very patient, Evrin, and I deserve a proper fuck after today—"

The last of my self-control snapped as I pinned her arms above her head and began fucking her like I was possessed.

"Finally," Tallulah gasped, sucking down some air, arching her back to meet my thrusts.

Her breasts bounced with each movement, the pink in her cheeks traveling all the way down her neck, and a fine sheen of sweat coating her skin. Tallulah's black hair had escaped its tie, spreading out all over the pillow in a tangled mess, and her blue eyes were hazy and unfocused as her cunt tightened around me, another orgasm dragging her under with a raspy moan.

She was a perfect, beautiful *mess*, and she was all mine.

I tried to gather some semblance of control for the bite, but Tallulah didn't give me the chance. She grabbed a fistful of my hair and yanked my head down roughly, tilting hers back to expose her neck. My teeth broke her skin of their own accord, the coppery taste of her blood hitting my tongue before I'd realized what I'd done. But there was no going back now, and I didn't want to.

Not when I finally had Tallulah where I wanted her. Where she was meant to be the whole time. In *my* bed, carrying *my* baby, with *my* mark on her flesh, tying her to me forever.

My knot swelled while my teeth were still embedded in her skin, and her arms were wrapped tightly around my shoulders. I'd never felt more closely connected to anyone. The desperate longing inside me to feel *seen*, to be touched, to be heard… It vanished like it was never there, the mating bond settling into place, filling up the parts of me that had been lonely for my entire life.

It was fucking madness that it had taken us this long to get to that point—and the fault was all mine—but we were here now and I was never letting her go.

CHAPTER 28

We are for real getting up this time," I told Evrin sternly, taking a step back when he went to reach for me. "Evrin! They're all going to be wondering what we've been doing up here for two days."

Evrin snorted. "Tallulah, my love, no one is wondering."

I gave him my most long-suffering look as my cheeks flamed red. "Still, we should show our faces. Our friends will want to know we're okay."

"*Your* friends," he corrected, blinking in surprise.

"They're our friends. They care about you, too," I said firmly, knowing that Meera wouldn't have gone through to the human realm with just anybody.

He sighed, flopping back on the bed, though a small smile played around his mouth that he was trying to hide. "I suppose you should put on clothes then."

"Fortunately, Meera brought me some." We'd had a steady supply of things dropped at the apartment door for the past couple of days, but no one had tried to interrupt us. I felt a little bad about it—surely there were questions that needed to be answered and plans put in place to make sure there was never a repeat of what had happened.

But maybe they realized that Evrin and I hadn't been ready to answer those yet. We needed time to just be together, to reconnect, to seal what we had first. My fingers idly brushed the raised scar of the mating mark on my neck as I picked through the bag of clothes Meera had packed for me, noting with a smile that she'd only packed things that were loose on top.

Eventually, I settled on a simple skirt, top, and flat shoes before pulling my hair into a low bun so my mating mark was on show. I quickly applied the barest minimum of makeup I needed to feel presentable in public, while Evrin rolled off the bed, draped himself in shadows, and called it a day.

I definitely envied his getting ready time.

"Do you need to siphon?" I asked, grabbing a sweater as we headed for the door.

He nodded, having already ducked out a few times to go top up the energy stores.

"Nervous?" Evrin asked, inhaling deeply as he tried to read the nuances of my scent.

"No, I wouldn't say nervous. I guess I'm a little worried. All of the things I've been able to avoid thinking about for the past two days are seeping into my brain all at once."

Evrin linked our fingers together, giving my hand a quick squeeze that had the tops of his claws leaving light indents on the back of my hand. "Don't worry, my love. There is a very capable group running this realm who can figure out these problems without us, though I'm sure our input will be appreciated."

I suspected Evrin was being sarcastic, but he'd soon find out how appreciated he was. He'd been incredible when everything had gone sideways, taking point and leading effortlessly from the small glimpse of him I'd seen from the cell and from Austin's words.

"There you are!" Damen grinned as he strolled down the hallway toward us. "I was sent to knock on your door. I lost a bet," he added with a laugh.

"Fortunately for you, we're already decent," I replied, nudging Evrin's arm. He almost smiled, though he certainly wasn't as relaxed as he'd been when it was just the two of us alone. I didn't think he ever would be, but that was okay. I had every intention of being his place of comfort and safety, just like he was for me. "We were going to try to make it to the dining hall before breakfast finished."

"No need—Allerick and Ophelia have set up a private breakfast. They were hoping you'd join them."

"Of course." I looked up at Evrin to make sure I hadn't overstepped, and he nodded in agreement.

After a brief stop off at the stores so Evrin could siphon, we headed for a small but grand dining room on the second floor.

"Oh wow, everyone's here," I said, blinking in surprise. There was a blur of pink, and then Verity was wrapped around me like a cherry-vanilla-scented cobra.

"I'm so glad you're here! You are okay, right?" She pulled back, scanning my face before her gaze snagged on my neck. "Ooh, we've got a mated lady over here! Congratulations."

I felt myself getting flustered by all the excited attention, but Evrin was more flustered, which had the unexpected effect of making me calmer. I wanted to be steady and supportive for his sake.

Verity moved out of the way for Ophelia to give me a hug, followed by Meera, then Austin. Astrid tipped her chin at me from where she was already seated at the table next to Iris.

To my surprise, Cora and Sebastian were there too, sitting rather sheepishly at the table.

"Are you okay, Tallulah?" Cora asked, eyes filled with tears. "I'm so sorry. I didn't know—"

"I know," I assured her, giving her a shaky smile, though I clung a little tighter to Evrin's hand as we took our seats opposite them.

Did she know that Lochan hadn't survived the event? I glanced nervously at Astrid, who was staring impassively back at me—I was pretty sure that was her affectionate face, though. She pursed her lips, nodding ever so slightly, which I took as confirmation. Though I suspected that even if Cora knew that Lochan was dead, she didn't know that Evrin had been the one to strike the killing blow, and I was more than fine with that.

The table was piled high with a mouthwatering array of food, including an impressive selection of human-world vegetables from Meera's garden.

"The first thing you should know is that we've moved you out of Elverston House," Ophelia said apologetically, sitting at the head of the table next to the king. "I'm sorry that it had to happen without consulting you first, but we had ten terrified Hunters show up and we had to put them somewhere."

"I've moved out too," Meera added. "I packed up your room."

"Thank you. Where are you staying?"

"Here." Meera gestured vaguely at the palace.

"We set aside the room next to Meera's for you," Ophelia said slowly, her eyes dropping to my neck.

"I'll be moving in with Evrin." I shot him a quick, reassuring smile, and he rested a warm, comforting hand on my thigh.

"To Carneath," Evrin grunted for the benefit of the curious Shades in the room. Selene nodded in approval before leaning over to give Austin a whispered explanation.

"So, they'll be staying here?" I asked, as we all began piling up our plates. "Those Hunters?"

Allerick grimaced. "No decision has been made yet. When given the option to immediately return—most of the portals are active again—they all wished to stay rather than risk the wrath of..."

"Our grandfather," Austin supplied, giving me a knowing look. "It sounds like he's gone rogue. It could be an interesting time for the Hunters Council if he pulls his funding. You might find them a lot more willing to cooperate," he added, raising his cup to the king, who looked thoughtful.

"What of Aither?" Evrin asked darkly.

"Still in the Pit," Captain Soren replied.

"Legally, his situation is somewhat murky," the king muttered. "At least in the eyes of the Council of Shades. Since you're both alive and well—"

"No thanks to him," Austin snarked.

"—he's arguing that he shouldn't be punished, and should in fact be *rewarded* as there are now ten more Hunters in the shadow realm. Obviously, that won't be happening, but the Council of Shades will likely go back and forth on semantics for months. That he stole the caspite orb is undeniable, and he will certainly spend a lot of time in the Pit for that alone." Allerick looked across at Evrin. "Roan was offered the junior position, but he denied it."

"He did?" Evrin's hand tightened a little around my thigh.

"He requested a redo of his challenge with Caius."

"And lost," Evrin surmised, though he sounded relieved. We'd discussed our families a little over the past couple of days, and I knew that there were years of unresolved tension between his brothers. It sounded like progress was finally being made.

For a while, we ate, and the conversation was light as everyone attempted to give Evrin and me time to adjust to all the information that had just been dropped on us. There was clearly more to come, though. I could feel it in the air.

I had my own news to share at some point. While Meera, Austin, and Selene all already knew, it seemed as though they hadn't told anyone else.

Allerick cleared his throat. "There is something else you should be aware of. A delegation from the Hunters Council came through yesterday to personally apologize for Lochan's actions, and to insist that their intentions when sending a negotiating party through had been good. Sebastian and Cora have reiterated the same, though of course we're aware that they could all be lying."

"Lochan also said that," I put in. "For what it's worth."

Allerick nodded once. "Nonetheless, if talks are to resume, then we need to have a lot more control over the process. For now, Sebastian remains as the Hunters Council's representative, but we would like him to collaborate with one of our own ex-Hunters, in order to form a more balanced party, able to have more nuanced discussions—both with the Hunters Council and the Council of Shades."

"That sounds smart." And then Sebastian's words back to the Hunters Council could be more directly supervised, which seemed wise.

"We'd like that ex-Hunter to be you, Tallulah," Ophelia said gently, giving me a hopeful smile before wincing. "I swear this won't be like the last time I asked you for a favor."

I laughed out loud at that. "No more dates. I'm taken."

"No more dates," Ophelia promised. "And I'm sorry for how all of that panned out—especially with Aither. I swear we vetted them. I didn't see that coming."

"He would have been fine with it if Tallulah hadn't chosen me. That hurt his pride," Evrin cut in smoothly, his thumb stroking gentle circles over my leg. "How can we be assured of Tallulah's safety if she accepts this role?"

I melted a little at the concern in his voice.

"Everything will take place here in the shadow realm—there will be no negotiations taking place in the human realm," Allerick assured us. "But aside from that, we'd like you to participate in the discussions too, Evrin."

Evrin's fingers twitched slightly, but he seemed too stunned to speak.

"You have the most knowledge about how movement between both realms could best be facilitated," Captain Soren added. "The in-between is both a problem we haven't been able to solve, and potential we haven't yet explored. There's no one better equipped than you to work on this."

"I couldn't agree more," I murmured, smiling up at him. Evrin nodded stiffly, though I could tell he was overwhelmed by the offer more than anything. He *wanted* to be more involved in things, he'd just never been given the opportunity before. "Evrin is perfect for this. In contrast, I am vastly underqualified. I don't have any relevant experience to draw on."

"Who else could do this better than you?" Meera asked with a gentle, encouraging smile. "You're compassionate, you can talk to anyone, you stand up for what you believe in, and you're not afraid to dream big. Really, Tallulah, you're *perfect* for this."

I rested my hand on top of Evrin's, gripping it tightly. "This means a lot, you guys. If you're sure about this... We won't let you down."

"We know you won't," Ophelia replied confidently.

"Does the job come with maternity leave, though? I'm going to need to take some time off in a few months—"

I was sure they could hear the shrieks of excitement from the human realm.

EVRIN

EPILOGUE

Y ou're quite sure this is normal?" I asked the Healer, pacing back and forth at the foot of my mate's bed as she let out another low moan of agony.

"Quite normal," both Meera and one of the Healers assured me, both of them focused entirely on my wife, as they should be. I'd never felt so helpless in all my life. Everywhere I stood, I seemed to be in the way of the support team bustling around Tallulah, and she was in agony and I couldn't take it away.

Never again. We were never having another child. Not if it meant her suffering.

"Ev," Tallulah groaned. "Why are you so far away?"

"I'm here, my love," I assured her, carefully stepping around Meera to get to Tallulah's side. "I'm right here. What do you need? What can I do?"

"Hold me," Tallulah demanded, breathing hard during her momentary respite from contractions. "I want you on the bed with me. Can we do that?" she asked, glancing between the Healers and Meera, who all hastily assured her that we could.

Carefully, I helped Tallulah shift forward before climbing onto the bed behind her and pulling her back against my chest, my hands coming to rest on her stomach right as it grew hard with another contraction.

"This has been the longest day of my life," Tallulah panted right as it ended, before promptly groaning in pain again. "Meera, I want to push."

While the Healers were here to help, Meera was the only one with birthing experience on the human side.

"I'm going to measure you, okay?" Meera said gently, ushering the Healers out of the way, and they ducked dramatically under the beams to avoid getting their horns stuck. The cottage really wasn't designed to hold this many Shades, and I couldn't wait until they'd all left.

This home was our sanctuary, and the only thing missing from it was our child.

Meera looked up, giving Tallulah a calming smile and a nod. "Alright, mama. You ready to have this baby?"

Tallulah tipped her head back against my shoulder with a breathy laugh while I did my best to contain my terror. "Hell yeah, I am."

"He looks just like you," I murmured, staring at my son in wonder as he nursed from his mother's breast. He had a funny little tuft of jet-black hair; clawless, dainty little fingers; and bright red skin that Meera assured me would fade into a paler pinkish hue in the next few days.

"His eyes though..." Tallulah replied with a tired smile, looking up at me. "Human babies don't have eyes like that. They barely open them. Flynn's are already so clear and distinctive, and they glow a little like yours do."

She looked down at Flynn—at our son—and her smile softened dreamily as he blinked up at her with vivid eyes. They were almost the perfect blend of Tallulah's bright blue, with streaks of my navy color.

"Will he ever be able to visit the human realm?" I asked. "Or does he look too different?"

Tallulah shook her head, her expression thoughtful. "I don't think he'll look too different these days. People will just think he's wearing colored contact lenses. Back in the olden days, when Hunters and Shades used to coexist... He might have attracted some negative attention then."

Before I could ask what contact lenses were, a faint tendril of shadows swirled around Flynn's tiny fist before disappearing into nothing.

Tallulah blinked twice before looking up at me. "Was that you?"

I laughed. "No. Our son might have a little more Shade in him than we thought."

Tallulah grinned before biting her lip. "You're not... disappointed, are you? That he looks like me?"

"Of course not." I climbed onto the bed next to her, pulling both of them carefully into my arms. "I don't think I could be happier if I tried, Tallulah. I'm not sure I am capable of ever feeling disappointment over anything ever again. You and Flynn... You're everything to me. I'm going to take such good care of both of you. I'm going to make you both so happy."

"I have no doubts about that since you already do," Tallulah replied, resting her head against my shoulder. "I love you so much, Evrin."

"I love you too. More than I can say."

THANK YOU

Thank you to everyone who has picked up this book and supported this series, I'm so grateful to you all that I get to do what I love every day thanks to you. An extra special thank you to my Ream subscribers, you guys are incredible.

Marcelle at Books Checked was not only the proofreader for this book, she was the heart and soul too. I couldn't have done this one without you <3

I also have to thank my PA, Nikki, for putting up with me, and my amazing, supportive, patient friends. Thank you for being the voice-of-reason Meeras to my panic-spiraling Tallulah.

Colette R. xx

P.S. To keep up with the latest news and releases, join my Facebook Reader Group or subscribe to my newsletter.

ABOUT THE AUTHOR

Colette Rhodes is a paranormal romance author from New Zealand. She loves to write about love in all its forms, and adores imperfect heroes and heroines who find perfection in each other. You'll often find her trying to justify her degree by including ancient history and mythological influences in her work.

If she's not writing, then you're almost certain to find her reading—ideally with a cup of tea in hand and a scented candle burning to match the mood.

Keep up with Colette here:
coletterhodes.com
@coletterhodes_author

ALSO BY COLETTE

SHADES OF SIN:

Luxuria

Superbia

Gula

Avaritia

Invidia

Ira

Acedia

STATE OF GRACE:

Run Riot

Silver Bullet

Wild Game

Dare Not

Saving Grace

THREE BEARS DUET:

Gilded Mess

Golden Chaos

LITTLE RED DUET:

Scarlet Disaster

Seeing Red

ON THE SHELF:

Scheme

Excess

KNOTTY BY NATURE:

(omegaverse with T.S. Snow)

Allure Part 1

Allure Part 2

EMPATH FOUND:

The Terrible Gift

The Unwanted Challenge

The Reluctant Keeper

DEADLY DRAGONS:

The (Not) Cursed Dragon

The (Not) Satisfied Dragon

STANDALONE:

Dead of Spring (MF - Hades & Persephone retelling)

Colette Rhodes
ROMANCE AUTHOR